YOUNIS A

A NOVEL

Without

بدون

TRANSLATED BY MICHELLE HARTMAN
& CALINE NASRALLAH

Younis Alakhzami
Without (Novel)

Translated by: Michelle Hartman & Caline Nasrallah

© 2021 Dar Arab For Publishing and Translation LTD.

United Kingdom
60 Blakes Quay
Gas Works Road
RG3 1EN
Reading
United Kingdom
info@dararab.co.uk
www.dararab.co.uk

First Edition 2021
ISBN 978-1-78871-080-0

Copyrights © dararab 2021

دار عرب للنشر والترجمة
DAR ARAB FOR PUBLISHING & TRANSLATION

This is a work of fiction. Unless otherwise indicated, all the names, characters, businesses, places, events and incidents in this book are either the product of the author's imagination or used in a fictitious manner. Any resemblance to actual persons, living or dead, or actual events is purely coincidental.

The views and opinions expressed in this book are those of the author(s) and do not reflect or represent the opinions of the publisher.

Text Edited by: Marcia Lynx Qualey
Text Design by: Nasser Al Badri
Cover Design by: Hassan Almohtasib

Without

Translators' Note

The novel you are holding, *Without*, began its life in Arabic as *Bedoon*. Though this was the working title that we, as cotranslators, used, we never took it for granted that this would be the final English language title. Indeed, we went back and forth debating many times: Should we call the novel *Without*? We knew that we would lose the nuance and richness that "bedoon" suggests in Arabic. We were especially attuned to losing the parallel between the protagonist's struggles with gender identity and nationality, and how both impact on belonging. After conversations with the author, editor, and publisher, we eventually agreed upon using our working title, *Without*, with the author's blessing. In conjunction with this decision, we re-read the entire manuscript with special attention to the use of the word "without." This led us to add three sentences to the very end of the novel, something neither of us had done as translators before. We felt that this would highlight the title and underline the word's importance. After extensively discussing this major change, we humbly presented it to the author, Younis Alakhzami, and he graciously agreed that it added to the transformation of *Bedoon* into *Without*.

While this might be one of the most major changes, it was not the only decision that we spent much time discussing and debating. What struck us both as cotranslators of this novel, though, was the fact that we actually agreed—and disagreed—on almost all of the same things. It is all the more striking because we were engaging not only a text full of characters but also the author of the novel. In reflecting back on this and the translation process, we realized that we worked off of each other but also negotiated constantly, at all times. Therefore, even if there was no visible conflict, the translation is certainly different than what it would have been were only one or the other of us to have worked on it. We have worked together in the past, in fact, but more in the capacity to read and comment on the other's work, not to produce a work together.

How and why would the finished translation have been different? As translators, we shape and produce translation not only by using particular words, phrases, and expressions, but also through a writing process that reflects who we are and where we come from. We know that we might have picked up upon and worked through some of the same things, perhaps even generally we might have worked similarly. But we also know that we do not always notice or focus in the same or even similar ways. As we revisit our translation process, we also have come to note that even though we experienced nothing we would call *conflict*, we had varying opinions on *why* we agreed or disagreed with something. This led to rich discussions, as well as translation attempts—and re-attempts—that we used to produce the novel *Without* as faithfully and respectfully as possible. What we were perhaps most adamant about was to produce different voices and tones for each of the different narrators of the novel's various chapters. Thus, we divided the work between us chapter by chapter, so each of us could fully immerse ourselves in a voice by delving fully into one specific character at a time. We hoped that this would allow us to tell that story in full, before starting over again in the world of a different narrator, which was rendered by the other cotranslator first and then reshaped together.

There are several elements of our translation that we would like to highlight for the reader to understand better the process of making an Arabic work into an English-language one. The first is the way we dealt with pronouns. Transition is the focal point of the story in many ways, and so it is not a surprise that it was the focal point of many of the challenges we faced in translation. Pronouns in Arabic are used more frequently and offer gender indicators more often than in English. There were many examples when the pronouns used for Ali(a) switched between she and he without missing a beat, often multiple times in a paragraph or even a sentence. This was difficult to capture in English with the same fluidity. We tried our best to guide the reader through these swift changes with ease. We noticed this in particular in the chapter narrated by Montgomery, where he wonders how Alia could ever have been thought to be female when he was so clearly male.

We did not always know Alia by that name. In fact, when we were introduced to this character, in Arabic, they were called Oula. In Arabic, the names Oula (عـلـا) and Ali (عـلـي) are closely related, not only in meaning and pronunciation, but their spelling is nearly identical. The difference is only two dots! Because the letter sound that starts both names does not exist in English and is approximated differently "Ou" and "A," we were aware that these two names do not look alike or sound alike in English, and also have no obvious connection in meaning. For the protagonist's choice of new name to be as clear and seamless in English, we chose to change the protagonist's birth name in English to another Arabic name, Alia, closely related to both Oula and Ali. We discussed this with the author and the three of us agreed early on that this was the best choice for the novel *Without*.

The most difficult issue for us in producing this translation was how we continually struggled with the terminology used in the descriptions of Ali(a) as an intersex, queer, and/or gender non-conforming person who is seen to be "unnatural" by those around them. We worked through this as sensitively and thoroughly as we possibly could. At times, we opted for more scientific terms than the vaguer terms used in Arabic, focusing more on their being an intersex person than as someone who was unnatural or flawed. Often we opted to translate terms more idiomatically than literally. For example, the word meaning "monstrous," to indicate something unnatural, sounds more inflammatory in English than in the Arabic original to refer to someone who is gay. While this term is negative, it carries a much stronger valence in English.

Similarly, we had to decide what to do when we encountered the much discussed and controversial Arabic word (شـاذ), which can mean gay, homosexual, or queer, but literally means deviant. Should we translate this word consistently in the same way, should we use the term deviant for these, should we use the word deviant at all? Because the word itself in Arabic contains multiple meanings, the implications of it are more subtle and readers can extract from it what they will. We made a general decision, which we both agreed upon, to greatly reduce the number of times derogatory words were used in the novel. We carefully judged each instance of such words: their context, who they were spoken by, and what was meant and implied in their use. We decided what type of word to use, for example: gay, homosexual, intersex, lesbian, "likes women" and so on. When appropriate we used expressions which have slowly become more frequently used in English like gender dysphoria, gender affirmation surgery, and so on. We made this decision, even when the literal word choice might not have always indicated this, because we hoped to convey that the text is fundamentally pro-intersex, pro-trans, while reflecting the reality of the Arab societies it is based in. *Bedoon* implicitly and at times explicitly critiques these difficult realities for queer, intersex, and trans Arabs. We hope that *Without* conveys this well and brings this important pro-trans Arab message to a wider audience.

Michelle Hartman & Caline Nasrallah
Montréal, 2021

Epigraphs

« Une vie de l'écriture m'a appris à me méfier des mots, ceux qui paraissent les plus limpides sont souvent les plus traitres. »

"A life spent writing has taught me to be wary of words. Those that seem clearest are often the most treacherous."
--Amin Maalouf

"Sombre is human life, and as yet without meaning."
--Nietzsche

"Questions are more essential than answers, and every answer becomes a new question."
--Karl Jaspers

Notices

First:

Not all of the events in this novel are real. This also goes for the characters—they are not all based on real people.

Second:

Some kinds of acute pain are too powerful, arrogant, and rude to be described, so forgive me if I was unable to do so.

Third:

I do not advise the faint-of-heart to read this novel. But if it so happens that you do read it, don't thank me, chastise me, or blame me for the changes you will experience, especially in your perception of those around you and the way you deal with them.

Fourth:

Jack Kerouac said, "Pain, love, and danger make you real again." This is a novel of pain, love, and danger.

Dedication

To darling A. A. A.,
Thank you for giving me your trust.

I pray for you when you are in the operating theatre.
I pray with you,
I pray you will have the strength to lift your broken
gaze and see the heavens above.

If only you knew how many times I've tossed and
turned in my sleep. Your suppressed mourning troubles
our consciences and shakes our very foundations!

Part One

Alia Ilwan

"If a man were responsible only for what he is aware of, blockheads would be absolved in advance from any guilt whatever.

But a man is obliged to know. A man is responsible for his ignorance. Ignorance is a fault."
--*Milan Kundera*

Alia
Khobar, Saudi Arabia

To be in love with a girl is in itself a crime. This is all the more true if she is a fellow student at your all-girls' high school in the Bayounieh neighbourhood in Khobar. These feelings are too sinful even to be inwardly acknowledged, let alone publicly expressed. Keeping them secret goes without saying. But what would happen, I wonder, were I to openly declare these feelings for my classmate Moodi? I was fully aware that there could be only one possible outcome. It was inevitable. Complete and utter doom.

Still, I longed to confess my secret love to Moodi. My feelings were at war with each other. They were relentless, threatening to suffocate me every minute of every day.

I love you, Moodi. I love you so much. I want to spend the rest of my life with you. I feel a boundless longing to be with you. I woo her beautiful spectre, as if in a lucid dream.

Moodi comes from the well-to-do Qa'ad family. She's a pretty girl with rosy cheeks, whose clothes give off the scent of traditional Arabian incense mixed with French perfumes. Her delicate, pearly white teeth are always busy chewing gum, and its minty fragrance trails in the air behind her, reminding everyone of how flawless she is. She's neither too curvy nor too slender, but perfection. She's an angel fallen from the sky one cool day when the flowers began to blossom, when everything took on a rose-coloured hue.

Anyone who claims she's merely human is a liar! She has creamy skin with pinkish undertones, full, rosy, and perfectly drawn lips. Whenever her luscious coffee-brown hair bursts free from her hijab, it cascades down over her neck and shoulders like a silken waterfall. There is no doubt that she's different from all the other girls I've ever known here in Khobar. She's not even like those beautiful girls from Aden or Taiz who I had the chance to see up close last summer, when, for the first time, I set foot in the land of my ancestors in the far south of the Arabian peninsula. I'm nearly certain that with all of the beauty God granted her—her unique refinement, the glint in her eyes, and her teeth as shiny as pearls—thousands would flock to her and try to win her affections.

But that sweet and happy young woman, who always has a smile on her face and pays little attention to her studies, pays even less to my emotions. She's indifferent to the looks cast her way by petite, Yemeni me, described by our fellow classmates as having "tomato cheeks." Since I'm well-spoken and diligent, they call me a nerd. No one can best me in the finer arts of grammar and rhetoric. I keep to myself most of the time. A smile rarely crosses my face.

"You look sad and subdued all the time, like an orphan," one of them told me. "Everyone agrees you always seem worried about something." Another tugged at my heartstrings when she whispered in my ear with a sly smile, "Anyone who looks at you would swear you'd fallen in love. Do you have a crush on someone?" I instantly feared she might have noticed my attraction to Moodi, and that she would gossip about me behind my back.

In any case, I don't blame Moodi for her indifference. Who could blame her, really? All the girls at school vie for her attention. Her teachers are drawn to her and give her passing marks even if she doesn't show up for exams. The school's headmistress once said, "You're as sweet as honey, Moodi. Your mother must be Egyptian!"

At night, in the shelter of my bedroom, when the universe is still save for the sounds of distant cars—young men racing to show off their speed and, quite frankly, suicide skills—I nestle my head into my pillow. I lure my eyelids shut and will sleep to come. But it never does. A vision of Moodi occupies my every waking thought—her laughter, her gestures, the flash in her hazel eyes, the outline of her symmetrical face and round, soft cheeks, polished and rosy like two apples. Her small nose that flares a little at the bottom does nothing to distort her beauty, not at all like her sister Bayyan's nose, which juts out of her angular face. Bayyan is one year older than Moodi and is enrolled in the science track at our school.

But Moodi acts as if she doesn't know I exist. She never spends any time with me, though I wish she would. She never even asks how I'm doing the way she does with the other girls. Our classmate Watfa is her best friend. They both agree that high school is the furthest they'll take their education. "By the time you finish, you'll be old and grey, and by then it'll be hard to have children and raise them properly!" Moodi would proclaim, always trailed by Watfa's agreement: "Education does nothing for a woman's future, nothing at all!" They've convinced each other that their marital homes will be more worthy of their time and attention than pointlessly pursuing an education. Like a broken record, Watfa repeats this whether or not it's appropriate. Men and marriage are the main topics of conversation for her and Moodi. This comes up once, twice, even three times a day, with no sign of abating. It's even the main course when we gather at teatime during the half-hour break between periods— "God will never be pleased with a woman who doesn't focus on her husband and home."

She doesn't let up: "Women weren't created to work and get tired. Our soft bodies aren't made for drudgery and toil. Women are made to raise children and care for their husbands."

She carefully examines our faces as she speaks, alert to who's on her side and who isn't. Her anger swells and her face brims with confidence as she swears by Almighty God that what she says is true; it's logical, correct, and indisputable. This is a righteous truth that cannot be invalidated, as undeniable as the light of the sun. Her argument culminates in one final proof, "That's why my father lives so happily with my mother. She's never once complained—not about him, not about her life."

Sometimes Watfa even cites Qur'anic verses and sayings of the Prophet she's heard her father repeat. "This is what Allah wants for us— *'And abide in your houses'*; and He also said that women must not wish to become like men—*'And do not wish for that by which Allah has made some of you exceed others'*."

Despite all this, and the fact that I've been growing increasingly certain that Moodi will never notice me or my feelings, I'm still inexplicably drawn to her. She affects me a great deal, though I know very well that at the end of the day—and at the end of the current school year, seven months from now—Moodi will go her way, and I'll go mine.

She's lodged herself deep within me, whether I like it or not. Every time I see her walk into the classroom, my heart skips a beat. It then proceeds to pound against my ribcage when her steps lead her in my direction. My chest tightens and my stomach flutters when I see her laughing and chatting with Watfa, cheerful as usual. I envy Watfa. Sometimes I even resent her and wish she would just disappear.

Though we've been classmates for two years, only recently has Moodi come to occupy my every thought and waking moment. I don't understand what's happening to me. All of a sudden, these complicated and conflicting feelings started growing inside me, and they fixated on her. Here I am now, unable to control either my feelings or the obsessions that follow.

The onset of these feelings for Moodi is not the only new fixture in my life. I've found myself becoming more and more drawn to the songs my father Abdel Rahman plays on repeat, especially those by Umm Kulthum, Abdel Halim Hafez, and Farid al-Atrash. Every Thursday, my father follows a special routine. He gets home from work at sunset, weary and exhausted. He takes a shower and sprays his clothes with his favourite cologne, a mixture of oud, sandalwood, and cardamom—or that's what he claims the secret ingredients are. He then reclines on the sofa in his room, my mother Jawaher right by his side. She'll have already made the necessary preparations for this weekly ritual. She cooks dinner extra early on Thursdays, so as not to miss out on sharing the entire evening with him. Then the whole house is flooded with Umm Kulthum's voice. Her distinctive rhythms set the stage for the night. I cannot recall one Thursday in all the years we lived in Khobar that started with any voice but hers. *Al-Atlal, Enta 'Omri, Fat al-Ma'ad, al-Hobb Kollo, Lelat Hobb, Ya Msaharni*, and *Aghadan Alqak*—these songs were our companions throughout those years. My father says *Fat al-Ma'ad* is the most beautiful song he's ever heard, "the lyrics, music, and performance." He sings along after Umm Kulthum's lengthy crooning, "*What good is regret... what use is reproach?*" In a euphoric daze, he exclaims, "God bless you, Baligh Hamdi, you're a composer like no other! What a genius... genius doesn't even describe it..."

He then calms down and finishes his thought, "If only the lovely Umm Kulthum had not sung it in the year of the Naksa."

The muscles in his face tense up when he reaches the part of the song where she sings:

> *The curtains of oblivion fell long ago*
> *If it's about past love and its harshness*
> *I've forgotten it; I hope you forget it too.*

He sways his head as he sings along, stopping only when he begins to lose his voice.

The ritual continues until the very end of the night. Before he climbs into bed and submits to slumber, he listens to one or two songs from Yemen, his homeland. He has a special affinity for Ayoob Tarish's *Wa Mfareq Bilad en-Noor*. "This song will be the main reason we return to Yemen," he often used to say, to me and to anyone else in the house.

> *You who left the country of light, the time has now come to reunite*
> *Loyalty to the homeland is calling, the time to heed that call is now.*
> *Do not stay away, enough distance, agony, and sorrow...*
> *Yemen awaits you with open arms.*
> *Stranger to the homeland, enough distance and travels*
> *Loyalty is religion, grace your families with your presence.*
> *Enough of letters, paper can be burned with fire,*
> *And money brings no joy to those who are longing.*

The songs of Abu Bakr Salem bring tears to his eyes and tug at his heartstrings, which were already heavy with yearning. They also nudge forward his plans to return to Yemen as soon as possible.

He would flip between two songs, each making him more homesick than the other.

> *If you fly, fly to the town of Aden*
> *Passions run high, I am too far, I am too sad.*
> *I cannot take this distance,*
> *Every day feels like a year,*
> *It is the paradise of the world,*
> *It holds all art dear.*

And:

> *If you love your home, get up and dust yourself off.*
> *For you, Mukalla, Sanaa, Aden.*
> *Yemen is sweet, even sweeter are its people.*

I rarely focused on the lyrics of the songs my father played. I barely paid attention to any single phrase. I always thought it so strange that my father sighed whenever Umm Kulthum, known as Kawkab al-Sharq, reaches the end of a verse. I couldn't understand it. But this all changed with the tidal wave of emotion that swept over me and fixated my thoughts on Moodi. Now, I'm actually drawn to those sentences and expressions that seem to stem from my own mind, from the feelings simmering just below the surface. I focus intently, anxiously, on Umm Kulthum's words:

> *Am I going to meet you tomorrow? How terrified my heart is of tomorrow...*

And:

> *Oh, you who forgets me while you are on my mind,*
> *Your spectre never leaves my sight,*
> *Comfort me and empathise with my situation*
> *And relieve me of all my worries.*
> *Far from you my life is torture.*
> *Don't stray far from me.*

And, every once in a while, my eyes swell with unwanted tears.

My mother has been attuned to these changes taking place within me. Back when I turned twelve and was still flat-chested, she grew more and more concerned. Later, she noticed my newfound interest in music just as she noticed my increased inclination toward quiet and calm. Not long ago, she was calling me silly and foolish. Now, I still haven't gotten my first period, and I'm late compared to other girls my age. This worries my mother, who claims time is running out because soon a suitor will come knocking, his family in tow, to ask for my hand in marriage.

No, it's fair to say that I hope the day my mother has been fretting about never comes. I'm in no condition, psychologically speaking, to picture a man sharing my bed and inching closer to me to "flirt with me, touch me, hold me, and enjoy my charms", as Watfa keeps repeating. Moodi always nods along in total agreement. But I cannot imagine a man breathing so close to me. The mere thought of it makes me sick.

But I do wonder, sometimes, why I don't have the same desires that Watfa and Moodi do. Why don't I care the slightest bit about men? Am I not a woman? I find it very odd that these feelings only come with puberty. When we were still in junior secondary school, girls started talking about boys. Is it safe to assume that they all hit puberty so early on? But when I hear my mother factually narrate how these things happen, I stop worrying. She knows best, after all. "They're just deceptive, early teenage feelings," she says, confidently brushing off my worries. "A girl only knows how she truly feels once she hits puberty and gets her period."

In my current state, I feel an extreme aversion to men. With every day that passes, I grow less and less interested in them, especially the ones with hair growing on their faces.

"My mother says that men without hair aren't real men."

"*My* mother says that the more hair a man has, the more of a man he is!"

I listen to these conversations in class and feel queasy. They make my stomach turn, and I feel I'm going to be sick. Mirvat, our Islamic Education teacher, hates men. She once told us, "I can't stand talking about them." She announced that a man has to be very clean and not let his beard grow out too much so that wispy beard hairs don't fall out onto the ground—or, even worse, get mixed into the rice when you're eating. "I don't like beards at all," she asserted. "They disgust me." Sarcastically, she asked, "Did God create hair for us just to let it grow?"

***

Back when I was in kindergarten, and during my early years in primary school, I spent a lot of time with my female teachers. I never really had the urge to play with the other girls in my class. Instead, I spent most of my free time between periods in my female teachers' offices. Sometimes I would even prefer to just stand there, behind their office windows, watching them move around. A hint of a smile would dance on my face whenever one of them noticed me and ushered me back to enjoy playtime with my classmates. When I went home for the day, I would stay inside until the following morning, when I got on the school bus. My mother was always worried about me, constantly cautioning me against leaving the house. This made me less willing to go out and play with the neighbours' children, who I viewed as monsters.

All this changed when I turned nine. That's when I threw caution to the wind and forgot my fear of being outdoors, beyond the high walls that surrounded our house. I firmly implanted myself within the group of neighbourhood boys. I started talking to them, playing with them, acting just like them, all the while completely avoiding the many girls who lived in the area. My mother didn't comment at first, and she didn't object either, as long as I had no budding little bulges on my chest.

My father was surprised at my football skills, especially considering I was playing with boys. In his opinion, I was better than them, dribbling the ball and scoring goals with great precision. Jokingly, he once said that his dream—that my mother's firstborn child would be a son—may actually have affected my genetic makeup. Perhaps I should have been a boy, as he had wished. He praised me, "The boys you play with can't kick the ball as hard as you can. You're the best player in the world. Better than Pele!"

When I turned thirteen, I was forbidden to play football with the boys. At the same time, I found myself involuntarily pulling away from my sisters Nuha, Suha, Anoud, and Shazza. I started to recoil from all the kinds of "girl talk" they shared. I preferred to spend time with my brothers Hamed, Assem, and the youngest, Mourad. I'd steal Hamed's bicycle and ride on gravel, tiled, and dirt trails, and on the pavement, sometimes falling on the asphalt and scraping up my arms and legs. Barefoot, with dark blood dripping from my skinned knees, I'd race my brothers up dirt hills, covered in grime and dust, oblivious to how filthy my clothes would get.

I cared even less about how angry my mother would be when she saw me, about the screaming fit that would ensue. I'd follow them up the trunk of the massive walnut tree in the middle of our yard. Even when my climb ended in a painful fall and bruises all over my body, I never cared. My mother would scold, "You're a girl, this is inappropriate!" And when she realised that her admonitions were going unnoticed, she would fly into a fit of rage and call me names. "Stupid," "scatterbrained," and other words she used went in one ear and straight out the other. And she didn't stop when her anger dissipated. No, she then resorted to other weapons in her arsenal. She would sit me down next to her, bring her face close to mine, and then, very calmly, with a smile, give me some advice:

"You're a girl, a lady, a delicate woman. Soon your womb will have fully developed and will be able to carry a man's seed. You need to take better care of yourself. If God forbid you were to break your hymen with your reckless behaviour, you'd never find a man who'd agree to marry you. You'll live your whole life without a husband, do you understand?"

But all her advice, everything she said, would float away on any passing breeze. She carried on, well-intentioned but naïve, "It's okay to play, but don't run around too fast, ride bikes, or open your legs so wide!" Again, I didn't listen. Looking to my father for support, she'd complain, "Your daughter is going to drive me crazy!" But none of it made a difference to me. I went on feeling that I was a different kind of girl. "I'm not like other girls, Mama," I would say. She would always shake her head, refusing to listen. Even Hamed backed me and confirmed, "This girl is more like a boy—ten boys even!"

When I turned fourteen, I started getting intense stomach cramps. They were irregular and kept coming and going every three or four days. This made my mother extremely happy. Joy returned to her otherwise morose countenance as she calmed my pain with analgesics, insisting that my cramps were the onset of period pains. "It appears you're one of those girls whose periods are very painful. You'll suffer, I can already tell," she would say gleefully, then murmur, "but the pain will subside after marriage. I was just like you."

But no blood flowed, and the cramps didn't go away. They accompanied me everywhere, like a shadow. I would sit in front of the mirror, feeling my face and the wiry hairs that had started to grow above my lip and under my jaw. "When you get older, you'll have light hair growing on your face, kind of like a beard," the Sudanese endocrinologist, Dr Abdel Ghaffar, had said. He'd started following my case when my mother began to feel there was cause for concern. But he couldn't find a convincing explanation for my condition. Obviously anxious and confused, he started scratching his bald head and making a sort of (+) sign on his cheek. He mumbled to my mother as I sat there watching. "There's nothing to worry about with your daughter Alia. This is normal. Her body is secreting an excess of male hormones, which is expected for her age group. This will all go away when she hits puberty." I was fifteen at the time.

The doctor's words confirmed what our General Sciences teacher had told us in class: all our confused teenaged feelings of love, passion, and attachment to each other were transient and would fade away, disappearing with time. She also gave us the following advice: "It's possible for a girl to like another girl, or for a boy to like another boy, during your teen years. It's easy for feelings to get mixed up between ordinary, natural love—like the love between siblings and friends—and that other, unnatural love, which is the forbidden kind. So, girls, you must remain on your guard and be aware of everything happening around you. Don't hesitate to tell your mothers if anyone makes you feel unsafe." Then, resorting to stronger language, she warned us, eyes bulging, "And don't you ever, ever, go near boys. At this age, they're nothing but rabid dogs that will ravage the flesh of anyone they come across. They're like wildfire, consuming everything in their path."

Even at an early age, I'd never been emotionally drawn to boys. I always felt a profound interest in girls, and, as I grew, so did this interest. Two years ago, I met an Egyptian girl at school. She was in the year below me. Nasma. She was as gentle and breezy as her name suggests. She had ivory skin, rosy cheeks, and slender fingers. I was completely taken by her. One morning, I mustered up the courage to talk to her for the first time, and she stole my heart with unnerving ease. There was magic in her smile and in the pink of her cheeks. But soon after, she left our school and Khobar entirely, to move to Jeddah. I was miserable for days. She haunted my dreams for a long time.

When my sister Anoud, who is three years younger than me, got her period, I began to despair. She was only thirteen! I grabbed my journal from the bookshelf and started to scribble in it furiously, cursing the state I was in and imploring God to save me. It was He, after all, who had decided to make me as I was. No one else.

It's not fair, I wrote. *Why do Anoud and all my other sisters get to live their lives free of stress, while I have to deal with all this anxiety?! Why have I been sentenced to this torture?!*

But I immediately felt guilty and tore out the page, afraid of God's retribution.

***

Sometimes, when I'm alone in my room, I picture myself talking to Moodi. I conjure up her face and tell her about everything I'm hiding deep inside, all the conflicted feelings I have for her. But even in this fictional world, she doesn't care. She won't even offer the solace of a curt smile.

I pull my notebook out of the drawer and write:

I don't know what's happening to me. I don't understand. I can't even explain it, let alone confide in anyone. Deep down, I wish I could be like all the other girls. I wish I had the same thoughts and desires as they do. But I don't. I can't. I always feel so detached from how they talk about their feelings. But why? It's probably those male hormones the Sudanese doctor told us about...

Starting a new paragraph, I write:

I wish I could think and feel the way that Watfa, Moodi, and my sisters do. All this confusion is torturing me! I feel so alone... I struggle to join conversations. I've gotten so used to talking to myself that my sisters call me crazy. But in reality, I have no control over this confusion, and the only solution I can think of is to wait for my period to come and puberty to hit... it's already so late...

I go on writing:

But despite all this anxiety tearing away at my insides, I'm a girl who fears God and believes in Him. I do strongly believe that soon He will pull me out of this daze. I pray to Him five times a day. Because I haven't yet had my period, I fast the whole month of Ramadan. I even perform all the extra, optional prayers. My sisters Nuha and Suha can't always fast during the full month of Ramadan because sometimes they get their periods, which prevents them. But I'm different. I hope I get it soon so that I can be normal like them...

Then I delve deep into a sea of supplications, stopping only when the darkness is defeated:

O Allah, it is Your mercy that I hope for, so don't leave me in charge of my affairs even for the blinking of an eye. And rectify all of my affairs for me. There is no God but You.

O Allah, I appeal to You for the weakness in my strength, and my limited power, and the lack of support and the humiliation I am made to receive. You are the Most Compassionate and Merciful, the Lord of the weak.

Still, despite all this, I once again fall prey to these contradictory feelings that relentlessly attack me. Furiously, I underline the words I've written:

I don't feel like a girl. I don't feel like I belong to the world of girls. I can't stand their conversations, and I hate talking about men! I won't get married: I'll live my life like this, without a man and come what may. My father will be angry and I know my mother will roar on about it, but it's my life and I'll live it how I want to. If it were up to me, I'd choose to be a boy.

Sometimes, when I think about the strict laws and customs here, my eyes can't help but well up with tears. It's depressing to think my fate will be the same as Moodi's and Watfa's.

These irreconcilable feelings surface sometimes more than once a night.

Occasionally, I manage to picture myself as a full-fledged girl, beautiful and natural with two swollen breasts, "a rose in a garden" to borrow my mother's words. But other times, I feel disgusted at the thought of being that sweet girl, adorned and perfumed with oud oil, lying in wait—at the end of the night—for her mate to appear and bite at her luscious flesh before he succumbs to slumber.

***

My father has always been oblivious to the details of what was happening to me. This was especially true after I stopped playing with the neighbourhood boys. He doesn't come home until late, and, when he does eventually arrive, he's always exhausted, too tired to speak. Even his breathing is laboured, and sometimes he grumbles about work. He's sick of his job. He complains that it's sapping his energy and health. During the workweek, from Saturday to Thursday, he never really speaks to us much. He doesn't give and take; he just sits quietly at the dinner table—if by coincidence he makes it home on time—and quickly finishes his meal before turning in, not to leave his bedroom until the following morning. He's only ever truly present on Thursday nights and Fridays. Otherwise, my father is more like a spectre that floats through the house. And although Ramadan is the month when he pays more attention to us and is more inclined to offer us his company, nothing really changes. The arduous day-long fast brings him home shortly before the call to prayer, at which point he's mostly quiet. If he speaks, it is usually about the "brutes" he works with or his cruel bosses who "claim to be Muslims and perform Umrah and Hajj every year yet are harder on their fellow Muslim employees than they are on Zionists!" His barrage won't even stop there. He claims that the bosses "ignore the fact that it's the holy month, the month of mercy and compassion", and indeed that their cruelty "actually intensifies during Ramadan—they spend their time chit chatting in air-conditioned offices, not caring that the rest of us toiling in the heat are also hungry and thirsty."

I, for one, do not understand how this weary, grumbling man who curses and swears when he's tired is the sentimental romantic who listens to Umm Kulthum every Thursday night. But all that aside, I love my father very much. I've been attached to him ever since I was little. He treated me like a boy all throughout my childhood. Those were the best years of my life. He left me wanting for nothing: he would always buy me new clothes to wear for football, and at the beginning, he ignored my mother's pleas to stop me from playing with boys and riding bikes. Standing behind her, he'd give me a knowing smile, and his twinkling eyes would wink at me to "go on out and play." But he later took a step back and retreated into his work—my mother had finally gotten through to him. He left me in her hands and diverted his attention to Hamed, Assem, and Mourad. My mother kept insisting that it was shameful for a daughter to confide in her father about the things that bothered her, but I still wished he could be there for me more. I've always had a longing to talk to him in particular about what's going on with me beneath the surface. I've wanted him to know about my feelings. Him, not my mother. There is something in me that makes me sure my father would be more understanding. He knows more about life than she does. He's the one who has struggled; he's the one who life has crushed; he's the one who has met with countless types of people, and he's the only one who is educated. He studied accounting and got his diploma, unlike my mother who didn't even finish elementary school. But my wish still has not come true; he has kept his distance.

It is with great pain that I listen to my classmates talk about the attention their fathers lavish on them. I cannot reconcile the way they depict their fathers with the way I see my own: these fathers take summer trips outside of Saudi Arabia with their daughters, buying them whatever they want, sometimes even surprising them with gifts—a watch, a bottle of French perfume, a gold bracelet, or perhaps some money. If they get sick, their fathers are the ones to rush them to hospital... But as my father has aged, his changed image has cemented itself further, and I now realise how diametrically opposed it is to the images my classmates draw of their own fathers. At home, we've gotten used to hearing him complain about work, and he has made it abundantly clear that he can't stand hearing us complain about school. He barely even gives my mother space to air her concerns. He is bossy most of the time, and moody, too; he could have a frown on his face and then just as quickly shed that skin, a smile emerging from underneath. Just like a chameleon. He claims his arduous job is the reason behind his mercurial moods:

"Isn't it enough that I work myself to the bone for you? My whole life is for you. All I'm asking is that you succeed at school."

Like a broken record, this is all he ever says. And that's on the rare occasion that he does speak to us. He's said it so often we've memorised it word for word. Sometimes he'll switch up the actual words, but the gist is always the same: "You need to get the highest marks at school. I won't settle for you ranking any lower than first in your class." Not only because I'm in high school, but also because I'm the eldest of his children, he'll gesture at me with his index finger, saying, "You must have a high GPA. I want to see you among the top students in the Kingdom. I want to see your picture in the papers."

Then, subdued, he'll lower his voice a little and continue, "I've invested all my money, all my time, all my energy in your education. I only ask that you excel and go to top universities. I want you to become doctors and engineers, or to run companies. I've devoted my whole life to you. Don't let me down."

Or he'll say: "I don't want you to end up like me, living on the sympathy and satisfaction of others. I want you to be free. Your degrees will open doors for you anywhere in the world."

Then he looks me straight in the eye and holds my gaze. "I'm speaking to you especially, Alia," he says, his voice struggling to hold back emotion. "You in particular must excel and win a spot at university to then go work abroad. I don't want you working in Khobar. Not even in Riyadh or Yemen, or any country in the Gulf. I want you to travel outside the Arab world. There's no good to be found in these countries. We break our backs day and night, wasting our youth, and they treat us no better than they do migrant workers. I want to visit you one day in the United States, Canada, or New Zealand."

But my father knows how far-fetched that is. How am I supposed to accomplish what he wants? I'm just a Yemeni girl in Khobar, a Yemeni girl who isn't eligible for any scholarship to study outside the Kingdom. Even getting into a Saudi university takes connections and bribery! And if my father's connections fail to secure a Saudi government scholarship, then he—the self-described sincere and dedicated worker who toils relentlessly—doesn't actually have enough money to afford university fees in Saudi Arabia, even if I do manage to get in. A few of his Saudi friends have suggested that he apply for citizenship, vowing to stand by him and help him through the process, but he has categorically refused to even consider giving up his Yemeni nationality—"no matter the temptation." He's repeated this time and time again, to us and to anyone who suggests it: he will not do it, he will not renounce his origins and forget who he was and where he came from. He claims that Taiz was the birthplace of all Arabs, the "origin of all mankind. Adam (PBUH) descended on Jabal Sabir." Standing firmly against my mother's insistence that he apply for citizenship and settle in Khobar, he always argued, "How can you ask me, someone with my direct ancestry, to beg for citizenship from my own descendants? My ancestors, princes in their tribes, never sought other nationalities even though everyone used to beg them to."

"I will act no differently," he would add. Then, his voice a little louder, he'd proclaim, "I am Yemeni, and only Yemeni. My people are the origin. I will not allow myself to be anything else." Quoting a song about Yemen by

Abu Bakr Salem, he might then recite:

> *You are civilisation, you are the lighthouse,*
> *You are the origin, the detail,*
> *Soul and art.*
> *Tell me, who looks like you, who?*

Afterwards, he always cursed the British, the occupiers who forced him to leave Aden, once they discovered he was part of the Workers' Party. The Party opposed the occupation, and my father used to distribute flyers that helped to incite rebellion against the British. My mother believes that my father adamantly refuses to apply for citizenship because he is certain that the Ministry of Interior will reject his application, despite the influence his Saudi acquaintances might wield. These acquaintances, according to her, do not have any real influence to speak of.

"Daughters follow their husbands, Abu Hamed," my mother says, objecting to my father's encouragement to study and work outside of Saudi Arabia. "Only sons are supposed to travel and work abroad!"

But my father responds in a derisive tone, "Easy to say when you're sitting comfortably at home all day. I'm the one who has to endure all the insults and humiliation."

I've strayed too far from my point. What I mean to say is that I'm living in a state of violent confusion. I'm at a standstill, unable to find a solution, unable to extricate Moodi from my mind or my imagination. The few hours during which I can watch her from afar in the classroom are no longer enough of a remedy; they no longer sate the frenzied feelings I have for her. I'm consumed by my desire to spend time alone with her. Just her and me. I want to possess her; I want her to be mine and only mine. I want to hold her tight against my chest. This restless feeling courses through my veins, night and day, so fiercely that I swear if I were to find myself alone with her, I would kidnap her and hide her somewhere secret, unreachable. So all-consuming and merciless are these feelings that I've come to fear them. I'm terrified that they will overpower me and force me to expose what I'm trying so hard to hide. And if I cave in one day and act foolishly, I will have single-handedly destroyed myself. Fires will rage in our otherwise calm and quiet neighbourhood. The earth will shake under my feet. And my parents will have no choice but to sacrifice me to purge themselves of their shame. Either they'll bury me alive or they'll ship me off to Aden, where my uncles are, so I can be married off the very day of my arrival.

I have to mention, though, that these strange feelings have generated some sort of positivity in my life. They've motivated me to take better care of my appearance. I apply light kohl around my eyes even though I hate kohl. I've started perfuming myself just like Moodi does, using the few bottles my mother has on her vanity. I've also started looking more closely at my reflection in the mirror, examining the contours of my face and the smoothness of my skin to ensure I'm beautiful and always look my best.

"You're the most beautiful girl at school, and what's more, you're the most hardworking and intelligent! Men will compete for your hand in marriage, you'll see. Just wait till you're done with your education. You're a rose in a garden." My mother always says this with great confidence, and usually I respond with a smile, "Surely you're referring to my university education, and not school?"

She whips out her customary answer, "Had it not been for your father's stubbornness, you'd be married with kids by now!"

Despite how cruel that image feels, I burst into laughter.

In the room I share with my sisters, I've gotten used to staying up alone in bed while they drift off to sleep. My thoughts always wander first to Moodi, then to my ambiguous future. Somehow the spectre of Moodi makes its way back to me without any effort. Once it finally dissipates, I always vow—just as I vowed the previous night, and the night before that—to purge her from the recesses of my mind at dawn, to restrain myself from making my way any further down that bumpy, perilous road, scattered with jutting rocks, that leads to nothing but pain.

Moodi will leave anyway, I tell myself. She'll disappear into some man's arms, and my feelings will wilt and desiccate with her disappearance. "I'm going to marry my cousin who works at the Saudi embassy in Kuwait," she says, elated. "He's so impatient! I'm planning to travel there to live with him. My life hasn't even begun yet. It'll only start after high school!"

I have to forget about her. Today. Not tomorrow, not the day after. How I wish I were him, though... Lucky is the man who will get to gaze upon this beautiful princess, day and night.

I'll forget about Moodi and focus on my studies. I'll do everything in my power to graduate top of my secondary school class. Getting good marks will help me along my path to choosing either of the two majors I dream of—philosophy or geography.

But the firmness of my nocturnal decision meant nothing. I spotted Moodi at school, saw her sweet smile and the twinkle of her hazel eyes. She was standing nearby, but I kept my distance, having separated myself from the rest of the girls. She walked up to me of her own accord, and I couldn't help but admire her stature and the soft glow of her face. She asked me—no, she begged me—to tell her how I felt. "I know what you're thinking about," she said flirtatiously, coaxing me to reveal my secret and assuring me she'd take it to the grave. She jumped for joy and pranced around when I let it all out and revealed the depth of my attachment to her. Had her sister Bayyan not suddenly appeared to yank me out of my perfect daydream, I would have danced around with her. I would have held her close and wept on her lap.

***

On our fifth visit to the Shahama Medical Centre in two years, Dr Abdel Ghaffar had no choice but to order an x-ray. Before that, he had actively postponed such a procedure, claiming it was "too early for such a step." The nurse turned on the device, which passed over my body, and the doctor then examined the results against a back-lit white screen on the wall behind him. He grabbed the images and brought them closer to his face, raising them against the light of the neon ceiling lamps. After returning them to the screen once more, he stared a while longer, his brows furrowing as he squinted. He put his glasses on and repeated the whole scene from start to finish, but with glasses, as if he were on the verge of a breakthrough or trying to figure out something that kept eluding him. He ended all this by confirming to me and my anxiously expectant mother that everything inside my body was normal. There was nothing to worry about.

"How can this be normal, doctor? Have you ever heard of a girl who still hasn't gotten her period at this age?" my mother asked him.

He examined the x-rays against the back-lit screen again. This time, he peered over the top of his eyeglasses, his neck strained, cheeks drooping, and lips pursed almost in disgust. "The truth is, she's one of the very few patients whose period is so late," he muttered hesitantly, noticing the signs of worry on both our faces. He quickly smiled and started shifting his gaze between my face and my mother's as he more confidently asserted, "But medicine has progressed, and treatment is available now, Umm Alia. There is no problem that cannot be cured by medicine these days. There's no need for stress or fear."

My mother's face brightened up a bit, a hint of a smile almost breaking through. Still alert, she pleaded, "Help us, Doctor. May God grant you good health. Please help us, we will always be in your debt."

She urged him on, as my eyes darted back and forth between the two of them. I felt a tiny bit of hope and was hungry to hear more. But on some level, I also intuited that the doctor was only saying empty words to reassure us.

The treatment failed. It collided with my body's stubborn line of defence and ultimately lost the battle. I took those pills for six full months without interruption, as instructed. But the thing we were all waiting for never came. We went to see the doctor again at the beginning of the school year to tell him about this failure. We were surprised to see that he seemed to have been expecting it. He sat there, that hopeful smile plastered on his face once again, repeating the same words about the strides medicine had made: "There is no disease that doesn't have a cure."

He asked me to keep taking the hormones for another six months.

"But they haven't helped," I said, beyond certain that the treatment was bound to fail.

"Usually this is a year-long treatment. I prescribed it for only half the duration hoping that you wouldn't need the full course."

It failed once again, and my mother rushed back to see him, on the verge of exploding with rage. He tried to calm her down, the smile on his face bigger than ever. Purposely deepening his tone to sound fully confident, he asserted, "Then we shall try another hormone, a stronger one."

He got up from his chair and left the office to check whether the hormone was available at the Centre's pharmacy. He returned a few minutes later and, still smiling, looked my mother straight in the eye. "This hormone won't disappoint you or your daughter."

He nodded encouragingly, trying to urge us along after he was unexpectedly met with my complete silence and my mother's cold response. He was vigorously trying to elicit some hope and reassurance, sensing that any remnants of these emotions had withered away.

"If we were to give this hormone to any camel, it would menstruate immediately."

"But not all camels menstruate, doctor," my mother retorted. Flustered, he flashed her an embarrassed smile, mumbling, "Well, I meant a female camel."

My mother flashed her own smile in response, only hers was both sarcastic and angry. "And the hair on her face?" she grilled him, as certain as I was that my persistent condition was too complex for this doctor to handle. He didn't seem to know what he was doing.

He muttered defeatedly, "She'll lose it all." The smile that both my mother and I despised was still bright on his face.

We kept quiet for a few moments as he continued to nod, trying to reassure us that he had indeed gotten it right this time. Then, with a very loud voice that was meant to dispel any hint of agitation, he ventured, "Trust me. This time, you won't be disappointed. Allow me this opportunity, before..."

"Before what?" my mother interrupted harshly, "Could you be implying the possibility of failure, by any chance?"

He was caught off guard by the speed of her response and her snide tone. He pushed his chair back a bit and took off his glasses, setting them down on the desk. "Not at all, God willing, it won't fail. This hormone hasn't failed me yet. Just yesterday, it triggered the period of a girl nearly your daughter's age," he mumbled.

"And where does this girl live?"

"In Riyadh."

I had to take that hormone for three weeks without interruption. I closely monitored the changes it effected in my body. My breasts swelled, quite rapidly this time, so much so that my classmates noticed and started to mock me playfully.

"You've gotten married and we're the last to know, is that it?"

"Only married girls' breasts grow that fast."

Even Moodi asked me what my secret was. "I want what you're having," she said, openly admiring what she saw. "I want my breasts to be like yours." My heart skipped a beat, and I responded with a smile. The neighbourhood boys I used to play with kept following me with their eyes, staring at me as I got on the school bus in the morning and as I got off it in the afternoon. They too were surprised by the changes in my body, incredulous that I was the same person who had bested them with my football skills. I'd hear their comments from afar: "Why don't you play with us like you used to? You're the best player in the neighbourhood," one of them said, another adding, "I swear to God you're the best player in the whole Kingdom!" A third moaned, "We don't have a scorer on our team anymore! We really need a scorer!" And a fourth repeated once more, "I swear you're better than Maradona. I'd testify to that."

On the outside, I smiled at the compliments and the recognition of my skill. But on the inside, I was hurting. I had long wished that God had created me male. I would've been playing in the best clubs in the Kingdom by now, Ettifaq or al-Qadsiah, or why not even in one of the two leading clubs, al-Nasr or al-Hilal? And why couldn't I be the best player in the Kingdom? What do I lack? If I were a boy and a famous player, our family could get citizenship much more easily. Alas, this was not on the cards. So I never let those musings get the best of me. I was, after all, just a girl.

There were so many times I asked myself: Why aren't we given the chance to pick our gender before we're fully formed in the womb? But every time, I'd quickly return to my senses and ask God for forgiveness, fearing His wrath.

I need to be patient. My mother says it, my father says it, my sisters and the doctor say it. I even say it to myself. I will be patient about a lot of things. I will be patient about my strange condition that keeps raising more questions that cannot be answered, about these toxins otherwise known as hormones, about the periodic cramps I get. I will be patient, as I have no choice but to be patient and wait: to wait for the gloom that follows me everywhere to lift, to wait for my period to finally grace me with its arrival and emerge from the fortified walls of its castle. Then I will be a complete young woman, like all the others, with the same dreams and desires.

In the bathroom, I take off my clothes and feel my breasts, which have swelled and gotten rounder. Other parts of my body have also been affected by the hormones; my hips are wider, my arms and thighs are smoother, and even my voice has lost a good deal of its huskiness and is now closer to that of a girl. Most importantly, I lost the hair that had been growing on my face, just as the doctor had predicted. Everything he said would happen did, except for the ultimate thing—the start of menstruation. My period continued to stand its ground and refused to comply with or submit to the hormones. Not even one lone red drop deigned to trickle down to offer me the transient illusion of hope. I wore out my private parts by wearing sanitary pads every day, at my mother's recommendation, "so that what happened to your sister Suha doesn't happen to you. She suddenly got blood stains on her clothes and blood even dripped onto the kitchen floor while she was helping me carry dishes out to the table." I kept wearing those pads till my body rejected them: my skin became irritated and itchy for days.

***

The Moodi I see in my nighttime dreams is different from the real Moodi, or even the one I daydream about. And on this night in particular, she was even more different than usual. She looked beautiful and utterly serene. She walked into my room suddenly, without knocking or asking permission. I only noticed she was there when she sat down on the small sofa opposite my bed and started leafing through a textbook. At first, she didn't say a word. She just looked at me with that bewitching gaze of hers and only broke the spell with a wink. She was radiating freshness and beauty, and the air was thick with the scents of oud and incense—and, of course, the characteristic smell of her minty gum that caressed every last one of my brain cells.

I thought, *The beautiful Moodi is in my room*. I almost couldn't believe it! I sat up straight and, just like that, we were facing each other. Flirtatiously, she said to me, "I came to study with you." She was like an angel that had just appeared before me, and she had deliberately worn a sheer white robe that left little to the imagination. This seduction paired with her divine magic made me both braver and more hesitant. As I inched toward her, our knees touched, and she shifted back a little, a smile dancing on her face. My heart had reached the limits of what it could feel: it could be no happier and beat no faster. I pulled the textbook from her grasp and set it on the stool by the bed. I took her palms in mine and kissed the pearly white surface of her hands. She closed her eyes, giving in to the drug-like bliss that was washing over her. I stood up, and she followed my lead, her eyes still closed. We were facing one another. A distance no longer than the length of a ruler separated my body from hers. I moved even closer. She did the same. At that moment a fire erupted in my body, and I shuddered with violent desire. I held her and my fire pierced her body. I felt a tremor course through her, and she shuddered in my arms. I trailed kisses along her neck as I moved toward her lips with an insatiable lust and hunger. I used to laugh at my father when I'd see him doing the same thing with my mother on one of those Thursday nights, wondering what the rush was for, so long as there was plenty of time. And now here I was, doing the same thing with Moodi! It seems that lust leaves lovers no room for patience. Trying to calm myself down, I slowly followed the scent trail the oud had left on her, starting from right under her earlobes, moving to the base of her throat. The scent only got stronger the further down I moved from her throat toward her chest, and the unbridled desire raging within me only increased in urgency. I was just about to reach her breasts when my entire body shook and yanked me out of my dream; I was burning up with a real fever and a sharp, splitting headache. My body was drenched in a sea of sweat that had completely soaked my bed, and the sound of my breath was so loud and harsh in the darkness that I feared it would wake my sisters.

I looked at the alarm clock on the small stool beside me. It was 3:00 in the morning.

It wasn't the first time I'd had such a dream. But it was the first time I'd felt that fever, that headache, and those severe cramps in my lower abdomen.

Quickly, I got up and stumbled into the dark bathroom. I tried to catch my breath. I felt around between my legs. There was a warm, mucus-like fluid that had shot out from inside me. I had felt it ejaculate out from within me when my dream startled me back to reality. I switched on the lights and saw that the fluid was thick and white, and I wondered whether it was a sign that my period was about to come. Or maybe it was a sign of female lust, the one I'd heard my classmates talk about at school?

In any case, I did feel some happiness, despite the brutal cramps and headache. I thought they must all have been the side-effects of that "camel hormone."

In the morning, I told my mother what had happened. She didn't seem too impressed. Her face didn't light up as I'd expected—her reaction was limited to a curt smile and a cold response. "Good. But we have to wait for the blood. Other kinds of discharge in girls are not as important." Then, an hour later, the matter took on new levels of importance as she added, "Women have a lot of different types of fluids. I want you to tell me about everything you find."

The dream recurred a few nights later. But this time, the object of my desire was Haifa, the Yemeni girl who was in the science track with Bayyan. Haifa was beautiful and arrogant. Other students used to say that she walked around with "her nose in the air" because of how rich her father was. Once, she pretended not to know me, which made me really angry, because I knew her mother was aware that my mother had a rich family in Taiz. Her mother had even visited our house more than once, and the last time was less than a year ago! But I'd never once thought about Haifa, not that I can recall... not to mention that she never even came to me in my regular dreams, let alone this type of dream. I don't understand why she showed up. I don't think we've even spoken more than once—only that time she walked over to me in the school courtyard and said, "I've underestimated you, bint Jawaher, you're quiet but you're a dark horse."

She said it and just walked away. I didn't understand what she meant at the time. I thought maybe she had the wrong person, or maybe she'd heard some gossip about me. It wasn't so much her words that irritated me as her arrogance, that haughty look she shot me. But even though Haifa was spoilt, she excelled at school. Nothing ticked her off more than someone, anyone, getting better marks than her. She was clearly envious of all the other clever girls, regardless of whether she knew them or not. So I controlled my temper and didn't respond to her remark. The end of the school year would come soon enough, I told myself, and with it our report cards. She'd combust of her own accord when she saw my marks.

In the dream, I hugged her from behind and kissed her neck as she swayed in my arms. "You can take your revenge on me now," she said, pulling her wrist free from my grasp. I pulled her to me forcefully, and she moaned softly and provocatively as she fell against my chest. Her breasts grazed mine as she deliberately rubbed against me, igniting a blazing fire in my veins—a fire which, once again, violently shook me back to reality, the fluid seeping out from between my legs. I felt the same cramps and intense headache.

What is happening to me? Why doesn't the dream ever go past this point? Or do all such dreams end this way? And why Haifa, out of all the girls I see every day!? Where did she sprout from? I knew I had latent rage and frustration toward her—was this my subconscious taking its revenge? Or had my subconscious put her in the same category as the other beautiful, charming girls, stowing her safely away to be summoned at will?

Doubtless the hormone is changing something in my body. Ever since I started taking it, this desire for girls I've tried so hard to hide has increased exponentially. On more than one occasion I've found myself staring at the most attractive of them, only to conjure up their faces later before sleep takes me away. Then their spectres would appear in sheer, loose-fitting dresses, languidly approaching me, femininity and tenderness oozing from their pores, just waiting for me to take them.

What on earth is happening to me?

***

Once more, we made our way to the Shahama Medical Centre, as the medication—despite its potency—was unable to trigger my period. My mother's patience was wearing thin, and by then even my father had become party to the cycle of questions and anxiety. I finally underwent a laparoscopy, a procedure the doctor had long been hesitant to perform because he was worried it would break my hymen. It was not Dr Abdel Ghaffar, the endocrinologist, who performed the procedure, but some other Egyptian doctor whose name I don't remember. I saw him for the first time then, and never saw him again.

Dr Abdel Ghaffar asked us to wait two or three days for the results. I spent those days in a constant state of fear and anxiety. The situation weighed heavy on my heart, which kept beating so fast I feared it would explode. Leaving the operating theatre, I had a faint hope that the surgery would lead somewhere. But this hope was very quickly dashed when Dr Abdel Ghaffar was late to call and inform us of the results. I had a very bad feeling about this Abdel Ghaffar. Not once did I find comfort in his diagnosis or his words. He seemed to speak only to calm us down, never saying much else. For some reason, I felt that, had I been under another doctor's care, I'd be cured by now. He was less a doctor than a raven. All he brought was bad news.

The longer we waited for his call, the angrier I got. For the first three days, my anger steadily intensified. It then turned to rage during the next three days, as we waited for a call that never came. The phone finally rang on the evening of the ninth day. We had just sat down to dinner. My father got up from his seat and picked up the phone after plopping himself down on the nearby sofa. He hung up mere moments later. The words he had said to the doctor were short and concise: "Yes... go ahead... yes... correct... Subhan Allah..." The only complete sentence he said during that call was a question: "What do you advise me to do, Doctor?"

After he hung up, he didn't budge, he just sat there quietly. He was staring into nothingness, the wheels of his mind churning, trying to figure out what to tell us, or rather what to say and what to hide. He remained silent for a long time. I was bursting with anticipation; the wait was agonisingly long. His strange silence made me break out in a sweat. Sweat filled my armpits, seeping out onto my clothes.

I was broken by this scene even before I found out what the doctor had said. I knew it would be bad news. I could read it on my father's face, which moments ago had been visibly happier. It was a Thursday night, after all. But his face had fallen suddenly, as if all the blood had been drained from it.

It did not bode well. I was sure of that. I couldn't wait a second longer, so I got up and stood in front of him, maybe half a metre from where he was sitting. I was about to ask for the news when he beat me to it, his voice morose and broken.

"He advised me to get you treated outside of Saudi Arabia."

I trembled in alarm.

"Why? What exactly did the doctor say, Abu Hamed?" my mother asked, before I got the chance to react.

My father was quiet again. Although only seconds passed before he started talking, it felt much longer. My mother had also gotten up from the dinner table and was making her way toward us. My father realised how much tension his silence had produced, so he said very clearly, meaning for everyone to hear, "The doctor said that Alia can only get treated in Europe. He said London would be the best place for her to go. I am now thinking of what our next step should be."

My heart dropped. I felt very confused, worried that what was wrong with me was very dangerous, bigger than any of us had expected. My mother sensed my agitation, so she pushed my father to tell us *exactly* what the doctor had said.

"We need more details, Abu Hamed," she insisted.

He nodded and grumbled a bit, feeling cornered.

"There's no cause for concern. All he said was that he's never seen a case like hers before, and that he doesn't know what exactly is wrong or how to treat her. He told me that he's consulted fellow specialists in other hospitals in the Kingdom, but they weren't able to reach a diagnosis either. That's why he took so long to call us back."

He paused a little before turning and speaking directly to me: "But he said the sooner we get you treated, the better."

He sat back down at the dinner table, but he quickly realised that we had all lost our appetites. He continued to direct his words to me, trying to pull me out of a misery that everyone had sensed, even my youngest brother, Mourad. "Don't be afraid. He assured me that the treatment exists in London. 100%."

He looked deep into my eyes. It seemed he had intuited what was going on in my head. Reassuring me, he went on, "I will do the impossible to get you treated. Even if I have to sell everything I own."

None of this was helping to calm me or my mother down. We needed to hear the exact words the doctor had said. We both felt that my father was keeping something from us, so we packed ourselves up on Saturday morning and went to visit the damned doctor, unbeknownst to my father. But we didn't find him. In his office, we found instead a young female doctor we had never seen at the Centre before. She seemed to be new there. The moment she figured out who I was, she frowned, and her face turned surly. She pursed her lips and shook her head, visibly uncomfortable and angry to see me.

"But I need to know the details of what's wrong with me so I can look for the right treatment," I said, my temper rising. Her strange reaction had made me very angry, especially as it was the first time we'd ever met her.

"The doctor told your father everything you need to know."

"But it's my body. Not my father's. The doctor was supposed to speak to me directly, so that I could understand precisely what he meant when he said treatment only exists in London. What treatment is this exactly?"

She frowned even more deeply. She furrowed her brows and clenched her teeth before she leapt out of her chair and stepped out of the office. Standing there, she looked me dead in the face and pointed her index finger at me accusingly, teeth pressed together, "You know exactly what the doctor meant, and let me assure you that what you're looking for does not exist in our Muslim community that fears God and the punishment of Judgment Day. You'll only find what you're looking for in those other godforsaken countries. Go there. You'll find what you need. The treatment for your disease."

She stormed off down the hospital corridor, grumbling, "I seek forgiveness from God, the Most High, the Almighty. I seek forgiveness from Almighty God for every great sin. I seek refuge in the words of God from His anger and punishment, and from the evil of His servants."

My heart beat wildly. I was gripped by a sudden fear. I felt my knees go weak, my feet rooted in place. I tried to lean on the chair for support, but

I fell to the ground. The room was spinning and the ceiling had moved or tilted—or was I levitating? My mother and I stared at each other in shock, completely caught off guard by the convoluted, incomprehensible words we'd just heard. Not to mention the inexplicably cold way we'd been treated. What could her words mean? What was she accusing me of? Immediately, I thought of my feelings for Moodi. My feelings for other girls. And I understood that there was a connection between those feelings and the words she had spit at us.

I collected myself and regained my equilibrium, and I asked my mother to take me home.

"I'm not going anywhere until I understand what that arrogant woman meant."

"We'll ask the doctor again later."

My mother was absolutely intransigent as I tried to drag her out of the office by the wrist. I couldn't get out of there fast enough. I did not want to face that doctor again. My heart was beating faster than it ever had before. A cold fear washed over me. I was terrified that, if she came back and found us still there, she would share more details about my case or would rudely kick us out, asking the security guards to escort us outside.

"Come on, Mama, we'll just come back later. We need to take the high road. This doctor is new, she probably doesn't know much. We're better off coming back later, when Dr Abdel Ghaffar is here."

Somehow, I managed to hold back my tears, though they were threatening to spill out of my eyes at any second. I'd cry later, when I was alone. I'd rehash everything that terrible doctor said, and I'd cry over my rotten luck and cursed fate.

I came out of that experience with more questions. They constantly niggled at me as I searched, in vain, for answers. I kept hearing over and over those last words she'd said to me. I did end up crying. I cried hysterically. I stayed up all night going over what she'd said, trying to analyse the hidden meaning behind her words.

Let me assure you that what you're looking for does not exist in our Muslim community that fears God and the punishment of Judgment Day. You will only find what you're looking for in those other godforsaken countries.

Then I recalled her strange supplication. I didn't understand its purpose. How could she consider me a devil before hearing about the torture I suffer every day? Why did she erupt like a wild animal when we are not the enemy? Why did she speak to us so crudely? What was stopping her from treating us like human beings and calmly explaining whatever she was insinuating? Am I not a patient in search of a diagnosis? Isn't it her job to explain the details of the treatment? Isn't it my right, to hear it clearly and frankly? The right of any patient, no matter the disease? She must know that I had no part to play in who I am! I had no choice. Isn't in my power to change anything. This is how God wanted me, for a reason only He knows. Does she not realise that the God she sought refuge in from me is the very same God who created me this way?

***

I didn't sleep that night. I stayed up until morning. I prayed until dawn and begged God for forgiveness. My tears fell all through the night, and I couldn't shake the feeling that some dark injustice had befallen me. I was sure that Dr Abdel Ghaffar didn't have enough knowledge in his head to find the correct diagnosis for my case, if there was any knowledge in his head at all. I was sure that my doctor had found no other way out of his miserable failure than to cry London. And he'd kept claiming that he was the "first and foremost endocrinologist in the whole Kingdom of Saudi Arabia"!

The day after the doctor called, the way my father looked at me changed. His eyes were suddenly full of emotion.

"How do you feel?"

"Like a candle burning at both ends."

I was crushed, deeply frustrated. I felt it in my blood. The desperation was written on my face.

He asked me this more than three times that week. Every time, I gave him the same answer, and his response was always a variation on the same idea, with "London" as its foundation.

"Hang in there. Your outlook on life will change after you get treated in London, inshallah."

"You're wrong. As soon as you get to London, you'll change your mind."

"I'm certain that your real life will begin as soon as you arrive in London."

There is something wrong with me that no one has yet been able to define. A conundrum that has yet to be solved. Still, imagining my life in London managed to bring me some sort of happiness. Trying to find some relief, I convince myself that there is something still hidden between the lines of everything unfolding, some sort of mystery. The screenplay seems to have been written for my eyes only, and because of it, I now have a new purpose in life, something to live for. This "London" I've heard so much about in such a short period has become my lifeline. I will be done with high school in less than five months, and then my father and I will fly to that mighty city everyone keeps talking about. The city of fog, the city of dreams—there is a secret wisdom, and only my Creator knows its purpose.

I carried my teapot and a tape recorder and went up to the roof. It was a cold night in February, with a full moon, when I decided to change my view of things and convince myself that everything I was going through was intended to help me, do me good. Only good things awaited me. The air was fresh, and a cool breeze softly tickled my face. I turned on the tape recorder to Abdel Basit Abdel Samad reciting Surat al-Baqarah. I sat there, listening closely, waiting for the noble verse:

Perhaps you hate a thing and it is good for you; and perhaps you love a thing and it is bad for you. And Allah knows, while you know not.

I breathed in and thanked God profusely for everything. Then I returned to my room.

That night, I slept more deeply than I had in years.

Bayyan

I couldn't help but notice the way Alia always looked at my little sister Moodi. Nor was I able to suppress my concerns about this, which inevitably seeped into a conversation with my parents. My father often talked at length about his fear of the deviance that seemed to be sweeping through the country's youth—its boys and girls. "Since the dawn of creation, all societies have been made up of normal and abnormal people," my father would say. "Some people are mixed up, and their feelings lead them astray, down a sinful path. This is especially true for families in which the parents are too distracted to closely follow the changes their children undergo as they grow older. In such cases, the parents fail to provide their children with the advice and guidance they need in the sensitive period of adolescence. So sometimes we hear about a boy who's been raped or girls who've been found secretly sinning together in the school bathrooms."

Like so many others in our country, my father had gone to university in the United States and learned a great deal about those dangerous relationships. He asked Moodi and me to be wary of behaviour like Alia's. So as soon as I noticed the way Alia looked at Moodi, I urged her to steer clear of the lesbian danger that Alia embodied. Two years earlier, Alia wasn't like that, but once she hit puberty, the change was undeniable. I just don't get how a girl could think about another girl that way. For the life of me, I can't grasp how a girl could desire someone like herself. What's more, I cannot fathom how such relationships could possibly lead to physical pleasure. I'm repulsed by the mere thought of two naked girls looking at each other, let alone lying together or locking lips! A disturbing sight indeed...

Even Moodi sensed a change in the way her classmate was looking at her. Her suspicions were confirmed when Alia started lining her eyes with kohl and wearing lip gloss. She'd started putting more care into choosing her clothes and perfumes. Before that, Alia had been completely oblivious to this type of thing. So Moodi decided to hang out with Alia only in a group, claiming she didn't care for the company of girls who try so hard.

Even my mother was afraid for Moodi. Feminine, seductive, flirty Moodi, who enjoyed spending hours looking at herself in the mirror. As she'd heard stories about homosexuality happening in schools and universities, my mother managed to convince my father to marry my little sister off right after high school. And thus Moodi was promised to our cousin, who was madly in love with her.

"Even if she makes it out of school unscathed by her female teachers and classmates, who's to say she'll be left alone at university?" My mother fed such ideas to my father, who was in fact even more worried about Moodi than she was. Bold, flashy Moodi: she cared only about being pretty.

"I completely agree. Besides, I don't think Moodi is too fussed about her studies."

But this fear I had of my sister's gay classmate haunted me even at university. I worried she would make advances on some other girl. And then, all of a sudden, after not having seen Alia for a year, there she was in the corridors of King Faisal University. A year earlier, I'd heard she'd enrolled at King Fahd University in Jeddah. Back then, I thanked God for that... but now here she was again, right in front of me. My heart sank and my pulse quickened.

She squealed in delight when she saw me. She had barely hugged me and kissed me on the cheek before she told me how glad she was to be back in Khobar, and how happy she was to see me.

I kept on monitoring her behaviour, trying to figure out whether she'd been cured of her disorder. When I asked her why she'd dropped her studies at King Fahd University, she said she'd suffered a lot because the Shi'a girls in Jeddah hadn't accepted her. They'd told her—or so she claimed—to go back to where she came from, where she'd grown up and where she'd "loved someone." I asked her more and more questions, there in the corridors of the university, but I couldn't figure it out.

Everything was revealed soon enough, though. Alia was unable to repress her shameful secret. I saw her brows furrow and her face turn gloomy when I deliberately described Moodi's wedding to her.

"Back at school, I used to think you really liked Moodi." My comment caught her off-guard. She faltered and was quiet for a few seconds, her cheeks flushed, her eyes quickly darting back and forth.

"Moodi is very likeable. All the girls used to like her, not just me," she said with painful consideration. Her voice broke, and I could hear her breath quicken.

Then I remembered what I'd heard about her quick divorce from her husband, Sharaf al-Awlaqi, and how every single person who'd told me about it fully blamed Alia and Alia alone for the divorce.

"He divorced her because he discovered she'd been fooling around," Haifa claimed. At the time, Haifa had been fully confident in her sources.

"What exactly are you implying?" I asked.

"She wasn't a virgin. There was a man in her life before she got married, and they fooled around. She got pregnant and had a secret abortion."

That story may have worked on others, but it most definitely did not convince me. I, for one, was certain that there was no way Alia had done that. Not the serious, disciplined Alia who never missed one noon prayer in all the years we'd been in school together. No, Alia would never dare commit that kind of sin. I was sure her divorce was related to her homosexuality, and that her poor husband found out about her condition too late.

"I hope Moodi is comfortable in her new life," she said, once she managed to pull herself together.

"She is. She says hello," I responded, starting to walk toward our car in the parking lot. My brother and our Indian driver were waiting for me there.

"Mashallah, is that your brother?"

I nodded.

"He looks just like Moodi."

May God heal you from this terrible affliction, I muttered to myself, waving goodbye.

I decided then that I would watch her every move and warn the poor girls who might get caught in her web. Alia possesses two basic qualities that could draw a lot of girls to her. One, she's smart and eloquent—all girls want a friend like that. Two, she has a pretty face, rosy cheeks, and an oddly husky voice, somewhere between a man's and a woman's. It draws people in.

My father, who had studied behavioural sciences, described Alia's situation: "The desire to experiment is ingrained in many of us. This means that the likelihood of people experimenting with homosexuality in a same-sex environment is high, even quite high, because there is no mingling between the sexes."

The story of her divorce only confirmed to my father and me that she did, indeed, suffer from this affliction. "She suffers from an acute case of homosexuality. If we lived somewhere else, I would have asked you to bring her to me so I could help her overcome this," my father said sorrowfully. "Based on everything I learned about cases like this when I was studying in the States, one is born either male or female. Anything else is invented out of people's own sicknesses and illusions. Never believe otherwise."

Is it rational to believe that God could have made creatures like her? When Allah created us, He made Adam male and Eve female. He didn't make anything in between. So where does someone like Alia, or others like her, come from? No, it's impossible that the Almighty God would have created people like this from birth. He is completely innocent—Alia and all the others choose to be the way they are. It stems from their own desires. If it were up to me, these people would be flogged, thrown in jail, and kept away from others so as not to spread their sickness any further. And if they continued to insist on being like this, they must be killed. Otherwise, God will have good justification for making the earth tremble beneath our feet with one loud blast as He did with the people of Lot (Q 38:15). Or for transforming us into despised apes as He did with the unbelievers (Q 2:65).

Jawaher

She emerged from my belly screaming so hysterically I couldn't believe it. They weren't the normal cries of a newborn, but intense wails, as if she were in extreme pain. She seemed unconvinced that she should leave the warm, dark protection of my womb and go out into the stark, bright world. I felt truly afraid for her as I snuggled her to my breast to nurse. She refused to calm down and wouldn't stop shrieking for many hours after she was born. She also rejected my right nipple and would only feed from the left.

It was a very difficult delivery, though all the women who'd gotten pregnant and given birth before me had reassured me that daughters were easier to deliver than sons. Of all my eight children, her birth was the most difficult. I hardly suffered at all during the birth of the four daughters who came after her, or my three sons after that. But while in labour with her, I saw death. I glimpsed the shadow of Azrael, the angel of death, hovering over my head. My heart pounded so violently I feared it might beat right out of my chest. She crowned for what felt like hours, and when I felt my resolve weakening, her head finally burst through the opening of my vagina, tearing it and the skin below. Dark red splotches spread across my face, I burst several blood vessels in my eyes, and my eyelids burnt like embers.

At the Shahama Medical Centre, the woman doctor pronounced, "Congratulations, it's a girl!" I wasn't very happy, and her father couldn't even feign a smile. "Thank God for everything." Abdel Rahman paused, then added, "Perhaps this is for the best... Whatever God grants us is for the best."

Because I'd been in so much pain during labour and the birth, and because it had lasted so long—from the dawn prayer until the delivery just before midnight—I was sure it would be a boy. In fact, I would have bet on it, after the many assurances I'd received that the most fool-proof sign that your baby would be a boy was the severity of labour pains. I could tell Abdel Rahman was pleased to see me in pain like this because he was also convinced that I had a boy inside me. He was impatient to greet his first child who would be his eldest—the son who would carry his name and be the 'crown prince.' When this child came into the world, he would have rightly earned his nickname, Abu Hamed.

But this was not God's will. Abdel Rahman was broken and hopeless. He experienced sharp chest pains, which radiated up to his head and gave him a terrible headache. When he brought me back home five days after I'd given birth, he told me, "The next one better be a boy. I don't want to be an old man when my son is still in school." Four more daughters flowed through my womb, one after the other. Nuha came two years after Alia, and Suha came a year later. Then Anoud a year after that. Shazza came two years later, before the female side of my ovaries dried up and three boys emerged in the next four years—Hamed, Assem, and Mourad! Eight children in ten years... just a decade passed between Alia and Mourad, the last of the lot!

When Alia was about seven years old, I noticed that she always migrated towards boys' toys. She didn't care about pretty, frilly dolls like other girls. She never once was interested in pink things, which other little girls her age couldn't resist. I watched joy spread across her face when she played with toy guns and cars, or any other boys' games for that matter. She'd go outside next to our house and be swept up by the neighbours' kids, spending her whole day playing with them. She often refused to wear girls' clothes. To see her, you'd never know she was any different than the boys. She would come back home in the evening, at the time of sunset prayers, curl her little body up in my lap and fall asleep. Unlike my other girls when they were little, Alia didn't spend much time on her father's lap. She preferred mine. When I expressed my concerns to her father, about how she played with boys, he calmly replied that there weren't any girls her age in the neighbourhood to play with. She was still an innocent child and had nothing to fear from playing with little boys. I used to feel sometimes that he saw her as his eldest son, and so he didn't mind seeing her play with those boys. At that point, I had not yet given him a male child who would bring him joy and distract him, so I felt I couldn't exert any more pressure on him to respond to my concerns.

Once, I visited her nursery for a parent-teacher meeting. Abdel Rahman couldn't be there because there were only female teachers and men were not permitted. One of them confirmed that my daughter didn't have the same nature as other girls—she was different. I was not at all shocked or surprised to hear this. I had discovered it before she had. A couple of years later, when Alia was in grade two, her Arabic and Islamic Studies teacher informed me that she was excessively attached to her, to the point that she always wanted to go home with her after school.

When I'm alone, my thoughts run away from me and I wonder if my own original desire to have a boy first somehow seeped into my daughter's blood and contaminated her with male hormones. Is what I'm seeing now the result of this desire?

Even as Alia matured, she still looked like a boy. Her breasts never developed, her waist didn't grow round, and she didn't start her period, even as she approached fifteen. The worst part was that she continued to act like a boy. I grew increasingly anxious. So that I could discover the truth and find some way to help speed up the process of becoming a woman, I begged my husband to allow Alia and me to go to the Shahama Medical Centre, even if only once. He rejected my first request, and also the second, asserting that everything was normal and that Alia was still a little girl. Six months later, he finally relented, after my pressing, urging, and insisting that our daughter's condition couldn't possibly be normal. But then the Sudanese endocrinologist we saw reassured us, confidently saying that Alia's condition was not unique—she was "not the first one like this who I've encountered in my long professional career".

I pressed him to elaborate further. "At what point am I supposed to worry, then?"

"Not until she turns sixteen, maybe even seventeen."

"Girls normally hit puberty before fifteen, so why is she different?" I asked, unconvinced.

"All bodies are different. Look at your hand, not even your fingers are all the same size," he answered calmly.

"Neither I, nor any woman in my family, has ever reached puberty so late," I retorted, undeterred. "Most women her age have already gotten pregnant."

"Previous generations ate only fresh and healthy foods—not like people these days."

Anxiety was visible on my face, but he simply repeated a different version of the same words he would resort to on all our visits. "Please don't worry, I'm the best endocrinologist in Saudi Arabia. I'm rated #1 in the Kingdom."

Even with his statements based on "scientific evidence," he was unable to convince me. And I was unable to persuade him to give us medicines—neither that time, nor the four subsequent times that we went to his office. But by our fifth visit, he had nothing left but to suggest a medical solution. We had run out of time and patience. Alia had reached her sixteenth birthday. He decided to give her oestrogen pills, for six months at first. "You won't need longer than that," he assured her. He was wrong. He added another six months after that, and it failed as well. She developed two tiny breasts the size of lemons and that was it.

At that point, I decided I had to try anything I could possibly think of myself—logical or not. I started off by making her wear the same underwear her sisters Nuha and Suha wore when they were menstruating. I even forced her to wear her sister's dirty underpants, soiled with her menstrual blood and smelling like rotten fish. Let the magic happen! *Maybe her womb will be impacted by the smell*, I thought, recalling female palm tree fruit that reproduced only when pollen reached it from nearby male stamens.

I made her drink herbs given to me by female relatives. I made sure her lower parts were exposed to the smoke given off by incense embers after I read out prayers and supplications. All of this failed. Alia submitted to my attempts, patient in the hope that one of them would work.

A year of oestrogen passed without any benefit worth mentioning. I decided to take her to the doctor once again. Alia objected, "He'll never be able to cure me." But I dragged her there by force, though like her I was sure that everything Abdel Ghaffar had to offer would fail. But I had no other option. At least not in Khobar.

We left Abdel Ghaffar with a different hormone this time, Clomid, which he called the "female camel hormone." He initially prescribed it for three weeks, and then another three weeks after that. His sole justification was, "your daughter's condition requires it." Even though it made her breasts develop into a mature young woman's, it failed to achieve its essential goal.

I was about to despair and accept this fate, at least until God decided that something should be done. Then one day it rained, heavily flooding the roads and the roofs of the dry concrete houses. I was sitting in the courtyard with my closest girlfriend, my neighbour Umm Mishari, watching the raindrops fall. A chilly drizzle was landing on our faces and revitalising us, when suddenly she had a crazy idea: "Marry her off, and her husband will help the blood flow from her."

Then she added jubilantly, like someone who'd stumbled upon a treasure, "Marriage will make the blood flow, trust me!"

I didn't reject her solution. One week later, after Alia had finished her exams, even before the results were announced, Sharaf al-Awlaqi and his family were at our house asking for her hand in marriage.

We certainly expected her to be upset. How could she not be? But then again, how could we have even broached this subject with her, when we already knew how she would react? Indeed, we saw a different Alia on the day we told her that we had agreed to the marriage and she was engaged. Intense anger was etched all over her face. She felt she'd been betrayed by the people closest to her. She wept with unprecedented intensity and protested what was happening. "How could this possibly happen without my knowledge or consent, when it's my life?"

When I suggested that her wedding be held in a month, her eyes burned incandescent red, like volcanoes threatening to erupt.

"You're talking about my wedding and I haven't agreed to get married."

"All of this is for your own good."

"I know what's good for me better than you do. I want to finish my studies. I don't want to get married right now."

"You can finish your studies after you're married. Sharaf is an educated man, he won't stop you."

"Mama, you know that I can't become someone's wife before I get treated and cured."

"Everything will change after you're married. Marriage will be your cure."

"I don't think so. That just isn't true."

"Actually, it is true. But in any case, it's the only way we can try to help you. Sometimes we hate the things that are good for us."

"Who told you that?"

"I'm your mother. I know the best way to cure you. All our neighbours say that marriage is the best treatment for someone with your condition."

"But I don't want to get married now. I'm not ready."

"After the first night, you'll change your mind. Trust me."

"I won't be what my husband expects. He won't find what he's looking for. My condition isn't normal. You have to understand that."

"Believe me, after the wedding night, everything will change. Then you'll thank me."

I kept insisting, but she just shook her head. She was still in a state of shock.

"What I need now is treatment, not marriage."

"Marriage is your treatment."

When she turned to her father for help, all she got from him was silence. His complicity in what she called a "conspiracy" provoked more of her anger. "You're trying to get rid of me and my problems," she said accusingly.

She called him out, reminding him, "You promised that you'd do everything in your power to get me treatment, even if you had to sell everything you owned. Aren't you the one who said that?"

He remained silent. She squirmed, and the veins in her hand swelled up. She continued to object, choked with sadness. "How can you expect me to travel to London, get citizenship, and live there, when you can't even keep your most basic promise?"

At the time, I knew nothing of this promise, but I connected it to the conversation with the woman doctor at the Shahama Medical Centre. I grew suspicious of what their words implied, as it seemed that they were hiding something from me. A secret. But, in the moment, I chose not to comment.

I told myself that no matter what this doctor had said, I couldn't really believe that my eldest daughter could be afflicted with what this stupid woman had insinuated. I couldn't even wrap my head around what she'd suggested. All I know and believe is that God created us male or female. That's it. He states this clearly in the Qur'an. This is how it is. It's not up for discussion.

Alia is a girl. There is nothing wrong with her. And I'll prove to the world, after her wedding night, that she is fully a woman and everything is fine.

I asked God's forgiveness for my unruly thoughts and for even daring to suspect such a thing about my daughter.

Abdel Rahman didn't answer our daughter's question. She stared at him, bleary-eyed, for a long time. Then she asked once again, "What about our agreement, Baba?"

His cold reply took her by surprise. "We've tried long enough. Sharaf is a capable young man, and he'll help you get treated if it's necessary. By marrying him now, you won't have to wait till you're done with your college education to get treated."

After this, she began to despair. She remained stone silent on the sofa, her thoughts churning. Not long after, she wiped away her tears, breathed in deeply and sighed like him, before nodding and shakily conceding, "Fine. If this is what you think and this is what you want for me, then invite Sharaf over to sit with me, so I can speak with him."

"After the marriage contract is signed."

"No, Mama. We do this before the marriage contract is signed or I run away from home."

I felt like this conversation might never end, and that I was starting to lose my grip on where it was leading. I knew I had to end it one way or another. I said as I was leaving, beckoning to Abdel Rahman to follow me: "We'll leave the decision to him, though it's not customary for the groom to see the bride before the wedding contract is signed."

I raised my voice a little and rebuked Abdel Rahman for his strange request, that she go to London and live there in order to get British citizenship.

"Why didn't you tell me about all this?"

"It doesn't matter now, Jawaher. I was trying to cheer her up back then."

"Are you hiding anything from me? What exactly did the doctor tell you?"

"I'm not hiding anything. I told you everything he said to me."

"Did he tell you our daughter was, God forbid, a lesbian? Tell me the truth, Abu Hamed."

"Are you out of your mind, Jawaher? What kind of doctor would say such a thing?"

"What about the woman doctor we saw?"

"You and she are both really off."

I wasn't really reassured by what he was saying. But I decided to take advantage of the opportunity and pressure him into signing the marriage contract the very next day, so that Sharaf would only be able to come to the house and talk to Alia after he was her lawfully wedded husband in the eyes of God and His Prophet.

Sharaf

When she sat down beside me that very first time, she was just as perfect as I'd hoped. She lived up to everything Umm Mishari had said about her. The mere description of her beauty had compelled me to agree to the engagement without even having seen her. I was drawn in by her rosy cheeks and full breasts.

"You seem like a sensible, educated man," she started, shyness creeping over her face in the form of a blush. I was taken by this gesture and by her reddish "tomato cheeks," as they'd been described to me. She really was the type of woman I'd always hoped I'd marry. This pleasant young woman—who would soon be the mother of my children—lacked nothing. Perhaps I might have hoped she'd been a little bit taller, but I realise that it is rare for beauty and stature to be commensurate in girls.

"You seem serious as well as sensible."

"There is something that I have to tell you. Please keep an open mind, I hope that you'll appreciate my candour."

"I'm all ears! You're legally my wife now, and I'm not like traditional men. I won't yell at you—I won't even raise my voice—as long as we speak to each other in the language of mutual understanding. I want you to be able to talk to me about anything."

"But what I'm about to say is no trivial matter. You must try to understand me and not rush to judgment too quickly."

I was caught off guard by this. I felt that I was up against something unfamiliar. This young woman sitting before me had broken with custom and asked to meet before the big day. She really must have something different to say. I sensed that my expectations might have been misplaced. She wasn't just going to ask me to let her finish her degree and put off having children until then, as girls these days are asking.

I smiled at her, nodding to encourage her to keep talking. With a half-smile firmly in place, I said, "Trust me, I'm a good listener."

"I've never wanted to get married."

This statement took me utterly by surprise. Two days before we completed the Qur'an reading ceremony that would seal our wedding contract, my mother confirmed that Alia was happily preparing for the big day. She'd heard it straight from Alia's own mother! What could have happened to make her change her mind overnight?

I figured that I should allay her fears. My instincts told me that she was like any young virgin girl, filled with fear of her wedding night.

"I know what's going through your mind right now, but you can rest assured that I am not one of those crazy guys who needs to show off their virility on their wedding night. Don't worry, we have all the time in the world—you and me—to decide when and where we do it."

She cut me off, waving her hands, "You're missing the point. Let me start again from the beginning. You should know, first of all, that I knew nothing about this marriage. They never asked my opinion. I wasn't even consulted.

I was shocked when I found out that the marriage contract had already been signed, I was legally someone's wife, and the Qur'an reading had sealed it."

Her words made me feel upset and empty. I faltered, not knowing how to respond or what to say. What *could* I say? This came totally out of the blue. I'd thought the most she might request was something along the lines of what my mother had said to brace for—to postpone consummating our marriage until she had begun her university studies, or, in the worst-case scenario, until she had finished the first year so that she could feel confident I wouldn't stand in the way of her education. But what I was hearing now was something completely unexpected, something strange.

She carried on, indifferent to my shock, as if she were trying to get it all out in one fell swoop.

"The truth is that I object to getting married on principle. I'm not rejecting you personally. I simply object to the idea of being married at this particular time."

"Is there someone else?"

The question practically jumped out of my mouth, perhaps triggered by the sudden rage that was boiling up inside me. I never even thought about how it would strike her. But my words seemed to have a murderous effect. Her face went bright red and clearly showed her anger. I wasn't sure, however, that she had the right to be angry with me, or if it were the other way round, after what I'd heard from her!

I thanked God that I'd managed to keep my cool, because I don't usually possess such fortitude or control. I reminded myself that I was in her father's house, and that it was my first time there as a guest. I trod carefully and chose patience over a rash and angry reaction. It seemed she had intuited what was going on in my mind. Her anger receded, and she feigned a kind of calm. Then suddenly she lifted her eyes to stare at me for a few seconds before lowering her gaze once again.

I sensed that the young woman before me was either challenged or was truly about to confide something significant. I thought it wise to wait a bit longer.

Calmly, slowly, she responded to what I'd said:

"God, no. I can assure you that there is no man in my life. Everything I have told you is true. I really have no desire whatsoever to marry. Let me be even more frank with you. I cannot bear the thought of marriage or even the thought of being bound to a man at all."

The novelty of what she was saying made me cackle involuntarily. What was going on? What was happening? I had to pinch myself to see if it were true. Was I actually hearing this from my now lawfully wedded wife, the woman whose virginity I had the right to take, the woman I could legally do anything to? Did she know that right now she was actually my wife? Was she aware of that? Did she realise that it's not even relevant for her to say that she can't bear the thought of marriage? What's done is done. Was this young woman sitting across from me in her right mind? Or had they found me someone completely insane?

I had to bring her back to reason. So I planted a fake smile on my face, even wider and happier than hers:

"I understand how you feel, my dear wife."

My words appeared only to anger her further. She wiped the false smile off her face and replaced it with a frown. She made no comment, staying silent, and I realised that I had roused her ire once again. But what was wrong with my polite words? I dare say they were even classy! Many people in our milieu would never have even thought to say them. Wasn't she legally my wife in the eyes of God, His Prophet, and our traditions? Didn't I legally marry her and accept all of her family's conditions? Including the one I was told she'd requested and insisted on: "not to prevent her from studying"? This condition was even written right into the marriage contract! She belonged to me now, even if she was unaware of this. Her father, who was her legal guardian, gave me her hand in marriage and signed the wedding contract on her behalf. He told me, verbatim, "I am marrying my daughter Alia to you, Sharaf, according to the laws of God, His Prophet, and Islamic customs." And I accepted her as my wife. There were dozens of witnesses. A few hours after the ceremony took place, my mother and the rest of the women brought her the dowry and many gifts, which cost me a fortune.

I carried on: "I see where you're coming from. You're still young. You're giving this way too much weight. All young women are destined to marry, either now or later, and all girls—or most of them, let's say—are frightened of the wedding night. I promise you that I will be as gentle with you as you want me to be."

She plastered that fake smile of hers back on her face. She shook her head. I understood this meant she was sorry that I refused to understand what she was saying. She leaned forward a bit and then sat up straight and stared right at me—her gaze more focused on me this time. Her face was resolute and her eyes were very beautiful and not at all small, as they had been described to me.

She murmured, "Thank you for that. But I want to be perfectly clear with you. I suffer from serious health problems and my body is not yet developed in a way that would make it ready for marriage."

I was so startled that I felt myself shudder violently. Her words made my skin crawl. This was much more serious than what I'd imagined. I could tell from her tone that all of this really had nothing to do with the pain of the wedding night.

Stunned and worried, I asked, "What do you mean?"

"I mean that up until now I have never once had a menstrual period. There is no evidence that I have a uterus like other women, and, as I told you, I do not feel the slightest attraction to or affection for men. Please try to understand what I'm saying. It goes far beyond what you're thinking at the moment."

Is this real or am I dreaming? What riddles is she telling me? How can a girl like this, who has just recently finished high school, say such things? How can she utter such words? How can she have this type of conversation, one that would be difficult even for someone many years her elder and with far more knowledge? Is she serious, or is this her way of testing me? Could she just be trying to get rid of me?

My anger flared up again, as I felt I had been much too tolerant. Was there more to the story that she was still hiding from me?

I caught a whiff of something rotten, some sort of trap. This was a real headache and had caught me off guard. Raising my voice, I asked, "Are you being honest with me or are you inventing excuses for some other reason you don't want to say?"

"Everything I've said is true."
But there must be some kind of secret in this. Surely she can't be telling me the whole truth.

"Have you found some kind of flaw that makes me unfit to be your husband?"

"Not at all. I've simply told you the truth."

"But I don't believe what you're telling me. You're trying to escape our marriage for reasons I don't understand."

The moment I said this, I thought about my mother and father and the huge efforts they'd made for this marriage. How could I go back to them with bad news when they were so happy? How could I tell them that my wife didn't want me as a husband? How could I tell them what I'd heard just now? I felt like I was in a surreal nightmare, one I was bound to wake up from soon.

I got hold of myself and once again clung to the notion that this was happening because of her fear of the wedding night; the girl was attached to her mother, father, sisters, and brothers, whom she would be leaving soon.

I was silent for a few minutes while the violent thumping in my chest slowly eased. I asked, "Be honest with me, please. I don't believe I've done anything wrong. If you had told me this before we were married, then it would be my fault. But we're now technically husband and wife, and we're supposed to celebrate our wedding in less than a month. What will I tell people?"

"I have been totally open and honest with you. I have nothing more to say. I'm asking you to understand my situation. I'm not yet fully a woman. I wish I were, but I'm not."

She went silent. Teardrops leaked from the corners of her eyes, dropping to the ground.

Things were starting to look really different. It didn't have anything to do with the wedding night. I left her like this for a couple of minutes. I was going to start off by asking what she wanted me to do, but she spoke again before I had the chance. "I'm begging you. I'm appealing to you as a good and enlightened man, to keep this a secret between us. My father is the only other person who knows."

Her words got me riled up again, after I'd only just calmed down. I went crazy, lost control of my temper, and roared at her, "He knew about this all along and still agreed to the marriage? So you're not honest, you're hiding secrets that you're too much of a coward to reveal! But I have my dignity and will not allow myself to be insulted by someone like you. I won't play games with you or bring myself down to your level."

I remained still and silent after that, my gaze darting between her and the furniture in the room around me. I inhaled and exhaled audibly, anger gripping my skull and making my whole head incandescent with rage. I asked myself the reason for this. What is happening? Why is this happening? A couple of days ago, I wasn't even thinking about marriage!

But my mother had begged me, "You're twenty-six years old—men your age are already married with children." I was the eldest child and the only boy in my family, with four sisters.

"I'm going to wait until after the girls get married."

"The girls will get married in good time. You getting married first will pave the way for their good fortune."

But I was only using my sisters as an excuse. What I really wanted was to return to the beautiful land of Shabwa in Yemen and get married there. But Umm Mishari came along saying, "I found you a lovely girl this time. Her origins are from amongst the best families from Taiz in Yemen. The girl is a beauty and her father is kind, educated, and works for Aramco. He was a senior employee at Black Cat Engineering and Construction in Aden, where he called the shots. Then he became a well-known fighter against British colonialism in Yemen, and his Saudi colleagues at Aramco here responded to his request for help. His children are all very bright and go to government schools. The girl's mother comes from the wealthy Bani Hammad family in Taiz."

"In fact, I wanted her for my own son, but unfortunately he is too young for her. I'm one million percent sure that someone is going to want to marry her soon, and I thought to myself that you should be first to meet her."

"She's a polite and obedient girl who doesn't leave the house except to go to school. She is observant—she fasts, she prays, and she knows the Qur'an. She works hard at home, and she knows how to sweep up, clean, cook, and serve without complaint."

"If you're planning to go back to Shabwa, this girl will make you proud and look good to your people there."

I was easily swayed by her words. It did not take her long to persuade me. Soon I was convinced of what a good person she was and my father dragged me right into the formal engagement process. Then, even more quickly, I found myself at the mosque, facing the muezzin who was reading the Fatiha for my marriage ceremony in front of a group of witnesses. In the blink of an eye, I'd renounced bachelorhood.

And now here I am asking myself—what is this comically painful soap opera I'm living in? It's turning my life upside down! Question marks are dancing around in my mind. I feel like I'm teetering on the brink of madness. I don't need this. I didn't go looking for it or seek it out. What's it all supposed to mean?

Anger raged through me as I sat there, faced with her cold-blooded silence. She'd said her piece. And I felt helpless and empty now that I'd said mine. I wondered what could be done in such a dire situation. My mind was dizzy with questions, spinning round and round.

I'm not the kind of person who would beat his wife. I don't like such scenes; I believe that you can deal with anything through conversation and goodwill. This is how I was raised, how I was taught to do things. There must be some basis for what Alia was saying, and most likely it was true. Or perhaps she couldn't say the whole truth. But in any case, she was rejecting the marriage completely.

I felt myself getting closer and closer to a full-blown eruption, but in the end I decided to try to regain my composure. *Don't hate something, lest it be good for you*, I thought. Then, in a final attempt to diffuse the room's heavily electrified atmosphere, I murmured, "The truth is that your lovely rosy face would make any man want you as a wife." I continued, affecting a thin smile, "But I would never force myself on someone, no matter how beautiful she was."

I got up from my seat and carried on, "If all you want is a divorce, I will leave you to live as you like. But I have to know if what you've told me is the whole truth or if there is anything else. I promise you I will keep this between the two of us."

She stood up. "This is the whole truth, with nothing left out. I'm prepared to take you to the Shahama Medical Centre with me. The doctor there can tell you all about my condition and the hormones that I have been taking for more than a year, that couldn't fix me."

"I'm not going to call you a liar—I'll take your word for it. But I blame your father for hiding something that he shouldn't have from my family and me. I don't understand why he did it. What exactly was he trying to accomplish?"

"I beg you not to put the blame on him. Perhaps he didn't believe what the doctor told him. Maybe my mother and Umm Mishari convinced him that getting married would solve the problem, because medications couldn't."

She appeared to be speaking sincerely. I left her in the room after handing her the wedding band that I had planned to slip on her finger in front of our families that night.

"I know you'll return the dowry you've received, but I am asking that you keep this ring as a remembrance. Even though I really detest the situation that you and your family have landed me in, I have to say that you are unlike any girl I've ever met. Your mind and spirit are worth more than theirs, and I hope that we might have a future together if you're cured one day."

Head bowed, she said, "Hundreds of girls wish for a man like you, and anyone who marries you will be lucky to have you. If one day I become a woman, I would be happy to be your wife."

We exchanged clipped smiles, and I remembered a piece of advice I'd recently read: "If the wind blows your tent down, know that fate intends you to build a palace instead." Perhaps there was a reason that God made things this way.

I gave her the ring and entrusted her with the responsibility of informing the crowd gathered outside what had happened. Subdued, we went out to join our families. I told my mother and father that I would wait for them in the car. Confused, they exchanged questioning looks. This was not the scenario they were expecting. My sisters and hers were all wearing their fanciest dresses. Balloons and rose petals were scattered on the ground, and there was a huge cake adorned by a single candle gracing the table, surrounded by bottles of mineral water and fizzy drinks.

I stood silently outside the door, trying to overhear what was happening. What I had loved about Alia was that strength, persistence, sharp intelligence, and clarity she possessed despite her young age. I'd loved everything about her, really—her eyes, her round face, the exquisite colour in her cheeks, and her slim body. She really had impressed me.

I heard her explain things to them in her calm, husky voice. Then I heard my mother's thunderous wail, "You all were the ones who asked my son to marry your daughter. You sent Umm Mishari to convince us to join them in marriage and link our families. How could you do this to good, Arab people of noble origins? It seems you have no shame and don't care about what will befall you!"

She was right, no doubt. My mother cannot be blamed for having said this. But neither is Alia to blame. She too was deceived, just as my father and I had been.

My mother left cursing the day she'd agreed to this marriage, and even the very day she'd met Umm Mishari. As she was climbing into the car, she shot Alia a look full of intense rage, and roared, "God restrains only the monstrous!"

Abdel Rahman

"There is no honour in living outside the homeland, however difficult life in the homeland may be." *--Yemeni poem*

All the unwanted things happening to me are not the result of fate or misfortune, as my colleagues are wont to believe. No, they are the inevitable consequence of the way I shamefully abandoned my country when it needed me most. I left when I should have stayed, fought for my land, and defied the colonisers. This, I will never forget. I'm neither stupid nor cowardly enough to lie to myself about it. By fleeing the way I did, I destroyed everything that was beautiful in my struggle against colonialism and the English occupation of Aden. At least I'm brave enough to admit it.

The only reason my daughter Alia was born with gender dysphoria, as the doctors call it, is because God is punishing me for my grave and unforgivable mistake. I'd agreed to meet with the doctor following Friday prayers the day after this diagnosis. He told me things then that I never wanted to hear. For the life of me, I never thought such a thing could afflict any of my children:

"Your daughter is neither female nor male. Someone like her can't survive here. Nobody knows how to deal with her condition. If she were my daughter, I'd take her to London, where she might have better chances. You'll be able to seek treatment for her there."

I immediately understood what he was implying. He'd described her as having gender dysphoria in an attempt to skirt the issue of her abnormality.

There is no one in the history of my entire family who was born that way. I can't recall even one relative of mine telling me he'd had a homosexual child, let alone a freak!

I could swear that this was happening to me because I'd fled like a coward. No, my father was not the reason I left. I shouldn't believe the lies I tell myself. I shouldn't listen to the excuses I've tried to come up with to relieve my tormented, guilty conscience. They won't bring me comfort, no matter how hard I try. I'm nothing but a cowardly deserter, a traitor with no honour to his name. If only I could turn back time. But the dial doesn't work that way... *"Let's go back to the way things were... Let's go back in time."*

Those who truly believe in their cause don't give it up out of fear of captivity and torture. They don't run, even if they are staring death right in the face. No, they stand their ground: unafraid, unshakable. Omar Mukhtar, the Lion of the Desert, didn't back down, though he knew death was approaching. Neither the martyr Abboud nor the hero Qahtan al-Shaabi fled the battlefields in Saba' and Himyar. But me, I took off like only a humiliating coward would. I yielded to my father's warnings and threats too easily. I didn't stick to my principles. Can I even call them principles, when they were more like shifting sands, unstable beneath my feet?

"They've discovered what you've done. You need to leave right away. If they get their hands on you, they won't stop at killing you. They'll come after the whole family," my father said, his voice thick with reproach. He blamed me and my involvement with those people who rejected the British occupation.

He was furious that the British had raided his house in search of the revolutionary flyers that I'd been distributing. A vein was popping out of his forehead, and anger shot through his eyes as he continued, "The British have brought us nothing but good! They paved our roads, built our schools and our hospitals. They made us feel like actual human beings living in a civilised, organised, and beautiful country. Did Aden look anything like it does now? Were it not for the British, whom you and your fool friends are fighting, would Aden have become such a paradise? Do you want to return to a life of misery? Is that it? You didn't live through famine, deprivation, and untreatable diseases like we did."

"But they plunder our goods and control our livelihoods!"

"You're a fool, nothing but a fool! You tell preposterous lies!" he roared.

He grumbled and started pacing. As I looked at him, I noticed how heavy his body had become. The English had contributed to making his stomach so fat it drooped over his thighs.

"You thoughtless imbecile, where were all these resources before they came? Why didn't you and your stupid heroes discover them instead? Do you stand against them because they discovered all this bounty that you were too blind to see? Is this how you repay them for offering you a better lifestyle? By meeting kindness with abuse? Were you dropped on your head? Were it not for them, you wouldn't have these schools and the Queen Elizabeth Hospital. It treats us for free. Could you and your group of lunatics ever dream of building such a great hospital?"

"But they're infidels, occupiers, usurpers!" I yelled back.

He screamed at me, his whole face throbbing with rage, "We'd be better off ruled by infidels—even Jews—who provide us with all the necessities of life than living under people like you, you and your miserable Workers'

Party that knows nothing about life! You're nothing but a gang of savages who don't understand what's good for your country and what isn't. Would you and your group of fools have been able to make Aden this beautiful and organised? You live in a damned fantasy."

Then he shouted so loud, it wouldn't have been physically possible to raise his voice any louder. "I swear to God you're idiots. I can't even describe the level of your stupidity! I'm telling you—no, I'm swearing to you by God Almighty—had those riches you and those rascals keep talking about fallen right into your laps, you would've stolen them all. You and the likes of you... You would have stolen every last bit and left nothing for the people. I can see so clearly the type of country your lot would have governed. You stupid, errant children. Your country would have no schools, no hospitals. It would fester in sickness and disease. You accuse the English of plundering your country's riches, but just watch: you'll be the ones who plunder everything that's good, every last bit of it. At least the English left us enough to live a decent life. I thank God that we fell under the protection and guardian-ship of the British, as I'm sure a million others in the country do too. Most people are satisfied, so who are you to decide what our lives should be like? God save the Queen, and may He curse you all. I wish I'd never had such a foolish son."

He paused for a moment to catch his breath. Then his barrage resumed, "This is not the time for me to open your eyes to the mistakes you and your idiot friends are making. The military is already onto you. They showed up at my doorstep looking for you and those flyers of yours. I was the last to learn about your secret affairs. You hid this from me, you idiot, instead of telling me. You have never taken my advice. No... And I had to hear this from the British! You're a stain on my reputation, and you've embarrassed me in front of them. It's a good thing they trust me and took my word for it, otherwise they would've searched the house and found your stupid flyers. But you can't stay here any longer. Forget it! You either flee Yemen before they kill us all or you go to jail. I'll turn you in myself, leading them straight to your door. Let them do whatever they want to you. I'm not willing to lose the rest of my family for someone like you. Reckless... crazy..."

"Baba, I won't run away. What about my reputation in the Party?"

I said this in a final attempt to dissuade him from what he'd set his mind to. But I already knew I had to leave. After what he'd said, even I was convinced.

He waved me off: "God curse you and your party. I swear, if you don't leave, I'll kill you myself and deliver your stinking corpse to them. Then I'll tell them all about the people you work with. I'll have them make an example of you and leave your dead bodies to rot in public. Who do you think you are to make us drown in your dream, you deluded fools?"

This effectively ended our conversation.

I gave in, and he managed to procure me a passport the next day. How he did that in one day when the process usually takes no less than a month, I have no idea. Nor do I know how I left unnoticed through the British-occupied port of Aden. The mystery remains unsolved... My father must have had tremendous influence among the British. More than I ever imagined.

The ship sailed to Bahrain that day, and from there I reached Khobar.

This is all simply the price I have had to pay for such a spineless surrender. I did not *have* to yield to my father's words. Sacrificing my soul and dying a martyr in my own land would have been infinitely more honourable than fleeing and living the incomplete and humiliating life I lead now.

What did I gain by running away? Look at me now—I'm caught between a rock and a hard place: on the one hand, the Americans have monopolised the oil wells; on the other, the local bosses treat us no better than unskilled labourers. They despise me, belittle me, and fuel my sorrow and regret.

God must be punishing me. I committed a disgraceful act—just thinking about it makes the sweat drip from my brow. Why else would He bless me with not two, not three, but four daughters, born one after the other, once we'd had Alia? When Nuha was born after Alia, it became clear that I would continue to pay for my grievous sin for as long as I lived. Disloyalty to one's homeland is one of those great betrayals that God does not forgive. It's as bad as doubting the existence of the one true God. Then, when Suha came, and after her Anoud and Shazza, I knew for certain that there was even greater punishment lying in wait for me in the years to come.

But God did not want me to pay the price for that mistake alone. Or maybe He did not want me to be tormented over one source of guilt. He preferred to have me carry the weight of another additional sin, and so there was Alia... Alia, in all her ambiguity. With Alia, my guilt is twofold: her condition and how I've dealt with it. This guilt will sit, perched on my shoulder like a heavy burden until the day I die. It may even go with me to the grave, until the Day when all shall be raised from the dead (Q 7:14).

Poor thing, Alia, paying the price for a mistake she had no hand in. This happened through no fault of hers. Alia did not choose the cards she was dealt; my bad choices are to blame. I see her in pain, suffering every day, and I am unable to do anything for her. This guilt I live with is far worse than the pain of betrayal.

My wife, too, has paid the price. Oh, my Jawaher, she certainly deserved a better life. She has unwittingly been made to share the pain I've caused. Why else would the daughter of one of the most important merchants of Taiz live such a humiliating life with me? Did her parents give her away as a sacrifice because they feared my father? Could they not have refused his request, knowing that he'd crossed over to the British? Did he threaten them the same way he threatened me, making them submit to his will?

Jawaher is from the village of Tuba, in the al-Hajariyya region of Dhabhan. She is part of the famous Bani Hammad family, known all throughout Aden. She shouldn't have been dragged through the mud like this, when her father owns enough land and real estate for her to live like a queen. I was the one who sealed her fate. Before me, she lived with honour, like royalty, dozens of servants flocking around at her beck and call. They did the washing, cooking, and cleaning—she never had to lift a finger. She and her family had a fleet of luxurious cars, heavy red velvet curtains obscuring the view of passers-by. No doubt it was my father who forced her father to settle for me—penniless me, with nothing to my name but my reputation. And even that I renounced by fleeing so shamefully. My father was tough, a colossal man, dictatorial in both thought and action, though he came from meagre beginnings. He used to claim that his only service to the British was to produce the sheets used to bake French-style baguettes. But he didn't fool me. I have no doubt that he was an informant, which explains why everyone was so afraid of him—even important merchants and tribal elders.

When the occupiers came, my father forgot—or pretended to have for-gotten—the person he once was. He blended in with them fully. He left behind the master fisher and carpenter, the man who hailed from the beau-tiful island of Mayyun, which rests lazily on the coast of the Red Sea, close to Bab-el-Mandeb. The people of this area are known for their good nature. They spare no effort in helping others, and my father was at one point the most gallant and giving of them all. He refused a favour to no one; he was unsparingly generous and full of compassion. But all at once, abruptly, he shed this skin. The change in his character coincided with his move to Aden, and he later grew to hate any reminder of his past.

"I was a fool. I hadn't grasped the meaning of life," he would mutter.

Thanks to the British, he made his way up through the ranks of society. Fear forced his in-laws to let him marry Jawaher's older sister—and to promise Jawaher's hand to me, in my absence. They did not object when he shipped her off to me in Bahrain, no better than a common servant. He used a British boat to send her, just as he had done before, with me. When I laid eyes on her soft white skin, luminous and rosy, I held my father in a higher regard. I understood his strength, influence, and power. For Jawaher had the very features that were most attractive to Yemeni men—she could easily have been the wife of a prince, a wealthy businessman, or a minister at the very least. Instead, she became the wife of a poor, exiled man. She had married a coward and a fugitive.

"God save the Queen," he regularly proclaimed. He'd say it proudly, with all his might, repeating it over and over to every person who crossed his path. It was his magic spell, an utterance that opened closed doors, hearts, and minds. Only a select few could accompany the British on their ships and enter their private night clubs. He was one of them.

My father destroyed everything in my life. Had he not asked me to leave, I would now be a national hero in Yemen. When I was still there, I was no less worthy than the martyr Abboud or the hero Qahtan al-Shaabi. Had I stayed, I would have become a well-known leader everyone admired. People would have sung my praises night and day. But instead I have been sentenced to this cruel punishment of a life. Who knows! Had I stayed, I could have even been the first president of South Yemen instead of Qahtan!

I still don't know what my children's future will be. I don't know whether they will ever be able to return to live in Aden or Sanaa. I don't know what the coming days and years have in store for me. Neither Aden nor Sanaa stayed the same after the unification of the North and South: the situation got significantly worse in both. Yemen is no longer the beautiful country it once was, and dear Aden is no longer a paradise, the city of hopes and dreams. My father was right about some things... it was as if he were reading the pages of a history that had not yet unfolded. He knew his people better than anyone. The British left Aden by sea, and corruption waltzed in from the mountains. Northerners migrated south in droves with bags full of money, and they ate it up whole, this city that had freshly emerged from war. They put their stinking hands on everything. They extorted sheikhs and princes, forced and threatened people to sell their lands and property for peanuts. Jawaher's wealthy family thus became poor, as if they had never owned a thing. Her father died of grief, and her family was displaced between Hodeida, Hadhramaut, and Mahra. Those who agreed to the unification of Yemen were fools indeed! Unity only begat division. It resulted in ruin. If I were them, I would have built a wall between Sanaa and Aden so high that it touched the clouds. I would have cut off the head of every person trying to enter Aden from Sanaa.

I mourn God's chosen land, paradise on earth. I mourn what used to be a haven for lovers, I mourn its coast full of migrating birds and aching souls. Thousands of others mourn it with me. Aden is gone and shall never return. The life I lead may be cruel. I may feel a permanent sense of alienation. I may be treated badly by everyone around me... but my life is still better, much better, than life in Sanaa or Aden. On every level. Even if I were to return to Yemen, everything has now moved to Sanaa: the government, all services, and all the corruption you must engage in to lead a decent life.

I decided to leave my job and extract myself from the hell I was stagnating in. I wanted to reclaim myself, to forbid anyone from ever ordering me around or mocking me again. But on the day I made that decision, the winds blew against my sails, and the ship was destroyed. One final mistake was the last straw, the one that broke the camel's back. My "foolishness"—the very same foolishness my father kept warning me about all those years ago—was the crowning jewel:

"You're a fool and you will die a fool. What do you want other than to make a decent living?"

And:

"Money is what makes a man."

After I quit my job, I squandered all my savings on a commercial project that I worked on with my close friend in Khobar, Abu Turki. Together, we established a company that would supply oil companies with pipelines. I spent every penny I had buying as many pipelines as possible. This was at the beginning of 1986, at exactly the wrong time: oil prices fell after Saudi Arabia led the price war that hit the market hard, and the economies of many countries, near and far, collapsed. Aramco's production and activity dropped. I couldn't handle the loss. I wept, and I implored God to stop punishing me, to stop doling out this torture that had been etched into my fate. But His wrath was greater than I had imagined. A few days later, I fainted, and when I regained consciousness, I was in a room at the Shahama Medical Centre, my children all around me. The doctor said I had suffered a heart attack that weakened my heart muscle. He told me to stop any strenuous labour before my heart gave out completely.

I was fifty-one.

But we are our own worst enemies, as they say. I ended up selling all the pipes I'd bought by the middle of that year for a pittance ... and just one month later, oil prices rose again and activity returned to Aramco. I was destitute. Poorer than I had been when I first reached Khobar. It was then that I became certain that my misfortune would haunt me for the rest of my days.

Two years later, more specifically on the first of July 1988, Jawaher, the children, and I were at the airport, making our way back to Yemen. We were headed to Sanaa; we had no other choice. Sitting there on the plane with them, I implored God to grant me some good in exchange for this misery. I prayed that He restore my health so I could have the strength to provide for my children. They were still very young and needed me. I associated my separation from my homeland with the ongoing punishment cast upon my shoulders. Indeed, not one joyous thing had happened to me from the moment I set foot on the sands of Khobar. My decision to return to Yemen was meant to break the curse: I was going home, to where people looked and sounded like me.

Alia and Jawaher were sad to leave Khobar. They looked back on their life there as lovely and lacking for nothing. Still, they were also happy to head back to Yemen. Jawaher was finally leaving behind the toxic environment that still persecuted her and Alia for leaving Sharaf, even though almost four years had passed since that incident. Alia saw this as an opportunity that could get her closer to London. She even rejoiced that God had perhaps decided to help her along the right path by taking her to Sanaa.

"I will fly from Sanaa to London. Just wait and see," she said with confidence and an accusatory look. By then I was unable to look her straight in the face. Not after I'd disappointed her and conspired with her mother to marry her off to Sharaf.

"I know you were trying to find excuses not to keep the promise you made me," she said more than a month after her divorce.

"No, not at all," I replied weakly. I could guess her response. She didn't need to say it.

No one is cleverer or more observant than Alia. Her high marks are far from being the only testament to her intelligence. She has an incredible aptitude for debate, persuasion, and reasoning, for analysing things and hitting the nail straight on the head. Her statement, however short, contained a bare truth. She had divined my exact motive.

But I had already tried to redress the damage that had been done to our relationship... I wanted to make up for my promise once the pipeline project succeeded. I had dared to forget that I would be hunted down for the rest of my life by the very Creator who had vowed to see all my attempts fail. He also seemed to be intent on hindering any attempt I made to bridge the growing rift between Alia and me. Otherwise, I'd be rich now, and she and I would be together in London.

Jawaher, who was sitting beside me, heard me humming the lyrics of an Ayoub Tarish song. We were one hour away from landing in Aden, and I was mumbling, "You left your land and it's time to meet again... loyalty to the homeland is beckoning, heed the call."

She noticed the tears quietly rolling down my cheeks, patted my thigh, and whispered, "Such is Allah; He does what He wills" (Q 3:40).

Alia
Sanaa, Yemen

The Saudi plane we had boarded in Khobar touched down at the Sanaa International Airport at 4 p.m. on the first of July 1988. It was the first time my siblings and I had ever set foot in Sanaa. We inhaled the fresh air as we emerged from the airplane, happily looking around to take it all in. The air was relatively cooler, and much cleaner than in Khobar, where there were frequent summer sandstorms: the sand would whip against our faces as the scorching heat and extreme humidity weighed us down.

I smiled as I greeted the Yemeni guards inside the airport. They were all chewing qat; some of their mouths were so full of the plant that there was barely any room for their tongues to move. But they managed it so deftly that they were still always able to make themselves understood. This was inevitably accompanied by green spittle in the air, on nearby faces, and on the open passport pages before them.

One of these guards spat out a mound of qat and stored it in a plastic bag. This reminded me of that time we had visited Aden and my uncle had done the same exact thing: he clumped together everything in his mouth and stored it in a plastic bag, only to put it all back in his mouth once he had finished his prayers. To describe this habit as disgusting is an understatement. It makes my stomach turn, I break out in a sweat, and I feel I am about to be sick.

The Yemenis are a simple people. Everyone knows it. They are definitely not the brightest. Wherever we turn, people describe Yemenis in the same way: they're simple, they never feel like working, and they're very much inclined to spend hours talking and chewing qat together. They laugh at each other's bulging cheeks: "Had it not been for this mind-numbing qat, Yemen would now be one of the greatest countries in the world!"

"I agree with them on that. Had it not been for qat, we'd have already restored our former glory, our land of ancient civilisation and storied history. Look at the splendour of Mount an-Nabi Shu'ayb in Bani Matar... See how its peak grazes the skies! We would have had exceptional doctors and advanced hospitals capable of treating the most complex cases..."

"In the olden days, Yemen was the most important country. This is common knowledge. Yemen is the birthplace of all Arabs. They migrated only after the collapse of the Ma'rib Dam. This is found—no, etched—in every Arab history book, without exception. Yemenis were the first people in the Arabian Peninsula. Whether you like it or not, the populations of Mecca, Hejaz, Oman, Manama, and Basra all came from Yemen. Which of these countries, near or far, can compare to our ancient Yemeni civilisations? Yemen was home to the great ancient kingdoms of Sheba, Hadhramaut, Qataban, Ma'in, and Himyar. Its history is so rich, so deeply rooted, of such ancient origins—who else could live up to even a tenth of that? No one! No one but the faraway land of Iraq. But Yemen was not only a land of civilisations, culture, and knowledge. It not only gave rise to the first humans: leaders, scholars, sages, and prophets. No, Yemen also was—and still is—the birthplace of art and poetry, sung or otherwise. Artistic expression spread throughout the Arabian Peninsula from Yemen. Indeed, had there existed any objective, impartial account of that artistic journey, it would be widely known today that Yemen was the origin of all artistry that spread throughout the Arab world—including Egypt—and even beyond."

We'd heard it all before, but my father was tireless. He would go on and on about Yemen, each time with the same enthusiasm. It was no different when we were waiting for our baggage at the airport. He was so full of energy and glowing with such happiness that it seemed the world couldn't contain his joy. He was smiling at everyone, left and right, as if he knew them all personally.

But staying in Yemen and defending its history and civilisation, "contributing to the reconstruction of the land of your ancestors, the land of Queen Bilqis," as he put it, was the least of my concerns. My obsession, my utmost priority and desire, was to return as soon as possible to the airport we'd just left and fly from there to London.

I was not born here. I don't have the same passion for this country as my father. Yet even he would have preferred we be going to Aden, his hometown, instead of Sanaa. Had that been the case, his joy and excitement would have multiplied tenfold. "Had we been returning to Aden, it would have reinvigorated even my weakened heart muscles," he claimed boldly. Sanaa was not the city where he'd been raised, the city he loved. In fact, he'd declared his hatred of it on more than one occasion, considering it to be the cause of the devastation that befell "God's heaven on earth." For years, he cursed the unification of the two halves of Yemen, seeing it as the worst thing that could have happened to the simple, good-natured people of Aden, who were completely devoured by the people of Sanaa and their money, mischief, and hostility.

He couldn't blame us for not being attached to this land. We were, after all, seeing it for the first time. No memories bound us to it.

I am only here temporarily. I have yet to reach the land I will call my own. Indeed, I have yet to set eyes on it! I was born in Khobar. That was not my city. I am now in Sanaa, which is not my city either. From here I'll go to London, but I have yet to discover whether it will become my own, or if my search will continue. At this moment in my life, I don't have a place; I remain without one. Without...

All these fleeting preoccupations did not stop me from enjoying the sights I'd heard about and was now seeing in person for the first time. I was stirred by the image of girls not covered in black from head to toe, and I was thrilled to spot a woman who'd left some strands of her hair free to blow in the breeze. What made me even happier was seeing a number of women chatting with men outside the airport. Pleasant scenes of that sort continued to unfold as we crossed the street, passing a car driven by a woman. Nearby, another woman was selling food in a small kiosk. After seeing this, I had no doubt that life was much easier for girls in Sanaa than it was in Khobar.

The car took us to our new residence, which my father had rented in the upscale district of Hadda, popular among politicians and diplomats. He'd selected it with care, worried we would experience a lower standard of living than we'd had in Khobar. He chose this area so we wouldn't be close to Bab al-Yemen, that led to the Old City of Sanaa, where he claimed there was "chaos, dirt, and counterfeit and illicit goods, including qat." The cooler weather thrilled me. Sanaa sits on mountaintops that soar above sea level, and temperatures never go higher than 30 degrees Celsius on a summer day. They may even drop to half that at night! Not to mention that rain falls abundantly in the summer, especially in July and August, giving rise to rushing rivers.

But my fascination at these new things, at starting a new life, quickly wore off. Not even three weeks had passed when I felt the glow in my chest die out. It was more of a fleeting flash of light; it had never really shone. I became more and more nostalgic about my life back in Khobar. Wherever I looked, I was met with stark comparisons between what had been and what was. Without even meaning to, I complicated matters by comparing the past and present, here and there. I compared everything really, from the standard of services, to accessible transportation, to the cleanliness of public places.

There, the streets are neatly and carefully arranged, and their edges are paved with interlocking tiles. They're spotless and shiny clean, mostly free of potholes, and lined with lush trees. Streetlamps stay lit all throughout the night until dawn. But here... The streets are run-down and full of potholes. There's no such thing as hard shoulders or pavements. The sides of the roads are rough and uneven, with no trees in sight. And forget about lighting— even if you were to find some light, it would be too dim to be of any use! Over there, public parks are actually green. Here, the only indicator that some arid land is actually supposed to be green is a sign that reads "public park." And the piles of garbage on every corner don't help. Also on the list are hospitals. In Khobar, hospitals are clean, with organised entrance and exit points, while here, they are more akin to grocery stores or restaurants in a popular market.

Soon, my father's behaviour began to change. Before, he'd always made a habit of putting off his hunger until he got home, repeatedly assuring my mother that he "never craved any food, no matter how delicious, unless it came from her own hands." But he soon became like the rest of the Yemeni people and ate his lunch in restaurants, especially the famous Al-Shaibani in the centre of Sanaa. And afterwards, just like the rest of the population of Sanaa, he would head out with one or more of his lunch companions to chew qat. The first few weeks after our arrival, after his guests had left, he would tell us that his spirits had finally been lifted. He continually affirmed that nothing is so harmful to a good soul as being away from one's country and worrying about the future of one's children.

Soon enough, though, he started to notice that he was finding comfort in these bad habits. So he decided to take a step back from his corrupt friends. He was sure that qat was the one and only culprit in their corruption: it had ruined the Yemeni people, stood in the way of their service to God and country, and tainted their values, morals, and above all, their minds. One night, he caught me by surprise. "There is undoubtedly a cosmic conspiracy to marginalise the Yemeni people and make them less relevant than their neighbours. The Yemenis came first though," he claimed boldly. Then, more hopeful, he continued, "But history repeats itself, and Yemen will inevitably come to rule the Arab world once again."

That was not the first time my father had caught us off guard with rhetoric we'd never heard from him before. He seemed to be theorising and philosophising, taking on the role of the learned historian who knows all there is to know.

In Khobar, none of the Arab men who wore the ghutra and agal ever bothered us. Only school bus drivers, for example, would seize any opportunity to steal quick glances at the female students' bare hands, or notice the roundness of their breasts and bums. But here, where any man might hang the Yemeni janbiyya dagger around his waist, regardless of social rank, they all seem to examine the softer areas of our bodies quite intently, as if to make sure we are sufficiently round.

I used to ride to school in a comfortable, vast, and air-conditioned government school bus. It picked me up right from my doorstep and drove me all the way to school or university every morning, and then back home again at the end of the day. The drivers were usually South Asian. Throughout all my years of schooling, I don't remember any of them ever running even one minute behind schedule. Here, however, girls seem to have to walk a good ten minutes to reach a public pick-up spot where they catch one of those small tanks that takes them to their destinations. Barely six people can fit in there, and only if they are all extremely thin—otherwise the space becomes too tight. What's more, the Yemeni drivers always insist that passengers squeeze together. As we got to know the way of life in Sanaa, my sisters and I begged my father to get us a family car before the beginning of the academic year.

***

As September rolled in, so did the school year. I struggled to get the Sanaa University Geography Department to transfer my credits from the three years I'd spent at King Faisal University. Ultimately, I succeeded, but only after immense effort. I had to meet the President of the University, Dr Abu Bakr al-Maqlahi, as well as his Vice-President, Dr Abdel Aziz al-Raqbi, in person to convince them that I was there to complete my fourth and final year at university. The recommendation I'd gotten from the Head of Department and Faculty Dean had not done the trick. Here, the President and even his Vice-President needed to be kept up to date about every last little thing happening at the university.

"It seems that schooling in Saudi Arabia isn't that difficult to keep up with," al-Raqbi said sarcastically as he looked over the top marks that I'd earned in all my courses at King Faisal University.

"Rather, it is the people of Yemen who are smart and hardworking, Doctor. We don't settle for anything less than excellence. We honour our country wherever we go."

My response took him by surprise. He looked up at me, smiling, nodding his head in approval.

"Mashallah. Not only are you beautiful, but you're witty, too."

After that, he went on for more than half an hour about the time he'd

spent studying medicine, specifically surgery, in Britain, "at the most pres-
tigious universities, Edinburgh and Liverpool." He talked about his work
and research in Canada, too, which I'd actually heard about before meeting
him—it seemed he parroted the same words to everyone who walked into
his office.

I sat there listening to him, full of apprehension. A fellow student had
warned me about the Vice-President. "Be careful around al-Raqbi. He's
a predator. He's stalked women, and he can't resist a pretty face," she cau-
tioned. "As they say, he's got one eye out the window and one eye out the
door!" Had it not been for that warning, I would have begged him to help
me get to Liverpool, as he himself had done.

If he'd known, whilst giving me those dodgy looks, that I wasn't fully a
girl and that I hated men, he'd have kicked me out of the University and
probably even Sanaa!

When I left the faculty orientation party that was being held the day before the beginning of classes, I got caught in the pouring rain. I was ecstatic
as I ran, thrilled with the feeling of my wet clothes clinging to me. I was
wearing a garment that was traditional to Sanaa, called a zanna. It was red
with a black square print. On my head I wore an asba adorned with a resh,
and around my waist, a silver Hadhrami belt. I wanted to stand out with
my style.

I wasn't pleased with my clothes because they weren't very comfortable.
But it's the done thing. I wasn't too happy about the Faculty building, either; it blended in almost too well with the residential buildings around it.
But I was glad to get to know my fellow students and the professors in the
Geography Department. I also ended up getting what I wanted. Al-Raqbi
approved all my transferred credits from Khobar, and here I was, starting my
final year of university, brimming with determination and a drive to excel.

Even if I had to give up sleep for the entire year, I would do it.

Halfway to the parking lot, I decided to stop running and slowed down. I was transported by the joy I felt at being soaked by the downpour. Had it not been for my father, who was waiting for me in the car close to the Faculty of Arts building, I would have stood under the cool rain all day. This is the one thing Sanaa has on Khobar: its unique weather.

***

One of the things I had set my mind to—other than getting to London as quickly as possible—was switching off the stubborn feelings of love and lust that surfaced, and very quickly spiralled out of control, whenever I encountered a beautiful young woman. And there had been many. But I'd been stung by these feelings before. So I resolved to deny them and never again let my heart get the better of me, no matter how beautiful the girl. Alas, I failed. My heart rebelled against my orders and refused to submit to my will. Now here I was again, getting caught in the web—too easily, I admit. Arwa came out of nowhere. Arwa with the soft, sun-kissed skin, her eyes a deep hazel like Yemeni Doan honey. She appeared in my life with no warning as we started the third week of classes.

She was sitting near me; we were only two seats apart. I was drawn to her by a strong, invisible force, against which I was powerless.

I was so taken by her that I couldn't stop staring. She noticed, but nonchalantly tried to ignore my stare, though it was so intent that I did catch her eye. It's possible that this made her uncomfortable, yet she still deliberately sat next to me the following week. We were both taking the same electives, Archaeology and Contemporary European History, as a part of our degree programs. I'd already figured out that she was studying toward a degree in

Arabic language and literature.

She smiled as she greeted me, "As-salaamu alaykum," and I felt my heart soar. It was beating so loudly I feared she might hear it.

"Wa alaykum as-salaam," I breathlessly greeted her in return. Shy and confused, I withdrew into myself. I broke out in a sweat—my body's typical reaction to such situations.

"Hello, Alia. That's your name, right?" She had a lovely voice. It made my whole body tremble.

"Hello. Yes, that's my name," I answered, still tentative.

"You seem different. You're not like the other girls."

I was startled by her comment. I really didn't want to have that kind of conversation so soon. Especially not with her. Right on cue, my heart started pounding with even more force. And though I liked her a lot, I found myself hoping we wouldn't sit together or have another conversation for the rest of the school year. After all, I would graduate in less than nine months. As would she and the other girls. Each of us would go her own way, exactly as had happened with Moodi. All I'd be left with was a memory of her that would disintegrate and disappear soon enough. But none of this was possible now. My staring had betrayed me, and in trying to ignore the pretty girls around me, I'd wound up with the most beautiful of them all. Here she was, casually lingering in my thoughts.

"Different? Different how?" I couldn't come up with a better retort.

"We all know you're a hardworking and diligent student. You're clearly determined to get the highest marks in your classes. All the girls have been saying such good things about you, about how you're the perfect student."

She paused for a moment, and then continued, "But we're all wondering if you have a life outside of university."

I smiled inwardly as my heart continued its wild pounding. Funny how when I tried to get closer to Moodi, she kept her distance. Now that I was trying to keep my distance from Arwa, here she was, trying to get closer to me. In the turmoil of that moment, I couldn't think of the right thing to say. I struggled to find words, but as soon as any appeared, they fell right back to where they'd come from. Arwa noticed my hesitation. Worried she'd overstepped, she apologised, "I'm sorry, I didn't mean to put you on the spot. Perhaps I was too blunt?"

She extended her hand to shake mine. It was a bold move, especially in that moment. But I quickly realised that I had gotten things mixed up in my head. I was only her classmate, after all! Why would I even think any of this was out of the ordinary? Where was this coming from? Trembling, I was suddenly overcome with the troubling sensation of having to discern which parts of my life were real and which were merely figments of my imagination. Why would my first thought be that Arwa was like me? Or that she'd appeared in my life to play the role of Alia to my Moodi?

I internally mocked myself for the absurdity of that image. Arwa could never be Alia. Nothing suggested it. Her voice was like birdsong, her skin clear and smooth, no stubble in sight.

"I'm Arwa Elias from Sanaa, originally from Taiz. What about you?"

"Alia Ilwan, also originally from Taiz, but I've only ever lived in Khobar, Saudi Arabia." I stretched out my hand, confused. Had she noticed how flustered I was? Did she notice the sweat on my palm?

"Nice to meet you. You're one of those emigrants, then."

She smiled faintly. I was trying to collect myself so I could face her and return the smile. "Emigrants!?" I asked, incredulous. "That's one of those words I barely understand. What do people mean by it? Who even made up such a thing?" My voice was gradually returning to me.

"Everyone says it. They use it to mean people who lived in Saudi Arabia and then came back to Yemen."

"But something in the way they say it makes me feel that it carries a hint of contempt for people who went to Saudi Arabia and returned."

Now it was her turn to stutter. She was caught off guard by my response. She could very well never have considered that the word carried any meaning other than the obvious one... So why did this rouse such a strong reaction in me? She quickly apologised, saying she didn't realise that the term insinuated anything.

"And what insinuations would you be making?" I asked, my tone serious, as if this conversation really were getting to me. I was caught in a sort of grey area between hope and certainty: hope that the way I spoke would be attractive to her, and certainty that she would hate me because of my abrasive attitude and never speak to me again. My heart sided with hope. My mind, with certainty.

Had I really become so malicious? Had I learned the ways of Moodi?

"Emigration... living abroad."

"No, that's not it. Would you call someone coming from Kuwait or Iraq an emigrant, too?"

She shook her head, shock and admiration spilling all over her face. "Mashallah, you're right. I never noticed that."

"So it's a word that's used only for people coming from Saudi Arabia, as if the hatred that some people have for Saudi Arabia has been projected onto the Yemenis who live there. Keep in mind that it was often circumstance that forced us to leave in haste in the first place, before we were imprisoned or killed! We've become second-class, maybe even third-class citizens, unwelcome in our own country."

Her eyes flashed. Perhaps she'd figured out that I really was different, like she'd presumed. This made her scoot even closer to me. Had I known this was all there was to it, I'd have played the same card with Moodi long ago.

"Why are you taking Contemporary European History if you're studying Geography?" She knew everything about me, then.

"Geography and History are siblings—cousins, rather. And I have a personal interest in history. I actually didn't set out to study either of those things; my first choice was Philosophy. But this is how things worked out. I guess it's just fate."

"Why Philosophy? God, it's so boring." She said this with a laugh, revealing pearly white teeth with a slight gap between them that made her all the more beautiful. At this point, my heart rate had returned to normal.

"I don't know why exactly. I just remember that, one day, I stumbled on an old book by the philosopher Anis Mansour. I found his thought process really fascinating. Granted, there are a lot of parts I didn't understand, but it was quite deep, with multitudes of meaning. That made me want to be a philosopher. To write like Anis Mansour."

"So you've been smart and different since you were a kid!" she exclaimed admiringly.

Her compliment made my heart race once again. "Why are *you* taking Contemporary European History, then, since you study Arabic?" I asked in return. Laughing, she retorted, "And how do you know I study Arabic?" She'd caught me. That's a slip I could never forgive myself for. With that, she must have noticed how interested I was in her. "Even my own father asks me that," she murmured. "I'm taking it because I want to know more about European history. I want to know why they've made so much progress while we're still here, tethered to the earth." She let out a small chuckle, and I laughed along with her. Trying to gloss over my previous blunder, I added, "That's also a major reason why I'm taking this course." "Why haven't we spoken before?" she asked, perplexed. I had been about to ask her the same thing.

That was the very first time we'd spoken, but it was enough to make her schedule lunch with me in the cafeteria the following day. She talked about her life in Sanaa, and I told her about Khobar.

Arwa had a wonderful magic about her. All the girls would clamour for her attention, racing to sit next to her and engage her in conversation at lunch. Still, even the charm of her character couldn't compare to her jaw-dropping beauty. At least that's what I thought. She'd taken my breath away from the very first moment I saw her. From that moment on, my soul was tormented.

Arwa didn't have Moodi's big round eyes, but what hers held was unique—a charm so distinctive that looking into them whisked you far, far away. They emanated peace, transporting you to a quiet and beautiful place that's hard to describe. They plunged you into strange, unseen depths, where you'd wade around, tranquil and serene. There is a cool breeze there, in those clear pools, where clouds filter the rays of sun. There's the chirping of birds, a rushing river, and the chords of a distant guitar. The arches of her eyebrows were outlined with delicate precision and could draw you in entirely, such that you'd find yourself automatically praising God for the beauty of His creation. Her skin was rather bronzed, her cheeks and temples perpetually rosy—I could have sworn that she had the most beautiful, the smoothest skin I'd ever seen. Even her stature was perfect. Not too tall, not too short. Every single part of her appearance was a testament to the perfection of her beauty, which was only enhanced by her unmistakable intelligence.

Whether I liked it or not, Arwa lodged herself deep in my heart at lightning speed. She penetrated even its remotest corners and settled there, calling to the surface all the old feelings I'd buried. They emerged ablaze like a phoenix from the ashes, this time stronger than before. Mightier, wilder.

For a moment, this eruption of old feelings evoked the image of Moodi and brought about the inevitable comparison of old and new. Moodi, the seductive, pale, feminine girl with her frivolous mind and perpetual mint gum, and Arwa, the beautiful, slender, quick-witted and clever young woman. No, there's no room for comparison, I told myself. When I fell in love with Moodi, I didn't know any better.

With Arwa, I fell fast and hard. Her beauty was undeniable. I dare any young man at university not to notice her—anyone at all, really, even the lecturers, some of whom are old enough to be her grandfather. Still, I did try to resist my feelings for her. I fought against her invasion of my heart with all my might from the very beginning. I tried to come up with justifications and reasons to stay away from her, to keep myself from making the same mistake I'd committed in the past. I searched every corner of my being for any last trace of firmness, reasoning, or wisdom, but all of them had allied against me and crushed any remnants of resistance. In that moment—the moment my eyes met hers—my heart dissolved, like a sugar cube in water.

***

I still don't understand—nor will I, until the day I die—the divine wisdom by which Haifa appeared before us at that exact moment. Haifa: the very same coquettish schoolgirl from my past. Out of all the girls I'd known when I lived in Khobar, or even that year in Jeddah, Haifa was the one who showed up here, at the university in Sanaa.

It was a strange sight to behold; at first, I couldn't believe it. I thought it must be another one of those dreams I'd had about her. Here we were, freshly starting our third month of courses, and she was standing there, saying that she'd just arrived from Khobar, that her father had decided that life there was bland and flavourless. He, like so many others, had returned to Yemen to join in the reconstruction efforts.

"But your father works in oil, and here in Sanaa..." I trailed off. Her distinctive laugh interrupted me. Though it wasn't sarcastic, her characteristically haughty look arrived on cue as she said, "My father doesn't *just* work in oil. He has other businesses. He works in real estate as well, buying and selling houses and villas all over the world. Now he also owns a large hotel in central London, which brings in a lot of money." My pulse raced. London again. Did Haifa know about my dream? Did she drop that into our conversation on purpose?

Even stranger than Haifa's sudden appearance was the fact that she already knew Arwa. In fact, they were old friends, "childhood friends," as Arwa explained. They'd grown up and gone to school together until Haifa left Yemen.

I couldn't chalk this encounter up to mere coincidence. There was definitely another reason she'd shown up. Haifa was the only one here who knew about what had happened between Sharaf and me. In Khobar, though, everyone had heard the story—acquaintances and total strangers alike. It took on such proportions that it became the talk of the town, the story on every woman's tongue. They used to get together and gossip about me, ultimately distorting the facts, even accusing me of adultery: "Alia got pregnant out of wedlock and had an abortion. That's why she got divorced so quickly!"

Haifa's mother was one of the women who visited my mother back then, seeking to quench her curiosity and find out what had *really* happened, straight from the source. I'll never forget the day. My mother cried until dawn because of that woman. She wept with an intensity I had never seen in her before, her heart heavy with sorrow. She blamed me for the scandal I'd brought on the family and stood there burning with the shame of hearing her daughter being called a "harlot" who "went behind her parents' backs." It hurt to hear this, and the pain of having such rumours circulating about me brought tears to my eyes, too. I cried even more over the sight of my mother writhing around and wailing. I wished death would take me right then and there so I wouldn't have to witness her agony.

So Haifa is here to spread the story again, and Arwa will no doubt be the first to hear it.

It didn't take long for Haifa to show up at my doorstep. Her curiosity must have been too strong. She claimed she was there just to pay a visit to my mother. The weather was mild that day, and she asked if we could talk alone, far from prying eyes. We took two chairs and sat down in one of the corners of the courtyard. With some hesitation, she asked, "What's going on between you and Arwa?"

This came as no surprise. I was expecting her to ask me that, especially after she'd shot me those suspicious glances the day before. What surprised me was the way she'd worded the question.

"Excuse me?"

"Sorry, that came out wrong. I mean, are you two close friends?"

"No... just classmates," I responded calmly. But I hadn't convinced her, and I definitely hadn't satisfied her burning curiosity. What did she expect me to say?

"Why Arwa, out of all the other students?"

Appalled at her audacity, I snapped, "And why not Arwa? What do you expect two girls at university to be other than colleagues, anyway? And so what if we did become close friends, would you have a problem with that?"

She decided to switch gears and attack me from another angle. She left Arwa aside for a moment and, with a suspicious glint in her eyes, said, "I know you used to like Moodi. Bayyan told me everything."

"Did you and Bayyan think I was gay, by any chance, and now you're afraid for Arwa?"

She was startled by how quickly I'd responded, and also by my tone. Perhaps she thought she was talking to the old Alia from school. Did she expect I'd get flustered at the mention of Moodi? Even before she got to my house, I remembered the rude and ridiculous comment she'd made at school one day. *I've underestimated you, bint Jawaher. You're quiet but you're a dark horse.* I was sure she would bring up Moodi, just as I knew Sharaf's turn was soon to come. Still on the offensive, I continued, "Even if you've forgotten, you can be sure that I haven't, nor will I, forget what you said to me that day at school."

She didn't utter even one word in response. Clearly, she remembered.

I never liked this girl. She was beautiful, that was undeniable. But I never liked her. I always thought that her name matched her God-given features— *Haifa* meant slender or tall, and she was indeed. And she no doubt also lived up to that famous saying about tall people, equating their height with stupidity. It surely suited her!

"I didn't mean…" she murmured, embarrassed. "We all get weird feelings at that age. Sometimes we misjudge people…"

People like Haifa shouldn't be given any room to manoeuvre, I thought. Refusing to budge, my voice dripping with sarcasm, I asked, "Do you want to talk about Sharaf, too, or should we switch tracks and discuss our marks in school, for example?"

She was completely taken aback by my attitude. I have no doubt that, deep down, she couldn't believe the derision coming from sad, quiet Alia, who barely ever spoke up. I was sure she regretted coming to see me.

Was what Bayyan did to me not enough? She ruined my reputation at university and made sure that all the girls avoided me for three full years! Was Haifa now in Sanaa to complete Bayyan's mission?

Her face flushed, and sweat beaded up on her temples as she conceded, "You're right. It's probably best we switch tracks. I'm sorry. I was just worried you were going to steal my childhood friend from me."

I cackled loudly, on purpose. I made sure to exaggerate my reactions. Haifa couldn't bear to sit there any longer, so she excused herself and left without saying a word.

Haifa would now be on her way to Arwa's house, no doubt, to tell her about my love for Moodi and the whole story with Sharaf. That is, if she hadn't already.

Maybe it's a blessing in disguise, I told myself, trying to picture Arwa's re-action. I was sure that once she found out about my shameful history, she'd get upset and decide to cut off contact with me. I would be the one to suffer. I tried to convince myself that it was God's will, that He was leading me away from a sinful path. By cutting off contact with me, Arwa would have offered me an antidote. Thus, she would have helped me find my way back to an easier life, free of love and free of torment. How I hate both of those emotions! How I despise falling headfirst into dreams that never turn into reality... and ending up back with the sad crooning of Umm Kulthum and *Enta 'Omri*, tears pouring down my face, in moments of intolerable pain and weakness.

I'd have to thank Haifa, then, not be angry with her. Perhaps she hadn't come to destroy me, as I'd first assumed, but to save me from drowning. Perhaps God sent her to rescue me. I should be thankful, not sad.

Go on then, Haifa, tell Arwa everything. Ruin her image of me. Convince her I'm the very model of depravity. Tell her about my scandal and dishonour. Say or fabricate whatever you want, so long as you ultimately help me push your childhood friend away from me. Help me refocus on my studies and retrace my steps to the path I promised myself I'd never stray from. I swore that I would never even pause to look around; I'd just carry on down that road leading to London. Take my hand and I'll be grateful to you forever. I'll never forget the favour you'll have done me... No matter what I secretly hope for, my decision is unwavering and firm. My relationship with Arwa will end sooner or later, and I am definitely better off if it ends now, before it takes root deep in my soul. Then it would be too hard to yank it out...

My intuition had not lied: it was not long before The History of Alia reached Arwa. The following morning, which was a Thursday, I noticed she was looking at me differently. She didn't come up and say hello as she usually did—though she'd repeatedly told me that I was older than her "both in age and maturity", which meant that custom dictated she be the one to initiate a greeting. But on that day, she didn't even lift her head to look at me. She seemed to be taking whatever she'd heard about me very hard. Her face was grey, and she'd forgotten to put on lipstick. She looked quite pale. Skipping over the preliminaries, I said, "I take it you've seen Haifa recently."

I made sure my face betrayed nothing, but she didn't even glance up. She contented herself with a thin, dry response, her eyes fixed on the ground.

"Why didn't you tell me about your divorce?"

"It never came up."

"Why did you ask for a divorce before you'd really been married?"

"It's an old story, a really complicated one, and it's neither the time nor place to talk about it. But I can assure you that whatever you heard is not the truth."

Then, before leaving the café, I added, "If you believe what she said, there's really no need for us to meet again. I wish you success in your studies and in life." I tried very hard to sound severe.

I was terrified by my own attitude. Where had all this resolute strength come from? My heart was pounding so hard I could feel it breaking through my ribs and jumping straight out of my chest. My knees went weak, trembling so violently I was afraid they'd cave in. I said what I said, but not without a heavy dose of fear. My courage was flimsy at best. I don't know how I mustered up the ability to fake it.

As I walked away, leaving her there, my body started burning up with a strange sort of fever. I knew how erratic my thoughts were; I would be unable to stick to any decision. All I could do was hope she'd be absolutely intransigent, get angry with me, and definitively sever whatever relationship we had, for good. My mind was made up. My heart, on the other hand—my strong, tyrannical heart—was beating with the hope that she'd run after me, begging for forgiveness.

I was overcome by remorse as I approached the lecture hall. My chest hurt and my heart was heavy with reproach for having been so cruel. *That sweet girl didn't deserve what you did to her*, it was pleading. *Put yourself in her shoes, what would you have done?* But the click of her heels as she caught me up shocked me back to reality.

She gently tapped me on my shoulder with one of her slender, delicate fingers, saying, "Can I come round to your place tonight so we can talk?"

Her head was slightly bowed, and her cheeks were flushed, as if strawberries had been kneaded into her skin. Her breath was racing. The fear and confusion that seemed to be weighing heavily on her shoulders broke through my last resolve. Tears sprang from my eyes. I jolted away from her and practically ran into the lecture hall, nodding that yes, she could come visit me. My heart had triumphed over my mind once again, I noted.

No doubt she loved me. And I loved her. But what was the nature of her love for me? It didn't matter. The important thing was that her feelings kept her up at night after what she heard from Haifa. They pushed her to trail behind me after she heard the indifference in my tone. That was all that mattered.

It's not every day that we experience such delicate, romantic moments, all heightened emotions and sincerity. They rarely happen, but when they do, they break through every last inhibition and penetrate deep into our hearts. I should have reacted differently... Upon seeing her bowed head and lowered gaze, I should have let my books fall to the floor and swept her into my embrace, holding her against my chest that was overflowing with love. How many times have I paused to reread such scenes in the Abeer romance novels I had loved? How many times had I pictured myself in such a situation? And now here I was, living that very moment, completely frozen and unable to react.

***

I sat down to prepare myself mentally and physically for the night ahead. It was cool inside the room, but the mild temperature did nothing to stop me from sweating. My thoughts were scattered. What would I say to her? To what would I confess, exactly? What was I being accused of? Should I tell her that I'd never felt like a fully-fledged girl, that there was something wrong inside me that no doctor had yet been able to detect? Or should I confess my unnatural love for her, and tell her about the crazy fantasies I had about her late at night? What about the dreams I used to have about Moodi and Haifa, should I tell her about those? Would she understand my predicament, or would she recoil from me and get it into her head that I am indeed gay, just as Haifa must have told her?

I took a hot shower, put on some perfume, and tried to collect my thoughts. But as soon as I was in the presence of her beauty that night, all was lost. She came to me like an angel, her lovely face surrounded by a halo of light. She was dressed in tranquil hues of pastel pink, and she had left her silky black hair loose, free in the breeze. The sight of her left me speechless. Her presence had single-handedly unravelled my plans and my heart itself.

She insisted that we talk alone, far from my siblings. I led her to the courtyard, to the same spot I'd taken Haifa. As she sat there speaking calmly and spontaneously, apologising for the "rash" words she'd said to me at university, she looked like a full moon shining in the night sky. She started talking about her life and her poor father, who "doesn't like Haifa's conceited father, so arrogant about all his riyals." He hadn't needed to work a day in his life, as he'd inherited all his money from his father.

"He's so nouveau-riche," she said. "He treats people according to how much money they have in the bank." She then took my hand and held it in her palms, caressing it gently. She asked me to be clear and frank with her. "It's time for me to know everything about you. We're like sisters now."

Sometimes, when things feel just right, a person can lose all restraint and give away every one of their secrets. That night with Arwa, I felt completely at ease. I was under her spell. I told her my whole life story, including the feelings I had in my childhood and early teen years. I told her about Moodi and the hormones. I kept expecting her to say something, but she didn't. At one point while I was speaking, she was focused on my lips as they told my story, and for some reason I thought she was about to interrupt me to confess that she felt the same way about me that I'd felt about Moodi. *That's why I put on my best clothes, doused myself in this sweet perfume, and wore all this beautiful jewellery*, I imagined she'd say. But she didn't.

I moved on to Sharaf. She continued to listen calmly, attentively. I told her all the details about what had happened between him and me, about that marriage that could probably go down in the Guinness Book of World Records as the shortest marriage in history. She laughed and apologised again for believing Haifa. "We all know what Haifa's like. She doesn't care about anyone else. She only cares about herself." I told her what Sharaf's mother did afterward, how she insisted on going to the Shahama Medical Centre to meet Dr Abdel Ghaffar so he could confirm I wasn't lying. I told her how the doctor refused to go into the details of my case, citing doctor-patient confidentiality, and how as a result she baselessly accused me of getting pregnant out of wedlock and then aborting to cover up the scandal. I told her how Sharaf's mother said she wanted revenge for the offense to her dignity and pride, so she publicly spread this lie to everyone—it even made its way to my aunts in Aden. Laughing, I then told her what that female doctor had said, how she hadn't given me the chance to speak, and how I'd left her office in a panic, feeling as if I'd committed a sin that was punishable by death.

Arwa asked me to speak about my feelings in more detail. I gave her every last one. And when we got to my passionate dreams, she laughed, "So you're saying that you feel like boys do?"

I wasn't sure how to respond to that. But I was so affected by her presence that I gave in and didn't hold back. Calmly, comfortably, I said, "Maybe... All I know is that I'm not like you. I'm not like other girls. I was born different and—"

"I'm not going to lie," she interrupted, smiling and shaking her head gently. "We do talk about you at university. We all think you must have high levels of testosterone, from the little hairs on your face. By the way, why do you use a razor to shave your moustache? Why don't you try using halawa wax? The razor only accentuates it."

It wasn't the first time a girl had given me that advice. But I always ignored it and tried to change the subject, to avoid delving deeper into the discussion.

"I'll try."

She laughed and said she'd made two mistakes. The first was believing Haifa. The second was holding my hand. "I wasn't aware that I was touching the hand of an unmarried man," she joked.

"I'm still a girl, so I really need to ask you to keep all this between us."

"But Haifa needs to know the truth!"

"I don't want her to know."

"You're sure you're a man?"

I felt like there was something else lurking behind that question. She'd asked it more than once, in more than one way. It almost felt like she *wanted* me to be a man. I mustered up some courage and said, both serious and joking, "If I were sure about that, I'd be at your doorstep tomorrow to ask for your hand in marriage."

She didn't seem to mind my saying that. She smiled shyly and didn't comment. This made it seem like it was what she'd wanted to hear. Then she started telling me about herself. She talked about her life growing up, her childhood and adolescence. She opened her heart to me and held nothing back. She told me about a female Arabic teacher who'd harassed her in middle school. This was shocking to hear, and it reminded me of a similar incident with my former teacher Mirvat, one month before my high school exams. I'd completely blocked it out until Arwa reminded me of it just then.

On the night in question, my teacher invited me and a number of other students to her small apartment in the teachers' residence, not far from school. She'd wanted the "clever ones," as she called us, to celebrate her birthday with her. "I want each of you to ask your mothers to cook something and bring it with you!" she said. And then, laughing, she added, "And don't you forget the gifts!" My mother cooked two dishes: a meaty Adeni zurbian and old Hadhrami-style chicken mandi. I put them into two insulated serving bowls that would keep them hot, and my mother picked out a bottle of perfume that I took with me as a gift.

It was a nice evening: our hostess had shed her teacher skin and with that she lost her strictness, becoming an ordinary woman, just like the rest of us. She was glamourous, but not overdone. She'd taken off her hijab and let her soft, wavy, black locks fall down to her neck. She also had bangs. I saw her in a different light that evening. Beautiful and funny, acting like she was just another student, one of us. I sensed that she was more interested in me than the others, as she kept urging me to eat more, to have some dessert: "Have some more. It will bring out the pink in your cheeks." Then she laughed, fluttering around the room like a bird. Every now and then she threw me a friendly look, winking and smiling as Abdel Halim sang:

> *Your heart is empty, my darling*
> *If you had as much love in your heart as I do, my darling*
> *If your days were being scorched by the fire of passion*
> *If your nights were sleepless like mine*
> *If you really were in love*
> *We would embrace our love and go far away from the eyes of the others*
> *Far away from all their eyes.*

We started filing out at around ten o'clock. But she asked me to stay with her awhile to help clean up. She sprayed a pleasant scent in the air and turned off most of the lights in the living room. She then lit a number of candles and scattered them around, lowering the volume so that Abdel Halim's voice wasn't too loud. We could still hear him, though, and she sang along as she swayed next to me:

> *Tell him... tell him... tell him the truth*
> *Tell him I loved him from the first minute*
> *Tell him I love him*
> *His love has me lost in his drowning seas*
> *In his brave eyes.*

She sidled up to me, her perfume very potent, when I was washing up in the kitchen. I suddenly felt her arms wrap around me from behind. I froze. A shiver of fear ran through me. I wondered if I was just having another one of those dreams. But then I felt her body heat against my back and her warm breath on my neck. "I know you're not like them," she whispered. "You're different. I can tell from your eyes, from your gaze. I can tell you're like me. You and I are the same. Don't be afraid. I'll comfort you, and you'll comfort me." Her hands moved up toward my breasts as she said those words. I let whatever I'd been washing fall into the sink and ran out of her apartment, terrified. I just wanted to get to my father's car. He was parked outside, waiting for me. As I hurried out, I heard her voice trailing behind me, "Come here, girl. I told you there's nothing to be afraid of!"

"Come back here, I was just testing you! My attentions are only motherly! Come back, let me explain..."

"Don't you dare tell anyone what happened."

Then her voice faded as I ran farther away.

I never told anyone about what happened. I had decided to push it down into my subconscious. When my eyes met hers at school the next day, I smiled as I said hello, no differently than I'd done in the past. I completely ignored the events of the night before. In a month I'd never see her again, anyway.

I later came to regret my fear and instinct to flee. It was unjustified. It's not like I was in the arms of some man... It was a woman, like me, like Moodi, like Haifa. Why did I panic and run away when my dream was finally about to become reality? Had I stayed a bit longer, I would've become better acquainted with those unknown, forbidden feelings. I could have at least let her hands graze my chest... I felt a deep pang of regret and started to hope that she'd invite me over again. But she never did. Even more regrettably, I dreamt about her one night, and it was the most beautiful dream in that series of nighttime fantasies. She let me fondle her breasts for a long time as she whispered in my ear, "Didn't I tell you not to be afraid... see how much fun we're having together?" This time, I only woke up when her fingers brushed against me down below. And I didn't even have that strong of a headache or cramps. I could have acted out those dreams in real life. I could've experienced so many things I'd seen only in my sleep.

Arwa's story was very similar to mine, but the difference was that she'd told her mother about it. Within a few days, the teacher had been transferred from Sanaa to Mukalla.

She slept in my room that night. On my bed, right beside me. She didn't show any signs of discomfort.

Our relationship blossomed after that. I even dared tell her that if I were to become a man, she'd be my wife. This escalated to a declaration that the time I spent with her was the best time of my life. Eventually I confessed that I loved her and was deeply attracted to her. She smiled at that. She said she was also attracted to me and that she wouldn't find anyone as "open-minded and ambitious" as I was. She said she would wait for me to return from London as a man. "I want to travel to London with you after that," she said. "I don't want to waste the rest of my years withering away in this dead country either. I want to really *live*."

The following evening, Haifa was at my house again. Arwa had told her what had happened between us. But this time, Haifa surprised me. She apologised for everything she'd said about me in the past. "You're a lovely and intelligent girl," she said. "You're tactful and clever. You deserve all the best in life. God will bless you and reward you soon. You'll see." Then, with a smile, she added, "I'm happy you're becoming a man. I think you'll be the best-looking man in Yemen."

I was completely taken aback by this. I couldn't make out what exactly she meant. Pre-emptively, I returned her smile and ventured, "I'm not sure yet whether I'm a man or not. All I said to Arwa was that I feel like a man inside. It's just a feeling."

She chuckled and gave me an endearing look. What was going on?

"I'm telling you, you're a man."

I didn't know why she was saying that, or why she was so happy. What was behind that smile and all that friendliness? She even said the words I'd so hoped to hear from Arwa: "If you want, I'll travel with you and help you through your treatment."

"I'll ask my father to book us a room in his hotel and a car to take us to and from hospital," she added, as if she were trying to prove the sincerity of her intentions.

Before she left, I begged her not to share my secret with anyone. "My lips are sealed," she swore. Then, for some reason, her tone turned serious as she told me that it wasn't right for me to be alone with Arwa without a chaperone, now that I was a man. She repeated it twice. Secretly, I laughed at how ridiculous that was. How was Haifa seriously saying those words to me? Haifa, who ever since our schooldays in Khobar had worn tight clothes and let her hair loose? Haifa, who hated the hijab and only joined us in the school prayer room because it was mandatory? She was the only one who used to excuse herself from prayer time every month, citing her period, which supposedly lasted a full ten days every cycle. Could she be serious, scolding me like that? How could she be, when she was fine being alone with me herself?

I must admit that I was at a loss when it came to Haifa. I never could understand her.

***

The most important step on my dream journey to London was ranking first in my degree course. The people in charge of the Geographic Information Systems and Remote Sensing Department then had no choice but to appoint me as a teaching assistant. Some tentatively expressed their disapproval; they had a lot to complain about.

"How could she be appointed? She's an emigrant!"

"She's only been here one year!"

"A teaching assistant? She's a woman!"

Ultimately, this changed nothing.

I knew the only thing I could rely on was my marks. No one and nothing else would have my back. At the university and in Yemen more generally, it's almost standard procedure for them to prioritise someone who knows or is related to the University President, the Vice-President, or some government minister. They could have very easily appointed someone with those connections instead of me. But I was steadfast in my determination and adamant about standing in the way of each of their attempts to thwart me. I even spread the word of my appointment among students and employees before it was officially announced. I did this on purpose, and I repeated time and again to anyone listening that my marks were much higher than those of the person who ranked second. "The difference is as great as the drive from Sanaa to Aden!" I'd comment. "No—even greater, actually," I went on. "The distance between al-Hadidiya and Mahra!"

The department officially announced my teaching appointment on the 1st of July 1989. This date, 1 July, would long continue to carry special significance.

It was a beautiful evening. Arwa rushed over to my house so we could celebrate together. My mother cooked mukhbaza for us, a dish in which tanoor bread was lathered with organic ghee and fenugreek, and she also made a date fatteh with flatbread and some bint al-sahn. Had Haifa not showed up unannounced — "I came to congratulate you and celebrate with you!" she proclaimed—I would've danced with Arwa just like she promised we would if I got the job.

***

When I'd first arrived in Sanaa, I cut out a picture of the famous Big Ben, located at the north end of Westminster Palace in London, from a glossy magazine. I glued it to the last page of my journal, and underneath it I wrote: "Finally, I see you for what you are. September 1989."

I wrote this to have a concrete image of the goal I wanted to achieve. That day, I decided that, no matter what, I would make it to London within one year at most. Little did I know that this was pure delusion. I'd been looking at things through rose-tinted glasses that completely distorted reality. It took seven months for the Ministry of Civil Service to approve my appointment as a teaching assistant, which according to an employee at the ministry was "the fastest appointment they've ever made." The ten times I showed up to see what was taking so long, they all just nodded at me and evaded my questions, making comments that had nothing to do with what I wanted to know. "You children of emigrants have money. Leave these jobs for the rest of us... we need them."

Arwa, on the other hand, started her job as an administrator in the University Vice-President al-Raqbi's office in under three months, without having to go to the Ministry of Civil Service even once!

Eventually I unglued that cut-out and stuck it at the end of a new journal, this time writing: "Here I am, finally by your side. September 1990."

***

Once I stopped taking the camel hormones, I no longer had those intense recurring dreams about girls. I was free of them for a long time. Until one night.

It was not Arwa whom I saw behind the water tank on the roof of my house, but Haifa. Here she was again. And after such a long absence. She grabbed my wrist and pulled me behind the tank, planting a long, hot kiss on my cheek. I could feel her burning breath on my ear, her chest against mine. But this time, I saw myself in a different body: for the first time, I saw myself with a woman's breasts and a small penis where my vagina should have been—or maybe I had both organs at once, the penis coming out of the vagina. I can't recall the image very clearly; it was dark, and I was trembling with fear and desire. Then all of a sudden, a voice came out of nowhere. It was Arwa calling out my name, and it sounded like she was very close. I started, and Haifa laughed, inching her face closer to mine. "Do you like her more than me? You know I'm the one who loves you. Not her," she whispered, before gluing her lips to mine.

As usual, I woke up shaking with fear, my body drenched in sweat. The pain was intolerable, so I rushed to the medicine cabinet and swallowed three painkillers. The pain only subsided an hour later.

***

A lot happened during those seven months I spent waiting for the Ministry of Civil Service to approve my appointment as a teaching assistant. The biggest change was that, at the end of September, we left the house that had witnessed so many beautiful memories with Arwa and moved to a new one. One month after our arrival in Sanaa, my father had sold a piece of land he owned in Aden, borrowed some more money from the bank, and bought us a house that was newly built. He was tempted by the location of this house, which was in the neighbourhood of the vocational school at the intersection of Khartoum and Sakhr streets, at the very heart of the al-Bahara, or al-Kamim, district.

That was what changed his mind and made him divert from his initial plan of buying a plot of land and building a house from the ground up. That neighbourhood was the most sought-after in all of Sanaa. Residents of the city dreamed of living there, especially since a large mall was located at its centre. Not to mention that living there would put a large distance between my father and his no-good companions. But one day—one that I am not likely to forget—my father, the man with a failing heart, decided quite madly to offer the workers his help and join them in painting the courtyard wall. He held up a heavy can of paint, but his muscles, which had been feeble for some time, did not respond to this sudden movement in time. He collapsed all at once and fell to the floor, groaning and crying out in pain. He was never able to carry his weight and stand on his own two feet again. He was fated to use a crutch after the doctors confirmed that he had moderate paraplegia that could yet worsen. He was only fifty-four years old.

This thrust all his responsibilities on my shoulders and, just like that, I was the one in charge of the house and everyone in it. This was at the beginning of September 1989. I cried a lot that night. I hid in the far corner of our roof and wept as the images of my past life flashed before my eyes in a reel of painful, miserable memories. Achingly, I wondered, *How many years do I need to wait for my bad luck to change? What do I need to do for God to be pleased with me and stop tormenting me like this?*

This new situation my father found himself in forced me to devote the only parts of my day during which I wasn't at university or the Ministry of Civil Service to learning how to drive. It was yet another painful experience that I begrudgingly endured, caught between the sixty-year-old instructor's harassment and the judging eyes of everyone around me.

"How could you allow your daughter to drive with her face uncovered, Abu Hamed?"

"What's wrong with that?"

"Your daughter is calling attention to herself. Do you know how many sick people will lust after her? At least have her cover her face."

"My daughter is as strong as any man. I'm not worried about her."

"Just marry her off! You won't be able to relax until you do."

"Alia will not get married until she finishes her PhD."

"Women belong at home. There's no shortage of men for her!"

"Alia will never marry a Yemeni."

This conversation unfolded between my father and our elderly neighbour, who had already expressed his wish to marry me off to his son.

It took me over a month to get my driver's license, a period in which I also had to endure harassment from the policeman who administered my driving test. He was my father's age. He took a seat next to me and started asking all sorts of questions. "Where are you from? Who's your father? Where do you live?" and so on and so forth, only to conclude his intrusion with, "Mashallah, mashallah. I'm ready to sell everything I own and have you live in honour and dignity in my home." Later, during the test, while I was swerving left, he laid the palm of his hand over the top of mine, claiming he was helping me stay in the right lane. I neither objected nor revealed my anger. I knew I had to keep my mouth shut and my nerves under control if I wanted to get my driving license.

That night, I cried again. Salty tears slid down my face as I processed how utterly helpless I had been; I couldn't have stopped the policeman from doing what he did at my driving test. His hand had been a mere slip away from my breasts, and had he actually touched my chest, I knew I would have kept quiet about that too. He had the power to prevent me from getting a license for as long as I was in Sanaa. Still, I vowed not to let these occasional distressing moments stop me from moving forward and accomplishing my goal, no matter how great the responsibilities I'd have to take on. Urging myself on, trying to strengthen my sometimes-faltering resolve, I promised myself, *I won't give up. If I do, I'll be holding myself back and resigning myself to a lifetime of misery.*

Patience, Alia, I'd go on. *Patience is the key to salvation. "Indeed, with hardship will be ease."* (Q 94:6)

A quote I'd read somewhere also brought me solace sometimes: "If you are experiencing delay in receiving something you want, know that God is testing your patience." I'll be patient for as long as You wish, my Lord. I have nothing left but patience. I've made it this far, haven't I? The road ahead isn't that long... You'll see. Nothing will stand in the way of my patience and resilience. I won't despair. There is no life with despair, and there is no despair with life.

Starting today, no more tears, I wrote in my journal. *I won't give up. I won't give in to misery. I am even more resolute than those of great determination. I am more patient than Job. I am more enduring than Jonah and Joseph.*

London is my goal. Nothing else. My one and only objective is to win a scholarship and get to London. I will achieve this, no matter what I have to sacrifice in the process.

***

Once I had my job, I then tried to find the fastest way to get to London on a scholarship. But the quickest route consisted of "waiting your turn," according to the Head of Department. To make things worse, he added, "It'll take a minimum of two years. There are others who are already in the queue." The next thing I did was sign up for English classes at the British Council in Sanaa—not only to learn English, but also to meet the Director and beg him to help me get that scholarship as quickly as possible.

"Here at the Council, we don't give scholarships directly to students. Our agreement is with the Yemeni government. We have five scholarships that they allocate to students. We deal directly with the Ministry of Planning, which in turn decides who will go. We have no role in the decision-making process." That's what John, the Director of the British Council, told me three months after I'd started taking classes. He was a tall, clean-shaven man in his fifties who had lost most of his sandy hair. His skin was pale and somewhat splotchy. His blue eyes were framed with thick spectacles. From the first moment I'd met him at the British Council, he gave me the impression that he was a good person, and this encouraged me to ask him for help. Once he'd explained their procedures, he smiled and asked, "Why London specifically?"

"London is my one dream in life."

This answer seemed to please him, but he chose not to comment any further.

I left his office feeling dejected. It had become abundantly clear that there was still a long way to go, and that I wouldn't be crossing the finish line as easily and quickly as I'd hoped. Sanaa is located at the foot of the Sarawat Mountains around 2300 metres above sea level. *There is less oxygen at such altitudes*, I thought... perhaps the British who live here have become infected by the same lethal dose of laziness and bureaucracy that courses through Yemenis' veins. Perhaps I'd need to search for another way to get to London. I wished I'd been born into one of the notable families of Sanaa. Then I wouldn't have to worry about any of this.

The next day, however, I realised I'd been too rash in my judgment. John called me into his office first thing in the morning, greeting me with a smile even bigger than the one he'd had the day before. "Before I say anything else, let me just tell you that I'm very intrigued by your dream of going to London. I've never met anyone so committed to their studies. It seems you've impressed all the teachers here and made a considerable impact on them. They came to my office and asked me to help you."

I was stunned by his words. I hadn't seen this coming. I felt a calm sense of euphoria spread through every cell in my body. "It never fails to surprise me that you're consistently the first person here and the last to leave," he said. It was true. I did get there first thing in the morning and left only at 7 p.m., closing time. "The staff practically have to kick you out!" he joked.

As he went on, I could feel my chest swell with pride. "Again, I need to emphasise that we at the Council don't have the authority to offer you a scholarship. What we can do is help you obtain it through the Ministry of Planning to fit your timeframe. But before I go into more detail, I need to ask you something. Are you the only one in your course who was hired as a teaching assistant?"

I nodded. "Yes, I'm the only one. There is no other teaching assistant in the Geographic Information Systems and Remote Sensing department."

He smiled. "Good. That makes things much easier. We can make this work by allocating one of the five scholarships we receive this year to a Master's student in your course." He asked me what the exact name of my specialty was and took note of it. "I need to stress this one last time: you must be the *only* teaching assistant in the Geographic Information Systems and Remote Sensing specialty. This is the only way to guarantee that no one else will be nominated for the scholarship. Are you positively certain that you're the only one?"

"100%."

"To increase the chances of this working, I'm going to try to get approval from Swansea University specifically, since it has a Memorandum of Understanding and established academic exchange with your university already. This will be very helpful. Swansea is a beautiful city, not too far from London, and you could always move from there to London if you wanted to."

As I sat there taking it all in, I could feel my heart pounding. I felt like all my efforts were finally coming to fruition, that things were finally starting to happen for me. It was as if two wings had sprouted on either side of my back and I was about to soar into the sky, joyful and buoyant. I wished my father were there with me, hearing what I'd just heard with his own two ears. On that day, I became all the more certain that my grandfather was right: the British were indeed a decent people, and my father was wrong to fight him on this.

"But the first move needs to come from you," John continued, his face turning more serious.

"From me?"

He nodded. Fear suddenly seeped into my joy. I was worried I wouldn't be able to deliver. Still, I looked him straight in the eye and confidently replied, "No worries, Sir. I'll do whatever it takes."

"You've already started to talk like us!" he chuckled. "It's very simple, really. All you have to do is ask your university to write a letter indicating that you're their candidate for the scholarship in Geographic Information Systems. Then leave the rest to us!"

As I walked out of his office, he called out from behind the glass door, "Remember—this is urgent. Do not delay!"

"Not tomorrow... today!" he added, emphasising how pressing this was.

Leaving his office, I felt anxious. What if they refused to write me that letter? I didn't have the best track record with them—the teaching assistantship appointment had already been so difficult to obtain. And I was still a new student; how would I get them to write me such a letter?

It was because of this anxiety that I didn't rush to the university right then and there. I needed to find a calm spot where I could be alone and collect my thoughts first, before going up against those people all over again.

That night, I prayed for God to help me face them the next day, to help me through what would surely be an unpleasant situation. I also asked my mother to keep me in her prayers. I'd often felt that the sincerity of her supplications had opened many doors for me.

Arwa was very supportive. "Don't let your anxieties get the best of you. I'm right here to help you. I'll march into their offices myself if need be," she said. I knew she was referring to al-Raqbi, the Vice-President of the University. She knew very well the effect her beauty had on him—and on men in general.

"I need a letter from the university that nominates me for a scholarship in the UK," I announced to Dr Shaker Mohammed, the Head of the Geography Department. He was a kind-hearted Iraqi man, always hard at work. People used to describe him as a bundle of energy. But over the past few years, his surroundings had managed to rub off on him, and he became just as Yemeni as everyone around him—and just as lazy, if not more. He had turned into a sedated version of himself, chewing qat at all hours of the day. Not only in his spare time, but also during work hours.

He looked up at me coldly. With a mocking smile, he said, "But you're still new here."

"I know, Sir, you're right. It's just that I need it to be able to complete my English courses at the British Council."

"I'm sorry my dear, we don't have any scholarships."

He spoke just like us, with the same Yemeni accent. He had truly become Yemeni through and through.

"I know that too, Dr Shaker. I'm not asking for a scholarship. I just need the letter as a formality. One that says that I'm the candidate for such a scholarship should one become available."

He smiled. "If that's the case, then I have no reason to object." He buzzed on the intercom to ask his secretary to print him the letter.

That was the first hurdle. It was also the easiest one, compared to the obstacles to come. The letter still had to be signed by three other people: the Dean, the President, and Vice-President al-Raqbi. He was the one I dreaded meeting the most.

Getting that letter signed was a veritable masterclass in patience. I was doling out fake smiles left and right. Just as I'd expected, al-Raqbi proved to be very difficult. He only delivered after asking me dozens of questions, making me wait through six full days of stalling. Arwa's intervention had, of course, been crucial: "Alia is the best student at this university, Sir. Please help her in any way you can. She deserves the best."

Then there was the response I heard from every person I came into contact with. They mindlessly repeated the same sentence, like a broken record—as if it were some kind of incantation to be uttered to every student: *There are no scholarships. There are no scholarships. There are no scholarships.* And it seemed they'd all agreed that this response should come with a sarcastic smile, one with no clear purpose. They also seemed to unanimously believe that approving a scholarship was some kind of charity, a blessing they bestowed upon us rather than our right as students.

I don't know if it was because of my fear of losing this opportunity or for other reasons, but my cramps suddenly returned. "Maybe they're here to give you that extra push to achieve your goal. This is how one's will is tested," my father said, sitting across from me at the table as we waited for dinner.

"That's what I thought, too."

Ever since I'd stopped taking the hormones I'd been prescribed, my cramps had subsided. In exchange, the small, thick hairs growing on my face multiplied.

"Don't despair, and don't let anyone take your dream away from you."

My father should have been a philosopher. He could have been very influential.

"If they do, I just might kill one of them."

"I have a strong feeling that you're just a few steps away from London. You'll get everything you want."

It took the British Council all of two weeks to send me the acceptance letter. I would leave to pursue my Master's degree at the University in Swansea, where I would also take English classes. I had no idea it would take so little time. But I also hadn't known that my efforts to get the acceptance letter would mean nothing if the Ministry of Planning didn't approve my scholarship! I was being dragged down yet another miserable path. Still, I patiently bore the pain.

The ministry in question was bustling with male employees. Only male employees. Any woman who walked in there had to endure their gazes, wondering what they were planning for her, as they examined the outline of her body. It didn't matter what she was wearing. Veiled or not; covered from head to toe by a black abaya or dressed in a regular woman's thobe—it didn't matter. Before she even put in her request, she would already have been scrutinised from top to bottom. She was delivered over to the eyes of these men the second she set foot inside the ministry's gate. Respite came only after she disappeared down the corridors or into an office.

Cynically, painfully, I thought, *Indeed it is a Ministry of Planning. But what type of plans these men have in mind... no one knows.*

"How is your name already attached to this scholarship? I've never seen such a thing," the Director of Human Resources asked me, incredulous. "Engineer Ahmed Balfaqih", his metal nameplate read. He'd put it at the front of his desk. His right cheek was so filled with qat that it was bulging, forcing his eye half-shut. It looked ridiculous and pitiful. I smiled, remembering the words of advice I'd received: "Smile at them. The wolves within them will turn into lambs."

"Actually, it's not that, Sir. The scholarship was sent in for a specific specialisation, not a specific student." I had my answer ready, as John had already warned me that they might ask that question.

"But your name is right here. Are you, or are you not Alia Abdel Rahman Ilwan?" He read out my name in English in a funny way. *Had the British remained here, this engineer would now have their accent down pat*, I thought.

"I am."

"So? How is it then by specialisation?"

"You're right, Sir. Your question is very clear and valid. Let me just explain the situation to you," I offered. "The scholarship was allocated to the Geographic Information Systems and Remote Sensing specialisation. And since I'm the only teaching assistant in that field, there was no one else eligible for the scholarship. The rest of the students, as you surely know, are competing for scholarships in Business, Economics, Sociology, and Medicine. They must have simply mentioned my name for this reason, nothing more."

But the wolf inside the Director refused to be tamed. "I'll look into it," he said. "Come back next week."

"Sir, couldn't this be done in a day, or two at most?"

Annoyed, he retorted, "Actually, it usually takes a month. Even two."

I didn't want to waste any more of my time arguing with him. It was the most irritating situation I could have been in. I simply cannot tolerate people standing in the way of what is rightfully mine. And it's not like he had a valid reason—he simply didn't like me, and so he'd decided to make this difficult. The worst part was that he truly believed that all the stalling and needless complications were well within *his* rights. These people love to act like they're the ultimate decision-makers when, in reality, they have no influence over the situation whatsoever. It's not like they're the ones providing the scholarship. They're not even contributing one riyal to it!

This Mr Balfaqih had left it by saying he needed a week to complete my request. But he took four. And after four weeks had passed, he coldly announced that my request had been denied. There would be no scholarship that was already in someone's name. Then came the inevitable comment I'd been expecting, "You children of emigrants have money. Leave these scholarships for the poor who actually need them."

When I told John that nothing had come of either the wolf or lamb, he laughed, "You must resort to the lion, then."

"How so?" I asked, confused. My anxiety was instantly visible on my face. He chuckled, but his tone grew suddenly serious, "Tell 'Mr Engineer' that if they don't grant you the scholarship, you will expose the fact that they unlawfully gave one to a relative of the Minister of Planning two days ago. Then he'll sign your papers on the spot!" He laughed loudly at his own suggestion.

"Are you sure that'll work with..." He cut me off with a wave, "I know this situation like the back of my hand."

John seems to be more acquainted with the ways of Yemenis than I am, I thought on the day I left the Ministry, signed papers in hand, a mere half hour after arriving.

Over the course of those long weeks that I spent going back and forth to the Ministry, I came across all sorts of people who seemed to suddenly transform from ministry employees into guidance counsellors, offering unsolicited advice. "You really want to travel to keep studying? Wallah, if I were you, I'd get married and stay home, not travel alone without a man. Emigration is desolation." Someone else started reciting Qur'anic verses I'd never heard before, claiming it was prohibited for a woman to travel alone without a male relative. These verses seemed to exist only in his own personal Qur'an. I cut many of these people off with a simple "My father is coming with me," to which they'd ridiculously respond, "I'm willing to marry you and travel with you." As if this absurd offer made any sense.

The day I left the Ministry, papers in hand, it was unusually hot, especially for June. I made my way to the British Council, then to the university, and eventually I returned home, along with the dying rays of the sun. I was absolutely exhausted. As I entered my room, I felt dizzy, the stress of the past few weeks catching up with me. I hadn't been sleeping and was extremely anxious. That engineer had brought me so much stress. There was one moment, when he was sitting there, haggling with me over my rights in that arrogant tone of his, that I was taken by an overwhelming desire to kill him. I was at the peak of my anger and despair. If I'd had a janbiyya fixed to my belt like a man, I would have pulled out the blade and plunged it into him.

As expected, I suffered through a bout of intense stomach cramps and headaches that night. This was always the case when I was physically exhausted. I'd experience levels of pain that made me hate myself and this life I was fated to live. I took three painkillers. I knew the drill. But I didn't completely give in to my suffering. I was aware that I was getting closer to that final page in my journal, where Big Ben was waiting for me. This brought me some solace, some sense of imminent freedom. Had I not had that hope, I would have locked my bedroom door and not gotten out of bed for a full week.

I didn't write much about this ordeal, but I did allow myself to describe that engineer in my journal with the most colourful insults I had in my arsenal. He evoked such hatred in me, more than anyone I'd encountered before in my life. He made me hate the Ministry of Planning, all of Yemen, and the people in it. He made me hate Sanaa—its streets, the shape of its buildings and mountains, its men and its women. I became more certain than ever that Yemen would never be my home; I couldn't belong to it even if it were the last country on earth.

After that, I stopped writing completely. I'd have more than enough time to write about my pain and suffering after landing in the London fog. And I'd need much more than my one journal: I'd need a few, volumes perhaps. But all I'll say is that the ten-month period between October 1989—when I'd hoped to arrive—and July 1990–when I actually did arrive—was one of utter misery. My feelings constantly swung between hope and despair, each pulling me in an opposite direction—my despair pulling me down to the most bitter depths of depression, while my hope was a weapon against fear and anxiety. And all this was unfurling against a backdrop of immense responsibilities too heavy for one person to carry. I had students to teach at the university, English to study at the British Council, hungry mouths to feed at home, and a crippled father who relied on me alone for help—I was the one who drove him back and forth to the clinic once a week. I became the family chauffeur, driving my mother and siblings around, and I was also in charge of groceries. On top of all that, I was forced to pay off my father's loans with the money I made as a teaching assistant. This depleted my salary, which would completely disappear before the middle of each month.

What little hair remained on my head mostly turned white, and my stomach cramps got much worse. The pain felt like knives slashing at my insides. Sedatives could no longer bring me any comfort. My stomach swelled, and the violent dreams that shook me to my core and woke me up at dawn became ever more frequent. And, last but most definitely not least, I barely saw Arwa. That was my deepest regret.

***

"Why London specifically?" I was in my room mulling over the question John had asked. *Why had I fixated on London, really?* Why, throughout all these years, had I not even considered another city? Dr Abdel Ghaffar had planted this seed in my mind when he linked my treatment to London, but why had I held on to it as the only possibility? Had I clung to the image I had of it from all the time I'd spent listening to my father talk about the British? Was it their highly organised way of life? The freedom of women, who are able to live their lives as men do? Their punctuality and dedication to work? Their cool and rainy weather? Their smiles and calm temperament? Or was it all of that together in one irresistible package? I didn't know. I couldn't tell... All I knew was that, had it not been for London, my life would've had no purpose.

When I decided to take a course on contemporary European history, I was trying to gain a deeper understanding of Britain. I read about all the Occupying Powers—France, Italy, and the UK—and I felt that the British occupation stood out from the rest. I saw in it one clear advantage over the others. Their original intention was to control the ports and sea routes and thus control trade, all the while harnessing the occupied countries' wealth for their own benefit. There is no doubt about that. But they also did contribute to the development of the countries they occupied. Why else would they have built us that hospital, or even the Gate of Aden? Why else would they have paved roads, set up schools, and introduced their systematic city planning to our lives?

My grandfather was right to say all that to my father. Had it not been for the British, our houses would still be built of mud, and in summer we would still sleep in the open air. When they came, they brought new ways of life. One could even claim that they taught us the meaning of life. Maybe they stole from us, yes. They even plundered our lands, sure... But here's a thought: they wouldn't have built hospitals and schools without anything in return.

I went to Aden some years ago. The British had already left, but the roads were paved and clean, souks organised, new buildings still standing. Just like my grandfather said, had it not been for them, Aden would've never become so modern. It would have remained the same old decrepit Aden, even today, and the famous port would've been a derelict ruin, the echoes of cawing crows reverberating through it.

***

I received my acceptance from Swansea University and the approval of my scholarship from the Ministry of Planning without the knowledge of anyone at Sanaa University. The day the official acceptance letter arrived from Swansea, there was a general state of shock and disbelief at the university in Sanaa. People's jaws dropped when they received the news. Al-Raqbi's shock was more visible than other people's—not only did his jaw drop, but his eyes, nostrils, and even his ears bulged and flared wide open as I gave him the news, along with the gifts I'd brought him. He was dead silent for a moment, too stunned to react. But then he leapt from his chair, a wide smile spilling across his face. He thanked me for the gifts and wished me luck. I'd given him a fancy bottle of French cologne, my head lowered in respect and appreciation.

"This is the least I could offer you in return for all you've done for me, Sir. You stood by my side and supported me," I said to him, just as Arwa had advised. "I will never forget this favour. I will remember this until the day I die. Without you, I wouldn't have won this scholarship. Thank you again and again, Sir. Inshallah I will make you proud and live up to your expectations. I'll continue to be a top student, I promise, and I'll graduate with honours and distinction."

"You deserve the best," he murmured with a smile. "May you return as Head of Department... and then Dean of the Faculty!"

I repeated this exact scenario with al-Maqlahi, President of the University.

Arwa headed to my house that evening to celebrate with me and say goodbye. It was an extremely emotional night, filled with conflicting feelings of happiness and sorrow. Our highs were high, and our lows low. My mother cooked the same food she'd made us before, but now for the last time: the mukhbaza with tanoor bread lathered with ghee and fenugreek, the date fatteh, and bint al-sahn.

Even though Haifa wasn't there to intrude, Arwa still didn't dance joyfully that night. A sense of imminent separation loomed large, and I cried on her lap as we said goodbye. It was the first—and would perhaps be the last—time she let me hold her so close. I wept copious tears. She stayed strong, fighting back her own tears as she begged me to get treated and come back quickly. "If you love me, please," she pleaded. Only half-joking, she added, "You have one year. No more. After that, whatever happens is on you."

***

The 1st of July once again made a significant appearance in my life. It was early that morning in 1990 that the plane took off for London, my father and I on board. I was a bundle of nerves as I handed my passport and ticket to the agent at the counter, terrified she'd find some reason to stop me from boarding the plane. My journey up to that moment had been so filled with difficulty and misery that I reflexively braced myself, expecting the worst. My anxiety followed me wherever I went, and I couldn't shake the feeling that this was all a dream, and I would soon wake. I could almost hear al-Raqbi's voice calling after me in the Departures area, telling me with that rotten smile of his that the scholarship had been cancelled, that I had to go back. But my fear quickly dissipated as the plane took off, soaring into the skies above, leaving everything else behind.

The psychological state I was in at the moment the plane took off is indescribable. I cannot put it into words. I was finally in the air, flying towards my ultimate dream. The only thing that dampened the moment was Arwa—her absence, the feeling that I had lost her. There was no shortage of men who would pursue such a woman. They'd do anything to win her over. And I knew that the promises I'd made, to her and others in Sanaa, were untrue. I'd never return. I was leaving with no plans to come back. I was going to tear up my return ticket and watch it float down the River Thames. I would never return to Yemen. If Arwa and I were indeed meant to reunite, it wouldn't be in Yemen.

I had an overwhelming desire to take out my journal and record that defining moment in my life. I wanted to preserve the wonderful feeling that was so hard to put into words. But my father was sitting right next to me. So my journal stayed tucked away.

Alia
Swansea City, UK

It was 4:30 in the afternoon when the Yemen Airways flight landed at Gatwick Airport. The sun was still shining brightly; one would think it was the middle of the day. Even before I got off the plane, my dizzying excitement buoyed me, and I felt I would never come down from this feeling. A serene happiness settled deep within me as I gazed at the tapestry of green from above. Now, whenever I think of this country, I recall that sprawling carpet of green. The thought of London also calls to mind the beautiful Hyde Park we hear so much about—even on Arab soap operas—and the harsh cold, the ever-pouring rain, and the white snowflakes that fall on Christmas Day. But the one feeling that's been carved into my heart and mind, the thought I associate most with my experience of this city, is freedom. I still find myself unable fully to grasp what this freedom means. Experiencing it is still a daily struggle. I was suffocated for so long by stifling customs and traditions. Constantly haunted by fear, excessive caution, and shame, how could I have felt otherwise?

I nervously fiddled with my hijab as the plane taxied slowly toward the jet bridge. I kept fumbling with it as if I were about to take it off. Had I been alone, I would've taken it off for good the very next morning. *I won't rush*, I told myself. *There's no need to hurry here. I have more than enough time to decide what I want to do, how I want to live my life, how I want to change.* I had three full years ahead of me: the first was dedicated to studying English and taking bridge courses like those I'd taken in Sanaa, but in English this time.

During the second year, I'd complete my Graduate Diploma, and during the third, my Master's degree course. A full thirty-six months. One thousand and ninety-five days. That's the time I had, and it was more than enough to create a totally new Alia. An Alia free of her issues, free of her fears and inhibitions. An Alia ready to set off on a wonderful, fulfilling journey.

I felt a bit anxious as I headed to passport control with my father; I could tell he was struggling to keep up with me. But inside I was jumping for joy. I was finally in London! I was really, actually in London. *It's not a dream or a fantasy anymore, Alia Ilwan!* I congratulated myself, recalling the sheer number of times I'd tried to curb my despair, which had become a dull, heavy companion in my search for hope.

Today is my true birthday. I will forget everything that came before. My real life starts today, on the 1st of July 1990. Twenty-five years of my life have passed, but I will not count them. Why would I, when they haven't counted at all?

I pinched myself for the tenth time. I had to keep proving to myself that I wasn't dreaming.

Things went smoothly at passport control.

"What is the purpose of your visit?" the customs agent asked me.

"I'm here on a scholarship from the British Council."

"Is this your father?"

And so on and so forth. Routine questions.

He gave us a friendly smile, and, as he handed me back the two passports, he said, "Swansea's a charming place. I go there on holiday every now and again. It has one of the loveliest beaches in the country. I think you'll grow quite fond of it. You may find that you never want to leave!" Before sending us off, he added, "Best of luck with your studies."

His kind words and gentle smile helped ease the tension building up in my chest. His polite manner impressed me, and, as I breathed a sigh of relief, I realised just how worried I'd been about entering the UK.

For some reason, I instinctively started to compare this with the way we'd been received at the airport in Sanaa, back when we returned from Khobar. This made me feel oddly self-righteous. Had the time been right, I would have asked my father what he thought about our polite welcome. *Look, Dad. Look. Here are the British people you fought against. See how they treat others? Do Yemenis treat people like this?*

I collected our two suitcases, and we left the airport for the tube station—as I'd been advised. I almost got lost amongst all those trains, but John's golden advice saved the day: "If you need help, ask. Always ask. British people love to help others, and they won't complain even if you ask several questions." The tube took us to the famous Piccadilly Station in central London. As I made my way through the station, I just stood on the platform for a moment, stunned, trying to take it all in. The ceilings were so high, and thick iron pipes crisscrossed above us in a grid. Hundreds of people bustled around. I looked up at the large clock ahead. It read a quarter past six.

On one side of the hall, the British Council had set up a small kiosk. It was empty, but there was a note with my name on it taped to the small stand. The note had instructions on how to find the nearby Best Western. The sun was still shining as brightly as it would normally be early in the day, and it wouldn't set before ten p.m. all summer. As the days stretched endlessly into each other, the nights would grow shorter and shorter.

When we got to the hotel, a representative of the British Council was already there waiting for us. He was holding an envelope with two train tickets to Swansea for the following morning, as well as some documents related to my enrolment in language courses at Swansea University. It also contained five hundred British pounds meant to help me open a bank account and settle into my university residence.

My father was very happy with all of this. Happier than me. He couldn't stop smiling. The happiness on his face spoke volumes, but he preferred not to say anything about the emotions bubbling up within him. Not a word. Aware of his past, I imagined that perhaps he was trying to avoid admiring out loud how ordered and pleasant he found everything around us. He jolted me back to reality when he invited me to go exploring with him, so we could, "get to know this London that we've heard so much about."

I grabbed the instant camera I'd bought in Sanaa when my trip was confirmed, and we headed out. The first thing I did was call a taxi to take us to see Big Ben. It was my first time riding in a car on the other side of the road. I felt nervous and a little afraid; it was as if we were driving into incoming traffic. It made me nauseous. My father's smile didn't falter, but I could see he was also tense. "The British are a very obstinate people," he said, still grinning. "They could've switched the driver's seat from right to left to be like most other countries in the world. But I guess this makes them feel special. Or unique. Haughty and proud."

It was my first time in a London taxi, those famous, old-fashioned, round black cars. I used to play with a toy one as a child.

When we got to Big Ben, I took dozens of photos. Passersby smiled in agreement when I asked if they could take photos of my father and me. We spent the rest of the evening strolling through the streets, then we had dinner and retraced our steps back to the hotel.

As we were walking in central London, I repeated to him that the British were good people, that they knew how to treat others, that I hadn't had any negative experiences with them. I'd said this before. He replied sarcastically, "That's because they feel guilty that they plundered our land and killed our people."

The day I told him that the British Council had decided he could accompany me to London and seek treatment for his paralysis, he couldn't believe it. He couldn't believe that they'd do this for him.

"What's in it for them?" he asked, amazed.

"I don't know, Baba. It was their idea. When I told them about you, they asked me to provide your medical records. I'm sure it's routine procedure. They must do it for everyone, not just you."

We had this conversation on the day I was going to the British Embassy to drop off our passports.

But, back then, he must not have fully understood what was happening. Or maybe he thought I was making it up, that it really was *me* behind this idea of getting him to travel with me. "I see what you're doing," he said with a knowing smile. "Don't worry about me, Alia. You go first. I'll follow once you're more settled in."

"Baba, again, it was their idea. They were the ones who promised me they'd get you a visa so you could travel on the same flight as me. They also promised they'd give me a call in Swansea a few days after we arrive to tell us where you'll be treated. I didn't do anything. They'd already taken care of everything. There was nothing for me to do."

He nodded, tears rolling down his cheeks. I thought I could feel what

was in his heart. He must have felt such regret for how he'd always rejected the British. If I were in his shoes, I'd be sorry, too. Had the British and
my father both remained in Aden, maybe he would've been able to find the
right treatment at the Queen Elizabeth Hospital, and he wouldn't have had
to leave his beloved Aden behind. But he'd been stubborn. He was afflicted
by the same reckless passion as the rest of his generation. Their wild and
self-destructive behaviour ultimately led to the demise of their country. I
wanted to ask him why he was crying, but I stopped myself. I didn't want to
reopen old wounds he'd long tried to heal.

My father fell asleep quickly that night. I was exhausted too, bone-tired,
but I couldn't sleep. I was so happy, it was almost like my body refused to
surrender. I stayed up for most of the night, replaying my life like a film reel.
I saw the faces of all the people I used to know. If only I could send them
a picture of myself through the ether. I'd show them the one of me in my
new clothes, standing in Hyde Park, or maybe the one of me in front of
the massive Piccadilly Station, or even in front of Big Ben. "Here I am in
London, my friends," I'd say. "Your old friend with the tomato cheeks is now
in London. The quiet little girl you knew has achieved a dream she once
thought impossible."

I thought of Arwa. Though, to be honest, she'd never really left my mind.
How I hoped she would wait for me... I remember thinking that I'd never
regret losing anyone as much as I'd regret losing her.

Before I fell asleep, I fumbled through the pictures for the one of me,
alone, in front of Big Ben. I glued it to the page I had reached in my journal
and captioned it:
You've been so elusive, but I've finally caught up with you. Were you bet-
ting that I'd lose the race? In the end, I won. – July 1990.

The following morning, we took the train to Swansea City. I'd barely gotten two hours of sleep, but I woke up full of energy, as if I'd slept a full ten hours. I was still so overwhelmingly happy that my joy fully masked my exhaustion.

It took us more than three and a half hours to get to Swansea. We took the train from Piccadilly to Paddington, where we got off to switch trains. We then boarded the one that would take us straight to Swansea. We passed through many villages and beautiful expanses of green, and the train made eight stops before we arrived at our destination. I took in all the sights and names of the places we travelled through, vowing to visit them all soon.

At each stop, many passengers got on and off the train. I watched these people go about their lives with great interest and followed the train's schedule closely: were these London trains really as punctual as people claimed? Not one minute late, not one minute early? Maybe if my father and all his comrades in the Workers' Party—along with all the other anti-colonialists— had let the British stay for another decade, Aden would now be a second London. We'd board a train as fast as this one. The first line would take us from the Aden-Victoria station north toward Ibb and Dhamar, then all the way to the main station in Sanaa (Piccadilly-Sanaa, perhaps?). All the other train lines would spread out from there: north towards Amran, Hajjah, and Saada; west towards Hodeida; and east towards Ma'rib, Shabwa, Hadhramaut, and Mahra. All the metro lines—blue, red, purple, pink, brown—would crisscross underground to and from these main lines, Sanaa-Piccadilly and Aden-Victoria, taking people to cities and villages all over the country. But my father and those like him are not the only ones to blame for the fact that this didn't happen. The British also shoulder some of the blame—most of it, in fact. If they're so intelligent, why didn't they think of flying the Yemeni opposition leaders to London and letting them roam the streets and parks? They could have seen for themselves what Aden might have become down the line. If only that had happened... if only... who knows?

But I saw how sad my father looked yesterday, staring into the distance as we strolled through central London. Those looks spoke volumes. I figured he must have been filled with regret— "if only I'd known"... Was he going to admit, now, that his father had been right? That he really had been as foolish as my grandfather had claimed?

We got off the train and stepped into a taxi that took us to the university.

We dropped by the university admissions and registration office. It was a Saturday, but the office was open and ready to receive us. There were people from many different countries. They were mostly European, but there were some Latin Americans, too.

The employee handed me the key to the room that we'd stay in for two nights. After that, I was set to move into the student residence for women.

"We've taken the liberty of booking a room for your father at a nearby bed and breakfast. It's less than three hundred metres from the women's residence," he said, smiling. Sending me off, he added, "Good luck with your studies!"

The world couldn't contain my joy. Those were undoubtedly the most beautiful and genuine moments of my life. My father shook his head slowly, a small smile of satisfaction spreading across his face. "I used to tell you that you were more powerful than ten men put together, but even a hundred men couldn't do what you've just done," he said, his voice calm and tinged with sadness. "I'm so proud of you. You can't imagine how happy I am that you've achieved your ultimate dream."

He caressed my head and tenderly pulled me to his chest. *My father has grown old so quickly*, I thought as I noticed that the once-black hair on his arms had now turned snowy white. Though he was only in his mid-fifties, his neck sagged, and there were deep wrinkles on his forehead and cheeks. Haifa's father is ten years older than mine, but the last time I saw him, I could've sworn that he was ten years younger.

"But my ultimate dream is to find a good doctor, Baba."

He let out a little chuckle. He then asked if we could take a short break from walking, and we sat down to rest on one of the benches in Singleton Park, which stretched from the university to the student residences we were heading toward. He asked me something I hadn't been expecting.

"Would you have ended up in London if I hadn't left Aden to go to Khobar all those years ago?"

I hadn't seen this question coming. I was surprised at its timing and at the look on my father's face. I didn't know how to respond. I think he expected my silence, because he went on, "The truth is that everything happens for a reason, and every action triggers a reaction. You must believe that the reason you're here dates back to my departure from Aden. I want you to know that everything is foretold. If we'd stayed in Khobar, for example, and not gone back to Sanaa, you wouldn't be here right now."

He took out a cigarette and started smoking. He remained silent for a good moment. But, before long, he resumed. I was still struggling to understand why he was saying these things. *It's the philosopher in him*, I thought, stunned by his words.

"And then again, had I stayed in Aden, I never would've married your mother. Everything is indeed predestined. Only God knows that which is unseen. Whenever I used to ask you how you were doing, you'd say you felt like a burning candle. It was your own internal glow that lit up your path. That burning sensation you felt pushed you to challenge everything on your quest to seek treatment. I was watching you from afar, always. And I knew you'd win out. You must stay faithful, never stop praying, and give thanks to God. Your prayers and supplications are what have gotten you this far."

He fell silent after that. He smoked the rest of his cigarette. "You're right, Baba," I said. Just those three tiny words. Nothing more. I didn't want to go any deeper into this conversation, which I'd already had with myself innumerable times. I didn't want to spoil the happiness that had finally become concrete. There was no way I could buy into his logic, that this sequence of events had inevitably brought us to the present moment in London. It was simply too much of a stretch.

After spending two nights in the visitors' lodgings, I moved into the student residence for women, and my father moved into his B&B. I'd drop in to see him twice a day, once in the morning to have breakfast together, then again after 4 p.m., on my way back from university. We'd have lunch together—which often was also dinner, since it was so late in the day. During the first month, I went with him four times to the university's outpatient clinic, where he'd been sent by the British Council. He needed to undergo preliminary tests so they could make a decision about the treatment for his paralysis and determine which hospital could best treat him. But the doctors were quick to confirm that it would be very difficult to perform any kind of operation, as his heart muscles were weak and might not withstand it. They advised him to stick to light exercise and avoid stress; they also gave him a list of medications.

That first month passed at the speed of light. My room was small, but the freedom I felt there was absolute. I'd sit at the window and contemplate all the beauty before my eyes. It looked out onto Singleton Park, those vast expanses of green crawling in all directions. In the distance, I could see the lovely Swansea Bay. To the far right, there were boats and yachts of different sizes and colours docked serenely in the marina. Only two boats were unmoored, moving very slowly towards their designated positions among the others. I was taken by a sudden urge to spend the night on one of them, waking to the sound of water. I summoned the memory of Arwa. She obliged and took a seat beside me. She lay her head on my shoulder. She was breathing very quietly, sitting there and taking it all in with me. How I missed her... Somehow, I knew that she would never be mine. She wouldn't be able to resist her parents' pressure to marry.

At the other end of the park, a group of young men and women were strolling by. They were laughing loudly as they made their way to a small bar my Brazilian colleague had taken me to two nights before. Her name was Lissi. She was beautiful and wonderful company, guzzling down one beer after the other— "I love it! It's bitter, but it does the trick!" she exclaimed, as she carried on drinking. She was telling me with great pleasure how happy she was to be in London. "I've finally escaped my controlling mother!" We had a lot of fun together. I drank orange juice and eventually helped her back to her room just before ten. As I led her to her bed, she whispered, "Free yourself of the insecurities your mother instilled in you."

At the end of the fifth week of classes, I took leave of my father for a day and joined my colleagues on a charming tour of Swansea. It was a Saturday, and we were all excited to discover our new home, happy to be living this new experience. Each of us was thrilled to be there, though some hailed from regions of Europe that were no less beautiful: Munich, Rome, Paris...

When we got back to the residence at four that afternoon, most of the group was already drunk. There was no local pub we didn't visit that day. I returned to my father, and they went back out for a nightcap or two.

They looked so free, drinking like that. It gave me the wild idea to try it out for myself. But I was too afraid, of too many things—not the least of which was the hijab on my head. It was enough to curb my desire.

But then I told myself, *The day will come, Alia, when you'll be just as free as they are to do whatever you want. You'll take off the hijab and, more importantly, you'll break free from the fear that controls you on the pretext of tradition. You'll set out to live a life full of beauty and truth.*

My English language professors at the university were all British, and they seemed to be perennially happy, with permanent smiles on their faces. Since I'd arrived, not one of them had walked into the classroom wearing a frown. This was in stark contrast to what I'd gotten used to in Sanaa. Professors could barely conceal the demons trying to scratch their way out of their eyes. The difference must be that the British did their best to weed the sadness out of their lives so they could be happy, whereas we kill the fragile joy in our souls so we can wallow in our misery.

It wasn't just their even-temperedness that attracted me. It was something more: their simplicity. We'd heard so much about these people but knew nothing about them. They were the kindest people I'd ever met. We used to call them "infidels", and over the generations, we'd continued to refer to them this way, without ever having lived among them. We never got to know who these people really were. We'd unflinchingly inherited this negative view from our ancestors without giving ourselves the chance to question it. What else had we blindly inherited—what misconceptions have yet to be unearthed?

From the first day I landed in London, I kept mulling over these questions. If these people were such "infidels," how was it that they lived such an orderly life? How are they so free, with nothing standing in the way of what they want? I found them to be very respectful of others and ethical in their actions, making way for those who were older, giving up their seats on trains or buses for women and the elderly. They might take a moment of their day to stop and help a blind person cross the street, they drove with caution, and they hardly ever honked. I couldn't believe my fortune at finally being in the UK.

"The British have surpassed us on so many levels," I told my father as we sat at the dinner table. "It's as if they're living on an entirely different planet. I don't know why we've condemned them... they're the most proper people I've ever been around."

"Don't let this influence you. Their world is only transient. Temporary. The Hereafter is more important."

I nodded in agreement, though once again I was unconvinced. Didn't the British also have a religion, revealed to them by the same God that brought us Islam? The principles of their religion don't differ much from ours, and theirs was even older. God cannot reveal a religion that is imperfect. They are not so different from us. They go to church on Sundays to worship God, just as we pray together on Fridays. And if God didn't love them and wish them well, would He have offered them all this beauty, and destined us to live in chaos? No, He would have sent them the wrath of the Ababeel birds, hurricanes and earthquakes, destroying them and wiping them out of existence. If we were so superior, He would have honoured us—the chosen ones, the good ones—and transported us to live in this land, which looks exactly like we imagine paradise: rivers and greenery, varieties of fruits and wines, the mesmerising faces of beautiful people, cool weather, and kindness.

I had to ask him the niggling question that I hadn't been able to get out of my mind, despite all my desperate attempts. With every passing day, I could see a growing conviction on his face that he had misjudged these people who were now doing everything they could to find him the treatment he needed. Because it was my last opportunity to do so, and my father was in a good mood, I finally asked him, "Baba, honestly, having seen what you've seen here... and knowing what Aden went through once the British left... If you could go back in time to the colonial days, would you do it all again?"

He laughed even before I got the chance to finish my question. It was as if he'd been expecting me to ask this, as if he'd sensed me building up to it. Scratching his chin, he said, pensively, "Imagine that you have a home with vast lands suitable for growing a wide variety of crops. All the best types of fruits and vegetables. Now imagine that someone comes into your home and suddenly says he owns everything there. You have to bow down to him, obey him, and surrender to him in awe and fear because he is brutal and all-powerful. You couldn't take him on if you tried. And then he starts exploiting your land, cultivating it, and selling your crops. He eats and drinks and gets his fill—not only his fill, but that of his children, his family, his friends, his whole country. Meanwhile, all he offers you is the bare minimum to quell your hunger and quench your thirst. The things he gives you make you feel like you're stuck in limbo. If someone did that to you, would you remain silent in the face of such injustice? Such theft and humiliation?"

"But before they came along, you didn't know a thing about your land or the crops that could grow on it!"

"But they didn't show up to teach us how to cultivate our land and harvest our crops. They showed up to plunder and pillage. It should come as no surprise to you that part of what they stole from us helped them build this university you're studying at, helped them pave these roads that you see here."

***

The days continued to bleed into each other at the same rapid pace. I decided to lay my internal struggles aside for a while. I'd think about them later. For now, I had to focus on my studies. It was crucial for me to pass this year's English courses with flying colours.

I was able to focus better once my father finally decided to return to Sanaa. It had been confirmed beyond any doubt that his heart wouldn't get him through surgery. A few days before he left, I took him to a well-known specialist in London, where I paid sixty pounds for a half-hour consultation, just to be sure. But even this specialist was quick to confirm the other doctors' fears.

It was with a very heavy heart that my father returned to Sanaa. It was a Friday at the end of August. I left university early and took the train with him first to Piccadilly Station, then to Gatwick Airport. As we said goodbye at the entrance to the Departures Hall, I tried to give him hope.

"Medicine is advancing very rapidly. Very soon, there'll be treatment for your condition. Hang in there. Mama and I need you. My brothers and sisters need you. I promise I'll send your medical records to more hospitals. I'll do my best to find you the treatment you need."

He held me close, tears spilling out of his eyes and onto his cheeks. "Don't worry about that, habibti. Take good care of yourself. My only wish is to see you again before I die."

"Don't say that, Baba. You'll live a long life and be there, in perfect health, to see me graduate, God willing."

He smiled through his tears and looked at me as only a father could, eyes full of love and tenderness. "I have a feeling you'll never return to Sanaa... But there's something I need to ask you. If, God forbid, something happens to me, you must take my place. Promise me you'll never leave your siblings to fend for themselves, no matter what."

That was the one thing I'd wished he'd never ask of me.

"I promise, Baba."

Seeing the tears in his eyes and hearing the weakness in his voice was heart-breaking. My own tears started flowing down my cheeks soon after. I was so close to asking him what Dr Abdel Ghaffar had said that night. I was prepared to beg him to tell me, to plead with him if he refused. But in that moment, I realised that whatever he would say was no longer of any importance now that I was finally here, in London. No matter what Dr Abdel Ghaffar had said, and my father had kept from me, it wouldn't be true anyway. Suddenly I wondered how many other poor people must have gotten tangled up with that doctor. Where had *they* ended up?

I took the train back to Piccadilly Station, where I had to wait more than four hours for my train to Swansea.

I got into a taxi and asked the driver to take me to Al-Saqi bookshop near Hyde Park. I'd heard so much about it back in Sanaa, and I thought I'd fulfil my dream of reading more works by excellent writers so I could write like them, if not better. Sometimes, I felt as if I'd been born to be a writer, or a poet perhaps. I picked up a few books of poetry by Nizar Qabbani and Mahmoud Darwish, novels by Ghada Samman, Yusuf Idris, and Ihsan Abdel Quddus, and a copy of *Gone with the Wind* in Arabic, which I'd forgotten to pack when I left Sanaa. Then I headed back to Piccadilly Circus.

I sat down on a metal chair, which I could tell had been recently painted silver. I put my books down next to me and started reading Nizar Qabbani's *I Married You, Liberty*. I allowed myself to be swept away by his literary prowess, but exhaustion soon caught up with me, and I let the image of my father filter back to the surface. I saw the streaks of tears on his face as he said goodbye, asking me to never abandon my family. *I hope I don't disappoint you, Baba*, I thought. I didn't know if I could keep my promise.

I pulled myself out of my thoughts and started to observe the relentless flow of human traffic all around me. There were so many different types of people. I wondered whether they were all carrying their own grief, all these people walking right by me. Some moved faster than others. Some had smiles on their faces, others furrowed brows. There were both able-bodied people and also some using crutches. Young and old. What were their stories? Is everything that happens to a person really predestined, written, unchangeable? If so, if we all lack free will, then what are the criteria according to which joy and sorrow are distributed amongst us? Why do some people hardly suffer, while others have enough hardship to last a lifetime?

I stopped myself and begged God for forgiveness. These are matters for Him, not for us earthly beings.

Mere moments later, I had a wild idea. I rushed into the nearest bathroom, took off my hijab, and stuffed it into my handbag. I shook out my hair and combed it, then walked straight into the first pub I saw. The Jewel Piccadilly. I ordered a beer—the same brand for which I'd seen ads plastered everywhere.

"A Carling, please."

I gulped down my drink from a large pint glass. I didn't taste the bitterness that Lissi had described, but when I got to the bottom of the glass, I did feel a sense of calm liberation wash over me. It was exactly how I'd imagined I would feel. Soon after, I asked for a second pint, but this time I took it outside and sat on one of the chairs scattered around on the patio, like I'd seen others do. *I have to start living like the locals*, I told myself. *Soon I'll be a local, too.*

A group of pretty blonde girls was standing in front of me, another group of even more handsome boys next to them. Like me, they all had beers in hand. They laughed, speaking with thick British accents I couldn't understand. To my left was a man in his forties, drinking a dark lager and reading a newspaper. He had a suitcase next to him. There was also an older lady on my left, probably in her sixties, also drinking beer. She had brought her little dog, who was pressing quietly against her legs. I could spot another, bigger pub, a bit further away, bustling with people. Most people had luggage in tow and were passing time before their journeys, just like me. Hundreds of people were walking in the street in front of where I was sitting. Coming and going. Some took their time, and some were rushing, probably running late. Others were strolling with a boyfriend or girlfriend, and most were dragging their suitcases, big and small, behind them. They'd cross the street when the light turned green and wait patiently when it flashed red, even when there were no cars in sight—with the exception of some impatient teens of course... I saw people in jeans and short shorts, people in suits and ties, children in prams, and buses stopping to let passengers off and on. Every now and then, I'd spot some joggers crossing the street and heading toward the green spaces and public parks.

Every spot was buoyant with life, and there was something beautiful in the constant hustle and bustle. Everyone was free to do as they pleased. People minded their own business and didn't meddle in what others were doing. Everyone was just free... free to do as they liked.

Here, you belong to yourself. You do whatever you want. You aren't implicitly controlled by customs and traditions that you inherited without having a choice in the matter. I saw a girl kiss her boyfriend on the lips before they each went their own way. At the entrance to the station, a man in his fifties with a long white beard was playing the guitar. He'd left his guitar case open on the ground in front of him, ready to receive the coins jingling in passersby's pockets. Someone had even thrown in a five-pound note. A pretty young woman was handing out flyers to people, perhaps an ad about some new French perfume or a new film now showing in theatres.

What a wonderful life.

Some people are born in the wrong place. I'm sure it's true. Something goes wrong somewhere, and people are fated to belong to a specific part of the world. It is then up to them to make the considerable effort of figuring out which place they actually *want* to belong to, and then moving there. Correcting the errors made by fate. Sometimes this happens on purpose: God deliberately wants us to toil and struggle to achieve the happiness that was originally our destiny. Those who succumb to their fate lose everything and eventually die without even realising that they didn't lead the lives they were meant to—because they didn't try. They didn't search for the true meaning of their lives. My own life is a prime example. And I'm definitely not alone.

I had no choice but to leave both Khobar and Sanaa. There was no way I could stay there, knowing even the little I did about my condition. It simply wasn't an option. When Dr Abdel Ghaffar mentioned London, it could only have been a sign from God. He guided me to the beginning of my solution, but it's up to me to fight to realise it. There are probably many people like me, who have been sent such signs, but in order to get somewhere, they need to be open to receiving and understanding them. As I sat there pondering these issues, I spotted an elderly Indian man crossing the street, holding his granddaughter's hand. He too must have received a sign and realised that his past life was not the one he was supposed to be living. And thus he decided to live out the rest of his years here. I thought that perhaps an African man I spotted sitting beside me was in a similar situation. He might have realised that he didn't belong in his country and thus decided to see if he could fit in with life here, in Britain...

Suddenly, my gaze met his. I'd been sitting there daydreaming about all these questions and must have inadvertently been staring at him—mistakenly thinking I was staring into the distance. He noticed I was alone and shuffled in his seat to face me. Smiling, he said, "Hi. Where are you from?"

"Swansea," I replied, bewildered.

"Are you alone or with someone?"

I grew more and more perplexed. I could tell from his eyes that our conversation wasn't going to end there. All at once, I stood up and said with a smile, "I have to go. I don't want to miss my train."

I picked up my bag and hurriedly collected my things.

"Hey, you! You haven't even finished your drink."

"It's fine. I've had enough."

Suddenly I felt afraid. I tried to get out of there as quickly as possible. I had a gut feeling that he was following me. His hand proved to be faster than my footsteps: he grabbed my wrist and, just like that, I was jolted back to the present. I had fallen asleep on the chair and imagined the whole thing. I let out a little cry, attracting everyone's attention. A group of young men sitting next to me looked at me and laughed. "Are you alright?" one of them asked.

"Yes, thank you," I said, breathing a sigh of relief and thanking God that it was just a dream. A nightmare, rather. I felt like my father's philosophising had crept into my subconscious and made me ponder the deep meanings behind everything.

I checked the time, anxious that I might have missed my train. But I still had an hour to go. I went to the bathroom and looked at my reflection in the mirror, adjusting my scarf. Was God angry at these thoughts that kept hounding me? Was this His way of warning me? I had so many questions...

But I wouldn't go back to living in fear. No way. I hadn't come all this way to be afraid. Lissi had told me to free myself of the insecurities my mother instilled in me. I knew she didn't mean my actual mother, Jawaher; no, she was talking about the whole environment I'd grown up in, everything I'd been told was right and wrong, the traditions I'd been raised with. I'd try to rid myself of it all, but I knew it wouldn't be easy. It's no snap of the fingers to let go of such ingrained notions, especially after twenty-five years.

I finally got on the train. It would be another three and a half hours before I reached my destination. Enough time to think about how I would change my life and live without fear. Would I take off the hijab? Perhaps the time had not yet come for that...

I debated with myself:

If you keep it on, don't you think that'll prevent you from seeing yourself as a boy?

Right. But until now, I'm still a girl.

Can't you try to imagine it somehow? Live it out?

Ha! With these breasts!?

I realised that even though I'd been in the UK for eight full weeks, I still hadn't set up a doctor's appointment to talk to someone about my condition and seek treatment. And when I told myself I'd make an appointment the following week, I suffered through a barrage of tough questions. Was it too early to start? Should I wait a while longer? Wouldn't they put two and two together and realise that I worked so hard to come here to get treated, and not to get another degree? What if the university finds out and notifies the British Council? Would they cut off my scholarship and send me back to Sanaa unchanged? Wasn't it best to wait another year, just until I was accepted into the Master's program and my status here became somewhat more permanent? Wouldn't it be wiser to reveal my secret then?

I mulled over these questions throughout the entire journey, without getting to the bottom of any of them. I regretted not having brought my journal along; I felt a pressing need to write this all down.

As soon as I arrived at Swansea station, I wished, once again, that I had the courage to take off my hijab and walk into the first pub I saw. I would sit there and just think... I'm all alone now. By myself. No one knows who I am. No one cares where I'm from or what my religion is, and no one will care if I violate the teachings of my religion. So why don't I start now? Why don't I just break free from all the restrictions in my mind and set off on my path to liberty? To borrow a phrase from Nizar Qabbani, perhaps I should marry this liberty. I opened his book and read:

> The executioner can't cut off my tongue.
> This is as true as the sky is blue...
> For liberty, resistance.

I was in bed when I decided that the time was not yet right for me to exercise my newfound freedom in this way. I was still afraid that word would travel to the university in Sanaa. What if they found out and decided to make me return to Yemen? I also made another decision: I wouldn't tell anyone about my condition before I finished my English-language courses this year and got accepted into the Master's degree course. I needed to make my existence here more permanent before I could think of anything else.

Part Two

Ali Ilwan

When Picasso was asked why some of his paintings were so confusing, he replied:

"The world today doesn't make sense, so why should I paint pictures that do?"

Alia
Swansea

The first time I sat down with Dr Bowles at the University Medical Clinic was at the beginning of March in 1993. I hesitated for a long time before taking this step, but my constant pain and cramps were not only affecting my mood and health, but also my concentration at school. This was what finally forced me to lift the mantle of silence. I reproached myself for my hesitation and also reminded myself that I was mainly in this country to get the appropriate treatment for my condition, so I mustn't waste any more time.

In the days leading up to my appointment with Dr Bowles, I read a huge amount of what had been written about conditions like mine. Everything here was accessible and clear. They gave different names to what I have: birth defects, a sexual abnormality, a sexual identity disorder, gender dysphoria. But none of this was important. All that mattered was that everything I'd read confirmed that I was more a man than anything else. Despite this, and despite my deepening certainty that I had originally been born male, I was nowhere near comfortable enough to talk about my condition. I was firmly convinced that the treatment I needed would not be approved, simply because I was not British. Conditions like mine aren't covered by the health insurance for international students. Worst of all, I could only be treated in London. And the only way for me to get treated there would be for the NHS to agree to cover the costs. Otherwise I would have to pay the exorbitant expenses myself, which I couldn't possibly afford. This was all the more true because most of the money I received from my monthly student stipend from the University of Sanaa, as well as the supplementary scholarship I'd won from the University in Swansea, went to my father to help with family expenses. But I had no choice but to try, and you never know, maybe...

Dr Bowles was extremely kind. Her face flushed and she scrunched up her eyebrows, shaking her head mournfully, reacting with empathy to what she was hearing. "My God, your story is fantastically odd. It's like hearing a myth or legend. Usually girls and young women come to me when they're having irregular periods. Once or twice, I've seen girls who've had sex with boys and were in a lot of pain afterwards. This made them hate sex, and they needed psychological help in order to get back on track. Once, a boy came to me asking for help to transition into a woman, but I have never heard of a situation exactly like yours."

"I've never felt like a woman, but I don't know to what extent I'm a man," I told her, taking advantage of her sympathy. But because I was so moved by her generous empathy, I suddenly burst into tears. I tried to pull myself together quickly, and she handed me tissues to wipe my face. "For my whole life, even before I hit puberty, I felt attracted to girls. I feel like I want to touch them, kiss them. I think that these are more a man's feelings than a woman's."

She paused, shaking her head and thinking, before telling me that she would help me in any way she could. One week later, she informed me that the only thing she would be able to do was transfer me to the psychiatric unit at the Hammersmith Hospital in London. Then she confirmed what I already knew, which was that there was no specialised hospital care for my condition in Swansea or all of Wells County.

Two weeks later, I received an email with the date of my first appointment in London. Dr Montgomery had scheduled it for Thursday the 1st of July 1993. That specific date—the first of July—has had recurring importance in my life. *There is surely some deeper message for me in this,* I thought. *It's not possible, indeed it's impossible, for this date to appear so persistently without some greater meaning.* But I would wait and see, or, as the saying goes, "The longer you live, the more you learn." That first appointment of mine was happening exactly three years to the day after I'd arrived in London for the first time.

I took the train from Swansea to King's Cross Station in Central London, and from there I took the pink line to the Hammersmith Hospital in the White City district. It was an old building that looked like an ancient Victorian house.

Dr Montgomery was waiting for me at the door to his rooms. He hastened to shake my hand, raising his eyebrows slightly in surprise, "I found what my colleague Dr Bowles told me to be truly unusual. It seems we're going to be spending a lot of time together." Noticing the confusion and even fear that crossed my face, he added, "No need to worry. There's a treatment for everything. Yours is not the first such case I've dealt with."

Montgomery
London

I couldn't tell her. I knew, but I couldn't just say it. How could I simply blurt out, the moment I met her, that she was male? There was no way she could be female—especially not with the structure of her face and the hoarseness of her voice. I couldn't just say it to her straight away, but testing her hormone levels did the trick: they very quickly proved that, for her entire life up until then, she was and could only ever have been male.

Still, I didn't confirm this to her until our third session together, when her lab results came back. By then, things were no longer ambiguous. The tests on her hormone samples revealed that she was male through and through.

Alia was eager to undergo the operations and wanted to get them all over with in one go, to emerge the very next day in a new body, a male body. But my many years of experience in the field had taught me to know better. I could not allow that to happen.

In cases like this, it's always difficult to discern just how much the person sitting before you will be able to accept the looming psychological turmoil, let alone the pain of surgery. When society has grown accustomed to seeing a person one way, putting a sudden and abrupt new identity into the world rarely goes as smoothly as patients believe it will. On the contrary, the shock can be violent. Before the surgeries, this transition requires several phases of psychological treatment that can last for many years, longer than might be expected. Even then, there's no guarantee what will happen. I've watched many people go through this.

"I'll stay in the hospital for a whole month. Even longer... if that'll do it!" Alia announced with such resolve, you'd have thought undergoing four operations at once were an easy feat. How did she not realise that this was pure fantasy?

She should never have been left untreated for so long. Her case should have been flagged early on. Facial hair and a low-pitched voice immediately indicate high testosterone levels. Cases like hers can be detected quite early, usually during puberty. But this is not a lone case, coming from a part of the world where sex is a rigid binary: there, you're either a man or a woman. Any less rigid, more flexible identity is quickly covered up or denied. I've come across many such cases. Most of the people involved were unable to talk to their parents about their situation and remained alone in their suffering.

Very few people are aware of how far science has progressed in this field. It has become easy to detect a baby's sex, even when the visible parts are not clearly defined. All it takes is some simple tests.

People flock to our hospital from far and wide, especially in the summer. They mostly come from Asia and the Gulf as soon as summer vacation starts, most often when the patient has reached, or is believed to have reached, puberty and has not yet started producing sperm, if male, or menstruating, if female. Sons are usually accompanied by fathers and daughters by mothers—rarely do both parents show up with the patient. Fathers most often storm out of my office, furious at the situation their sons have wound up in. They believe that their sons turned out this way because they were molested as children but kept quiet about it. They believe that this alleged molestation alone brought on their sons' "deviance."

"Don't be shy. Tell the doctor who touched you when you were little."

But again and again, without fail, the sons swear this never happened.

"This is not about deviance or homosexuality," I explain to the fathers. I then delve into a deeper description of the difference between homosexuality and gender dysphoria, or congenital identity malformations. Some fathers are understanding, while others beg God for forgiveness and stumble out of my office unconvinced—especially if their sons are about to become daughters.

Very few understand that their children were born with both male and female reproductive organs. They don't believe that the sex organs matching their chromosomes remain deep within the body, and that the more visible organs can be deceptive, as they alone do not dictate a person's sex. But my young patients quickly realise that something is wrong. And thus begins their journey of discovering their true sex.

"You should have told your parents what you were feeling, so they could have understood there was something wrong," I told Alia.

Tearfully, she said, "I did tell them, several times. It didn't help. Perhaps they too thought I was gay."

It wasn't the first time that I was awash with resentment, sitting there listening to the stories of a child wronged because of such misconceptions.

"Dealing with such issues should be easier these days," I tell Alia, as if willing her to relay my words to everyone she knows. "Everyone should be aware that not all intersex people are gay. Cases like yours exist. Some people are simply born with the wrong visible sex organs that don't match their chromosomal make up. How can this be considered deviance? Or a departure from God's laws, as so many fathers who've sat in this same chair have shouted?"

"I cannot blame my father, Doctor. He believed what the doctor who was treating me told him."

"And what did this doctor say?"

"I'm not exactly sure, but the female physician assisting him implied that they'd decided I was gay. That's why the doctor insisted that my father bring me to London. I don't think he meant I should come here to get treated... I think he meant that, here, I'd be able to lead an openly gay life, and I think my dad understood it that way, too. So he kept it a secret."

I asked her about the medical reports she'd received back then. I was shocked by her response: "They refused to release any of my medical records to us."

This is when the story began to make some sense. I can easily imagine this doctor's thought process. It was already too late when he realised the grave mistake he'd made. The damage to Alia's body had already been done. And because he didn't have the courage to admit what he'd done wrong, he covered it up with all these other claims. That scenario is disastrous enough— but if he actually thought that Alia's "diagnosis" was that she was gay, the disaster is tenfold.

I told myself that Alia was one of the rare lucky ones, because she'd made it here in the flesh. I've read countless stories of parents abandoning their children to avoid shame and scandal. Life has treated those cases... those children... cruelly and unfairly. They didn't have a say in what body they were born into. They are people who deserve care, compassion, and a listening ear. Their stories demand that we find a solution.

Treatment can be relatively simple if administered at an early age. At Alia's age, though... it will be infinitely harder on her.

One week before my appointment with Alia, a father came to me with his son, a young man in his twenties. He had two testicles and a small penis, but his testicles would not produce any sperm for the life of them. Nor will they ever, because this young man, simply put, is a young woman. A woman in a male-appearing body. Had he come to me at an earlier stage, at least four years earlier, he wouldn't have needed numerous painful operations. This young woman's suffering and pain could have been somewhat alleviated.

"What took you so long to come here?" I asked the father.

The man replied that his son had only told them about his problem one month earlier, "When we tried to force him to get married."

"Didn't you follow your son's development, step by step? Didn't you ask him if he'd started ejaculating when he reached puberty?"

But the father just sat there, shyly shaking his head. "We don't talk to our children about such things."

Still, I can't really blame them too much. Even here in Europe, where such topics are discussed more openly, there are still people who truly refuse to believe that some of us are born in the wrong bodies and need help. Instead, they ignorantly convince themselves that this is a kind of punishment. Parents are convinced that they have sinned, and that this punishment is to torture them. In all of this, do they never pause to think what the child had to do with any of it?

Alia asked me to start her treatment right away. She could not, however, have fathomed the scale of the suffering that was coming. She would not only endure one painful operation but up to four or five, maybe even more. She couldn't possibly have understood the amount of cutting and pasting her body would be subjected to. How could she have at that point even imagined the countless years of looming pain and check-ups or the toxins we call medicine that she would have to take for the rest of her life?

"When did you start feeling different?" I asked, surprised to learn that Alia was 28 years old.

"I'm not really sure, Doctor. But I always knew I was different, as far back as I can remember. I was probably eight, perhaps a little younger."

Alia needed to go through extensive counselling before being fully ready to transition. Some of my patients were unable to adapt to their new post-transition lives as quickly as we'd anticipated, and they'd displayed an eagerness not unlike Alia's. It had taken them a full year, sometimes even up to two years, to stabilise.

"We're going to have you complete several stages of therapy so I can be absolutely certain that you're ready for the next step. This could take a while, so brace yourself. It's a long journey. There will be painful surgeries. But before we get to that, you need to be mentally ready to transition from being a *she* to being a *he*. There's no need to hurry. Things don't always happen the way we'd like. We'll move together gradually, step by step. We won't rush to the finish line."

She nodded in agreement, a faint smile dancing across her face.

"I'm ready now, Doctor."

"You won't be ready until at least a year from now. Trust me. Don't underestimate the process."

I was tragically deceived once, and I was not about to make the same mistake again. It was a case that had, at first, seemed perfectly simple. A teenage boy came to me, and I discovered he was actually a girl who'd been born with a disfigured penis below her stomach. The penis was limp, with no life, only able to serve as a urinary organ. But she had a full female reproductive system in hiding: a vagina, ovaries, and a uterus. He was excited to learn this and accepted the transition into being a female with ease.

I was fooled into believing that she didn't need extensive counselling. She seemed even readier psychologically than physically to make the transition. But I quickly regretted my naiveté. We performed a mere four surgeries on her, and she emerged a beautiful girl with delicate features, fluttering around like a joyful young bird just learning how to fly. But less than a year down the line, she killed herself, because when this former boy became a full-fledged girl, all her friends abandoned her. I cannot repeat the same mistake twice. I knew better than to rely on the excitement radiating from Alia's face. Before going even one step further, I needed to be absolutely certain that she was psychologically and physically ready for what was to come.

"But I'm already twenty-eight. If I have to wait another year to start treatment, I won't be done with the surgeries until I'm in my mid-thirties!"

"That's right, but you mustn't forget that securing funding for your surgeries will take at least a year. And that's *if* the Health Services Authority approves the funding."

"Is there any hope that they'll approve it, considering I'm not even British?"

"I think so. I made it a point not to mention where you're from in my correspondence... implying that you're British. Keep in mind that the Medical Research Centre may fund half of your treatment as well. Don't worry."

"I don't know how to thank you, Doctor."

"We'll be the ones thanking you once you emerge from these surgeries and live your life as a man. Your success will reflect well on our reputation. You may not know this, but cases like yours present new and important challenges to us as doctors. We're determined to get you through it successfully."

Alia came to us much too late. I cannot imagine how this man lived twenty-eight healthy years in this body. I've never seen a case like this. Alia is a medical marvel. How did he tolerate the massive physical and emotional pain he must have suffered? How could he have borne it? How did he live all those years in a female body with such singular composure, grasping at the slightest thread of hope that he would one day come here to be treated? He deserved to be highly commended. No one else would ever know just how much he suffered. But getting here at such a late stage means that he will most likely need more surgeries than the four major ones. The doctors might not find what they need in his stomach for the complementary support operations. First, they will have to take off the breasts. Then comes the main surgery, which is also the most dangerous. They will remove the penis and testes from the abdomen, redirect the urinary tract, and stitch up the cavities, finishing up with the vaginal opening. This process takes six to ten years.

"You've been here for three years. Why did you stay quiet all this time?"

"..."

"You shouldn't have been afraid. Health care is confidential here. Your scholarship is a completely separate matter. You've unnecessarily wasted two years... I should think that your health and body were surely in better shape two years ago."

I stopped myself there. There was no need to depress him with such reproaches.

I told him it was a necessary first step to find himself some friends who'd been through this process, to help him truly understand what it means for someone to reintegrate into society as a man after having been perceived as a woman for so many years. This would especially apply to the social circles that had accepted him *because* he was a woman.

"They accepted you because you appeared female. You would never have gained access to certain spaces as a man. So people's reactions may be quite different from what you expect."

I told him not to be surprised if some of his acquaintances and female friends stopped associating with him as soon as they heard about his transition. I prepared him to expect blame and shame from some people, and even to be defamed and vilified. But I also told him not to pay these people any mind.

I once again implored him to listen to every word I said: every point I brought up was essential.

"From now on, you need to train yourself to be a man. The most difficult part is changing the feminine behaviour ingrained in you and becoming more masculine. When people transition, they don't adapt to this as quickly as we'd like, or as they'd like. Especially when it comes to interactions with others: women treat people more gently and tenderly than men do. You're used to acting this way because you were raised as a girl. But this might be awkward when it comes time to deal with men."

Confidently, he said, "Before I came here, Doctor, I read a lot about my condition and what I should do. Rest assured: I will be ready. I just want to live the rest of my life as a man."

After our third session, I started addressing him with male pronouns. By then, his tests were back. But it was only after two full years of counselling that I asked him what he'd like to be called. I told him it was time to issue that very important medical certificate that would change the course of his entire life. This document would serve as proof to the world that he was, indeed, a man. I had not wanted to get him unnecessarily excited by asking him this question too soon. I waited until I was completely certain that the Health Services Authority, with support from the Medical Research Centre, would cover the cost of the surgeries. His turn would come before ringing in the new year in 1998; that's when the funding would start. There were more than one hundred cases on the list ahead of him. Still, he would become a man within ten days at the most, on paper at least.

Tears welled up in his eyes when I told him that I was in contact with a lawyer who would amend his official identity documents in the UK, and that I would also write to his embassy to change his passport.

"What do you want your name to be?"

"This is the most important word I will ever say," he whispered, but he was prepared. It took him less than two seconds to answer.

"Ali."

Tears streaked down his face. Then they flowed with such intensity that neither his shirtsleeves nor the many tissues he was holding could absorb them. They dropped onto his thighs and even down to the floor of my office. His joy was contagious: I felt at once sympathetic and sad for him, and it wasn't long until tears were streaming down my cheeks as well.

From the first time I met him, I vowed that I would stand by him. I would do everything I could to help him because of how deeply dismayed I was by the injustice he'd had to endure and the patience with which he'd faced it. Ali's case is an extremely rare one. It is among the strangest and most difficult that I'd ever come across.

I bade him farewell and planned to meet him again the week of his first surgery: "I think David will be the one performing the operation. He's one of the top surgeons in Britain. Don't worry, you'll be in safe hands."

"I don't know how to thank you. All I have is words, and words are not enough to express my appreciation."

I hugged him, wishing him success in his future life.

Nasser
Leicester City, UK

When I first met her at university, I immediately noticed the stubble of her moustache. I'd never had an Arab colleague before, let alone someone from the neighbouring country of Yemen, which had been a large part of my childhood. I was raised on beautiful old Yemeni songs. I extended my hand to shake hers.

"I'm Alia, from Yemen."

"I'm Nasser, from Oman. We're neighbours!"

"Siblings."

"Indeed! I didn't even know that you were in our program. I didn't see your photo on the board with everyone else's."

"Right. I prefer not to put my picture up there."

Her low-pitched voice suggested that she had unusually high testosterone levels. I'd just started my doctoral studies at the University of Leicester in October 1995. She'd begun hers in the field of remote sensing a year before me. Our second meeting took place two months after that initial encounter. I invited her to meet my wife and daughter at our house in the modest little town of Loughborough, less than twelve miles from Leicester.

My wife Fatima was studying for a Master's degree at the Loughborough College of Technology, so I'd rented us a house near her college.

"Could you hint that she should stop shaving her moustache? It would be better to wax or pluck it," I told Fatima while we waited for Alia to arrive for her second visit, about two months after the first. We were celebrating Eid al-Fitr, which came at the end of February that year.

"I don't think waxing or plucking would work. Her moustache hair is as thick as yours." I'd expected her to say that.

"I also know that she doesn't wear a hijab. I guess she only puts on that hat because she feels uneasy around my Saudi colleague Meshal and me. Tell her not to wear it on my account. I don't care about these things. It will be easier for you to tell her... you two are friends now."

"She's told me she wears it because her hair is falling out. She suffers from hypothyroidism and high blood sugar."

"She has trouble with her sugar at such a young age?"

I'd always been a bit suspicious of Alia. She never really struck me as a woman. Her features seemed ambiguous. Her clothes, the way she walked, her voice, her hair... nothing suggested she was a woman, not in a normative way at least. There was something different about her. I feared she might be a lesbian—otherwise why wouldn't she have married yet? She came from a milieu very similar to mine. They don't let young women stay without a husband for very long.

"I suspect she likes women, so be careful," I warned Fatima, as the suspicion inside me gained traction.

It wasn't until two years later that my colleagues in the College of Geography and I found out that Alia Ilwan had become Ali Ilwan. I'd just gotten back from my summer holidays in my hometown of Nizwa in September 1997 when I found an email from the Dean of the College in my overflowing inbox. It informed us that the woman we had known as Alia had transitioned. She was now a man called Ali. He asked us to stand by Ali and support him psychologically, so he could make it through this very difficult stage of his life. He also said that Ali was currently in hospital because of a sudden illness and that he was going to need at least a month to recover and return to his studies. All of this had happened in the summer when I was away. The email had been sent in July.

I was horrified. This disrupted my entire day and evening. I wondered how this could have happened. Why hadn't she told us about this herself? Why did we have to hear it from the Dean of the College?

Suddenly, Alia struck me as a liar. He must have known all along that he was planning to transition. He just didn't want to tell us. Gender affirmation surgeries don't happen overnight!

Our colleague Meshal's indignation only made matters worse. As soon as he saw me, he started shouting, frothing at the mouth, so angry that his spittle flew around him, "How dare she spend time alone with my wife, knowing that she was a man?"

And just like that, all the time we'd spent together flashed before me in the blink of an eye. He must have known who he really was—there's no doubt about it—but I also don't believe that he would have hidden something so serious from us without a good reason. Alia must have had reasons to keep this secret. Why else would he have kept it even from Fatima?

"Did he really know?" Fatima asked the same question I had been pondering myself. The image of my wife sitting alone with him in our living room made me incredibly angry. Meshal didn't even know that he had visited our home no less than four times recently, and that I had left her alone with my wife and children for hours at a time. But all the while, I was not leaving *her*, but *him*, alone with my wife. My God! He must have taken us for complete fools! He knew that he was a man and, despite this, spent time alone with my wife. How could he?

These questions burned inside me. I swore that if I ever discovered that he could have told us the truth and hadn't, I would kill him.

"Woe is him..."

"Yes, he's known he was a man for more than two years," Meshal confirmed.

The fire in my chest burned more and more intensely, and I felt like my head was about to burst.

"We're her best friends, why didn't she tell us?" I asked, enraged. But I knew he didn't have any answers. He was just as angry as I was.

"Why didn't *he* tell us, you mean."

"It's going to take some time to adjust to this."

"I still don't know why he hid it from us. We'll have to wait for an answer."

"Where is he now?"

"Ha ha," Meshal laughed, shaking his head, a manifestation of his extreme disbelief. "He's with his fiancée, his future wife, somewhere. It's unbelievable. Closer to fantasy than reality."

"His *fiancée*? He also has a fiancée?" I asked, incredulous, as he stepped away from me at the peak of his rage. Pacing, he made the universal sign for crazy. "She got engaged to, I mean he proposed to, our Malaysian colleague Amira. She came over to our house twice when Alia was there. God help him if I lay eyes on him again! But what can I say? Birds of a feather flock together. Didn't I tell you the whole story is completely mad?"

He paused and turned toward me, shaking his head in sorrow. He then muttered bitterly, "Isn't that something?"

Ali had spoken about Amira more than once. He'd also spoken about Yasmine, an Omani woman who Fatima happened to know.

I stood there, rooted to the steps leading up to our college. Questions spun around and around in my mind—*How could he have done this? How could he have used us like this?* He knew that he was a man, and therefore he should not have spent time alone with other men's wives. He shouldn't even shake hands with them, let alone kiss them on the cheeks! But then I circled back to the other question buzzing in my head: *How on earth did she become a man?*

Before this, I had read about male-to-female gender reassignment surgeries. I can somewhat imagine, maybe even visualise, that transformation. You take off the penis and testicles and, in their place, make an opening to construct a vagina. This is still within the realm of imagination. But how is the opposite possible? Where do the penis and testicles come from? Unless he could get a donor... But... It's making me a bit crazy.

Meshal just kept cursing Ali, accusing him of cheating and lying. He walked away and had almost disappeared from view when he came storming back to say one last thing, the rage in his eyes like lava spilling from a volcano. "This Alia is a reason I might have to divorce my wife. She's stained me with shame. If my family hears this story, they'll bury me and my wife alive."

"You mean *he* stained you with shame," I said, adding to his anguish. He laughed hysterically, swearing and cursing the day he'd met him.

I asked him to wait a little bit, until we'd had the chance to meet him and hear the whole story. But he looked away and dissolved into his own fury. I was trying to tamp down the anger that was also burning inside me. It had shaken me to my core and left me unable to control my temper.

I still couldn't quite believe what I'd heard. The story was difficult to understand or even make sense of. It was almost madness, the plot of a full-blown blockbuster.

I considered my options. Should I swear to God, on my honour, to completely cut off any contact with Ali from this day forward, no matter what reasons or excuses he gave? Could anyone blame me if I did? I doubted it. He had made us live the ugliest, most outrageous lie, a betrayal that no Muslim man or woman should ever have to accept. Or perhaps it would be wiser to slow down and wait, not rush to judgment, and look into the details first before making any rash decisions?

I walked back down the steps that led to the college. I decided to apologise to the colleagues I'd promised to play football with that evening. I would just consider the day a write-off.

I stepped toward the wooden bench under the shade of a large walnut tree. It was cold outside, and clouds were piling up atop each other in layers. I took out a pack of Dunhills and started smoking and thinking, *How could Alia be a man with such ample breasts and a round behind?* Even Fatima doesn't have such a bum and breasts. So what if her voice was lost somewhere between soft and husky? That didn't necessarily mean it wasn't a woman's voice. A British colleague of ours, who's also writing her dissertation, has a voice closer to a man's, too. Hers is even huskier than Alia's, and she's definitely a woman—she's married and has a child.

I recalled the fluff growing on Alia's face and how she'd shaved off her moustache. Trying to escape from the hell of questions plaguing me, I joked to myself, *Ali has both sexes in one body—the upper part is male and the lower female.*

I went back to my car. Usually, the walk to and from my car was the loveliest part of my day, unless it rains. I'd cut through the magnificent Victoria gardens, with its green lawns and rows of giant, thick-trunked trees, the leaves of which had begun to fall. I stared at an elderly man walking his dog and at the children darting all around, their morning ruckus and innocent, bird-like laughter carried by the breeze.

People were reading books and newspapers on the wooden benches all throughout the garden. Squirrels scooted up tree trunks as soon as they heard approaching footsteps. I didn't feel calm at all; I was agitated, and scattered thoughts and questions raced through my mind.

I would have to discuss everything with Fatima. We would decide together how to deal with Ali from that day forward. I would ask her to call Yasmine in Muscat to find out if she knew what we'd just learned. Or at least to tell us more about Alia, who'd been her colleague in Swansea.

Smoking as I walked, I kicked a chestnut that was lying on the ground. A branch had fallen off a tree onto the path. I threw it to the side. I desperately needed to calm my nerves.

Do I really care if Alia has become Ali?

No, I don't. Nothing about this should make me anxious. Nothing in this life should worry me at all. This has been my philosophy for a long time: Nothing in life is worth it. Alia became Ali. That's it, end of story, case closed. Life goes on.

I laughed hysterically as I walked to my car, imagining Fatima's face the first time she laid eyes on the new Alia, on Ali. Her reaction would surely be like none ever seen before—neither on TV nor in the cinema, let alone in real life.

Then I thought about our second child, who had only been in Fatima's womb for four months, and I realised that I would have to break the shocking news to her gradually, for fear of disturbing the being growing inside her.

I put a cassette into the player and skipped to my favourite song, the one I like to listen to when I'm feeling down. I turned up the volume to try to dispel my rage, which was mixed with a deep sense of frustration, despair, and injustice. Muhammad Abdo warbled:

Open your mind, if you're stressed,
You don't need these sufferings.
God above can relieve your distress,
He has power over all things.

The song made me feel even worse, so I ejected that tape and replaced it with Salam Ali Saeed's. I don't know why, but it suddenly aroused a sweeping nostalgia for Nizwa.

I yearn for you, long for those who left the homeland.

I yearn for you, long for the birds in the trees.
Take me away, far away from everyone...

Amira

On the way to Nizwa by plane

If ever someone had told me that I would end up marrying my college roommate, my close friend who'd once even slept in my bed, I would've laughed out loud and questioned their sanity. But if that person had added that, one day, I would be flying with this husband to Nizwa in Oman, I would have sworn they were totally mad. I had never heard of that place in my life, and I only knew as much about it as my husband did about my hometown, Penang, in Malaysia.

Before I met Ali, I'd heard of Oman only through my limited interactions with a few Omanis I'd met at university. I'd heard of it by name and knew it was a Muslim country in the Gulf, near Dubai. I later got to know Yemen through Ali and Oman a bit more through our colleague Nasser. It's actually because of Nasser that we're on our way to Nizwa now.

Ali was asleep on my left, tired out by the long journey. We were returning together from London, where he'd undergone his sixth—and hopefully last—operation. We'd gone to Kuala Lumpur and then onto Penang, only to fly back out to Kuala Lumpur less than forty-eight hours later. From there, we set off for Muscat, where we're headed now. Nasser was waiting to accompany us to Nizwa. We were planning to live in Nizwa for at least a year.

Things had moved so quickly. Nasser called Ali and told him that the Nizwa University Faculty of Science needed a physics lecturer. It took only a few minutes for Nasser to convince him: "I think Amira's the right person, and the salary is quite competitive. Come on... it will be like old times."

Ali couldn't believe his ears. He jumped for joy at the idea, enthusiastically encouraging me to accept.

"But I'm working as a lecturer at the university here... I can't just drop everything!"

"I think you should ask for a leave, for a year or so. It's a good opportunity for you, and perhaps I can find work there as well. I really feel that we'll finally be able to just *be* together there. We've suffered so much, travelling back and forth between Malaysia and London. I'm really worn out."

"And my mother?"

"That's another good reason to accept."

He smiled. I knew what he meant. I felt the same way.

I could hardly tolerate my mother even before Ali came into our life. But once he did, she became downright inhuman.

"What do you want from this short little man? He isn't even one of us! We don't speak the same language. We don't bleed the same blood. There are dozens of people in our town who would love to be with you. You couldn't find anyone else to be your husband?"

"Ali is a good person. He's a gentleman, Mum. I've never met anyone as brave and strong as he is. He has all the qualities a woman looks for in a man."

"I don't know what you're talking about. Make no mistake, Ali is no different than your father—nothing more than a scoundrel."

"Shame on you. My father was no scoundrel, and neither is Ali."

"Oh yes they are. Both of them are good-for-nothings. Mark my words. Do I need to remind you that your cousin has been waiting to marry you for years? How could you have gone and betrayed him? How could you take up with this Ali?"

"My cousin is married, Mum, and he has a child."

"He only got married when he gave up waiting for you, and you know it."

"That's not true. Either you're delusional, or you enjoy buying into these delusions. My cousin never once told me, never even *hinted* at the fact that he wanted to marry me. Where is this coming from?"

"Oh, you're just as stupid as ever! Your degree didn't broaden your mind, it narrowed it further! You married Ali because he's sweet and handsome with those rosy cheeks. But you forgot that he's short—shorter than you— and much younger, too."

"Ali and I don't care about the age difference—or that I'm taller!"

Whenever she lays eyes on Ali, she flies off the handle. For some reason, she can't stand him, and she never misses an opportunity to let me know that I should leave him.

"If he were rich at least, I'd leave it alone."

"We love each other and that's all that matters."

"I don't understand, how exactly did this love develop? What happened between the two of you in London?" She exhaled angrily before carrying on, "I hope you don't plan on having his children. I don't want my grandchildren to have him as a father."

"Actually, I plan on having ten children!"

"You don't understand! He's Arab. Arab men divorce their wives at the drop of a hat and marry another just as easily! Arab men are no good—you used to tell me that yourself!"

"Sure. But Ali's not like other Arab guys."

"You're an idiot. You'll see."

I could never understand why my mother hated Ali so much. When she found herself alone with him one evening, she barked at him, "The girls in your country are gorgeous. Much more beautiful than Amira. Tell me why you chose her!"

"Because I love and respect her, Auntie."

"But you are much more attractive than her. Why don't you find someone who's as good looking as you are?"

"Love doesn't abide by those standards, Auntie."

"What kind of love is that, between two people who couldn't be more different? She's only getting older. She'll be elderly soon, and you'll still be a young man. You'll leave her or take another wife."

"I promise you, that will never happen."

That's when she really lost control. "If you think she's wealthy and has a lot of money, you're delusional. Amira is poorer than you."

How fate works is one of life's great mysteries. The directions it takes you can be truly inconceivable. Anyone in my shoes would say that my destiny—my relationship with Ali and what steered me to it—is, simply put, inconceivable. No one could possibly make it up. It's outside the realm of the imagination. But the strangest and most wonderful thing is Ali's story. Had it been filmed and shown in theatres, it would have grossed millions of dollars and won all the Academy Awards.

How did I meet Ali? It happened by chance.

How was I to know that the steady hum of my days was suddenly about to change? Destiny led me right where it wanted me, without even alerting me to the gathering storm that would trouble the calm, stagnating waters of my life, so quiet for decades. What happened was out of my control.

It was on an October morning in 1993 that I first met Ali, when he was still Alia, in my little office at Swansea University. At the time, I was working on my PhD, and I was also head of the university's Malaysian student association and supervisor of a Malaysian student residence. I empathised with Alia's situation. She was desperately searching for a room she could live in during her final year. On the day she completed her diploma, the university asked her to leave her residence, as it only housed female students actively enrolled in a diploma program. I was struck by her reserved manner, the way she moved, and how she looked at things. It was all a testimony to her calm, kind character. I remember thinking that she seemed lonely and was searching for a friend; I felt we could become friends, as I was trying to get to know people from all around the world.

I invited her to a party held in the residence where only we Malaysian students lived. One of the girls had just graduated and was moving back to Kuala Lumpur, which meant her room was now empty. I watched Alia closely. I noticed she was shy and hesitant—how she seemed poised to take flight from the groups of girls all around her. She no doubt felt out of place amongst us, as we were all of the same background. Not to mention, we were also speaking our own language, Malay, which could only have made her feel more alienated.

"Come and see your room. You can have it, but only if you like it. Don't feel like you have to be polite if it doesn't suit you," I told her, trying to cross the invisible barrier between us.

"I just need a place to come home to at night."

"Why? Where do you spend the rest of your day?"

"At the university."

Her loneliness, her isolation, became palpable then. I assumed she'd decided to be the kind of student who dedicated herself fully—and solely—to excelling in her studies.

We Malaysians consider students from China and Japan to be the most serious, because it seems like they're only interested in their studies. They study, and study, and then study some more. Their whole time at university is spent like this, eating with one hand and holding a book in the other. We joke that they can even solve difficult math problems whilst sitting on the toilet. Before they go to sleep at night, they review all the information they learned, bolting it into the vaults of their memories. Their minds are busy revising their lessons even as they're falling asleep. And the instant they open their eyes in the morning? They rush to the vaults to make sure all the information is still safely stored there.

But Arab students, like Ali, tend to be the complete opposite. Studying comes second in their lists of daily priorities. Getting together, laughing, socialising, and companionship usually take precedence. Exceptions are rare. Alia, however, seemed different. Although she looked Arab on the outside, her behaviour was more like that of the Chinese students. Perhaps this was because, at the time, she was a woman, but she stood out—she didn't act like other girls did. Was it because she came from a modest family background? That could explain why she wasn't good at removing hair from her face, why she didn't wear blush on her cheeks, and didn't moisturise her cracked lips. Perhaps that's why we didn't catch whiffs of perfume when she walked by, even though all the other female Arab students from Kuwait and Saudi Arabia were always doused in their favourite scents.

"You spend most of your time studying?" I asked her, astonished. She smiled tersely before responding in her husky voice, "I don't have a choice. There's nothing else for me to do."

"Don't you have a social life? Friends? People you know?"

"I do, I'm not completely cut off, but..."

I went silent. I opened the door to the room that I'd told her about. She smiled again, shifting her eyes to the floor. She brushed over what I'd said and told me, "The room is great. It will do nicely."
Alia's voice was unique. It was not the most refined nor the most delicate, but there was something compelling in how deep and hoarse it was.

I didn't want to pressure her any further to reveal what she was hiding. I let the conversation suspend itself there, allowing it to end naturally, inwardly hoping to pick it back up another time. But I was not left unaffected: I was completely taken by a desire to know the secrets of this unusual woman. I was convinced that she had more to her than met the eye.

The very next day, she moved into our five-bedroom apartment, into the room next door to mine. Our relationship grew deeper by the day. We lived together for over a year, and, with help from Yasmine, a mutual friend, I was able to pull Alia out of her isolation and total immersion in her studies. Yasmine had come from Oman to pursue a Master's.

Alia slowly became more vibrant and freer; she left behind her world and stepped into ours, into one that was full of laughter and fun. For this, all credit goes to Yasmine. Yasmine, with her sharp yet velvety voice, who couldn't bear to sit still for more than an hour at a time. She lived close by. She'd head to our doorstep and playfully ring the bell with mock impatience, and we'd know it was her.

"Hurry up, lazy bones!" she'd shout, trying to provoke us. Wherever she went, we followed.

Then we arrived at that cold historic morning. Yasmine had left around a month before, headed back to Oman. She'd finished her studies. A sense of peace and quiet had settled over our lives once more, and we rarely left the apartment. Then, with no warning, Alia turned my life upside down. It was the 19th of November 1994.

The night before that fateful morning, the electric heater in her room broke. I was getting ready to submit the final version of my PhD dissertation before my viva. It was viciously cold that night. I was standing in front of the printer in my room, watching the pages come out one by one when she walked in, shivering from the cold. I suggested that she share my room, and we could sleep in the bed together. It was Friday night, and I had planned to print off the entire dissertation and lay it on the table before bed. That way, I could wake up the next morning and spend all Saturday and Sunday revising with no interruptions. She said she had a secret that she needed to confide in me, and she hoped that we could have a picnic the next morning on the seaside in Swansea, so she could feel more comfortable opening up to me.

"Could we postpone and do it on Monday morning instead? You know my plans for the weekend..."

"I know... but I really can't put it off any longer."

Her response both worried me and roused my curiosity.

"Then why can't you just tell me now?"

But she insisted, on the grounds that she was exhausted. She said she couldn't arrange her thoughts properly when she was so tired, and that we would "need at least three to four hours to talk... it's too late right now." I could hear the obvious discomfort in her voice and see it in the trembling of her fingers as she spoke.

Thus we spent the next morning having a "picnic on the seaside in Swansea," just as she'd requested. I'll remember that picnic for as long as I live. It changed so many things for me. It changed the very course of my life. My suspicions were confirmed when Alia told me straightaway that she was hiding a man inside her body. These suspicions had become a shadow cast over us every time our eyes met. I noticed the look Alia always had in her eye; it was different from other girls'. She was something else entirely. And she'd only fanned the flames of my uncertainty with those secretive monthly trips to London. At first, she used to claim that she was visiting her endocrinologist to have her thyroid imbalances monitored, an illness she said she'd inherited from her mother.

I never once saw Alia dressed in feminine clothes—neither at university nor at parties. Her uniform consisted of jeans and a baggy shirt, with a men's hat. She also didn't have a skincare routine like we did. She didn't wear foundation, or any other type of makeup for that matter. No lipstick, no powders. I never saw her in earrings. Not once did she pull her hair up in a ponytail. Her life was almost suspiciously devoid of the colour pink. Her entire style was androgynous, all the way down to her shoes. The perfumes she kept lined up on her desk—as it had never occurred to her to buy herself a dressing table or a vanity—were borderline masculine. Most importantly, I never once heard her complain of period pains like the rest of us. Our cramps were sometimes so bad we had to stay home and miss lectures, and we were often prone to mercurial moods, especially on the first three days of our cycle. But she never complained. Not even once. She had never brought up anything related to periods the entire time I'd known her. What's more, whenever someone brought up their period pains, she would excuse herself and go to her room, just as she would whenever one of us started talking about the man of our dreams.

There was a strong, cool breeze that sunny morning. It felt invigorating. Alia hesitated and almost stuttered as she set the stage for her revelation.

"I'm very fond of you, and I consider you one of the people closest to my heart."

She grew silent for a moment to collect her thoughts before divulging the rest.

She'd had the foresight to have led me to a chair at the edge of the water, where it was calm and very few people would stroll by, especially on a Saturday morning following a typically crazy Friday night in the bars and pubs. Most people would sleep until noon.

She stumbled through her words, her smile never leaving her lips, "I have a secret that I can't keep from you any longer. Please don't react on the spot. Just let me say what I have to say, and then I'll give you space to process and respond."

Mute, I nodded my head, encouraging her to carry on. Then she spoke again, measuring her words more carefully this time. "Promise me that you won't be cross with me, no matter what."

"I promise."

"Promise me that, even if you don't like what you hear, you'll keep it between the two of us. Please."

It seemed that this really was serious.

"I promise. Just tell me, Alia. You're worrying me now."

"I'm sorry. This isn't easy for me at all. But I'll try. You know that people can go through all sorts of things in their lives... some get dealt a much rougher hand, they're born different, and they have to endure and suffer much more than others. I'm one of those whom life has wronged." She paused and glanced at me, to be sure I was right there with her.

"What I'm about to say may not be perfectly accurate, scientifically speaking, but I will try my best to put it in simple terms. I hope you'll understand."

"Some people," she continued, "are born gay. They're born different. They're just made like that—they didn't have a choice in the matter. It's their fate. Only God Himself knows the reason behind it."

Suddenly, I don't know why, I expected her to come out to me as a lesbian. I automatically replayed the previous night in my mind, but I couldn't remember her acting any differently than she usually did.

"I'm not one or the other, Amira, I'm something else entirely. I'm a boy...

a man. But I was born with two sets of genitals. I have female parts on the outside, parts that are temporary, and male parts on the inside, parts that are permanent."

I could feel my head spinning. I couldn't decipher what she was saying. All my years studying physics couldn't help me make sense of it.

Almost in reaction to the strangeness of her confession, the seagulls suddenly stopped squawking. The ducks and swans stopped swimming and diving under water. They seemed to be peeling their ears to listen to this odd conversation.

I continued nodding, indicating that she should carry on.

"I'm a man on the inside. The doctors confirmed this about a month ago. I need to undergo a minimum of four major operations to get the body I should've been born in."

I was shocked. I felt my mind scrambling to process everything.

Lost in thought, I remained silent, unable to speak. A number of different images and scenarios ran through my head. I experienced a flurry of competing feelings for this person: anger, sadness, pity, compassion. But I remained the very image of calm and didn't react. After having grown so close, I knew who she was deep down. I knew her truth, better than anyone. Still, anyone would have been bothered that Alia had hidden such a massive secret from them. How could she hide something like this from me when we'd been quite close for more than a year? I know she's very ethical, good-hearted, and generous, even with her limited financial resources. I won't rush to judgment; I need to take a moment to understand the whole story first. I was self-aware enough, however, to admit right then and there that one reason I found myself so calm was that I had a very special kind of love for Alia. It's difficult to describe, as she is a very special kind of person. Her combination of good-heartedness and mystery always drew me to her, calmed me, and made me open to whatever she said.

I wondered if I loved her as a woman with male traits, or if I had somehow unconsciously intuited that he was actually a man. Perhaps this was why I was not angered by what I'd just heard. I couldn't tell.

Was it that I had actually been hoping, deep down, that Alia were a man—with all the wonderful qualities she possesses, so rare to find in men these days—and I was pleased that she'd become one? *Maybe*, I mused.

The clouds above us parted at that moment, and the sun shone strongly down. Big and little boats were lined up inside the port that day. I felt the sun's warmth as it welcomed people shaking off sleep and moving from inside the boats onto their decks. The gulls regained their voices, squawking from the rooftops of nearby buildings, masts of ships, and sidewalks. The ducks and swans went back to swimming around again, too.

"How could the doctors not have known about your condition in childhood?" I asked, after he'd grown silent.

"Where I was born, where I grew up, we didn't have medical specialists who knew about problems like mine."

After this exchange, he carried on for more than an hour, telling me the story of his life, the "secret life" he had led, as he called it. He talked about Moodi and Arwa, the British Council, the British occupation, and his father. As I listened, I grew increasingly convinced that this was a person who life had truly mistreated, who was miserable and defeated. I felt even more empathetic because I knew someone else who had suffered like him. I would tell him later on about my relative who was ostensibly born a man, but who in reality was a woman. She killed herself when she couldn't face people after her transition.

"When will you start having the operations?" I asked.

"I'm still waiting for approval from the Health Services Authority to fund the first operation."

Pedestrian traffic slowly began to increase all around us and along the coast as people gradually came to life after the previous night's slumber. There were many elderly people, some of whom used walkers or crutches, their partners trailing along next to them. I watched a woman in her seventies light her roll-up and plunge into thought. A very old man walked out with his dog and his young granddaughter, who was speaking at the top of her lungs so he could hear her.

It was a lovely morning, and the sea was calm despite the cold gusts of wind that blew in our faces from time to time. I spotted Michael opening up his well-known pub for the day. Everyone in Swansea knew about Michael. He was an old man from Germany, and his pub was popular with the locals. He liked to introduce himself to every new person who walked through his doors as Michael Schumacher. He'd lived in the same spot in Swansea for over fifty years. There were only twenty years of his long life that had been spent elsewhere. "I'll only leave Swansea in a coffin," he used to say to anyone listening.

The same scene kept repeating itself, over and over. After a while, at the top of the hour, thirsty throats would begin to flock to the bar. As in all of Britain, after drunken Friday nights, Saturday was the biggest drinking day here in Swansea. People started drinking beer around noon, usually at the same time the Premier League matches began. Loud screams and chants poured out of the pubs. At times, you could hear the sounds of cursing, an altercation, or a fight, or all three mixed together, coming from the old man's pub, and the two cheaper pubs next door.

"Whatever you need, I'm here for you," I reassured him. "You deserve the best."

"I really appreciate that, but..." He sank into silence, tilting his body forward, thinking about what to say next. His hesitation was legible on his face. Nodding encouragingly, I softly nudged him to go on, "Carry on then."

"Everything that I've just told you is only a preamble to the main and most important thing—the reason I brought you here today."

His words snatched me out of my reverie, and I knew then that he was about to ask me to stand by him as he underwent the whole process. My first thought was how I would manage to do that when I knew my return to Penang was imminent... and, in any case, I couldn't stay past the coming January. But that's not what Ali asked me.

"Haven't you told me everything?" I asked him, surprised.

"Not yet, I'm going to say the most important thing now."

"Which is...?"

But he retreated and asked me once again to promise not to be angry or annoyed with him, no matter how shocking him confession—which "you may not accept," he claimed.

I motioned to him with my head, indicating, "I promise."
He whispered faintly, "I love you, Amira."

His words were like a bucket of ice being dumped on my head. I was shaken by what I'd heard, and I could feel a shiver run down my spine. I hadn't expected to hear that from her—or him, rather. I was completely at a loss. I felt my tongue stiffen as my mouth went dry. I felt the blood rush through my veins, my joints crack, my hair stand on end. I involuntarily leaned away from him as he remained angled toward me. It was as if everything was passing me too quickly, bypassing the speed of my every thought and expectation. I hadn't even recovered from the first shock of Alia being a man—and now this confession! How could I possibly respond?

For more than a minute, I was tongue-tied. Mute. Everything paused as the seagulls went quiet again and the swans stopped swimming, as if attuned to our conversation. Even the footsteps around us grew quiet. The air stood still. Still, quiet silence pervaded the area. Or at least that's what it seemed like at that moment—he let me be and did not utter one single word.

I couldn't stand this strange silence for much longer, so I put an end to it and said, "You've caught me by surprise, Alia. You're talking about love when you can't even tell what tomorrow will be."

I felt my voice break slightly under the strain of what he'd said. I glanced at him and he shifted backward, as if my words had both provoked and comforted him. He announced, quite assertively, "I assure you that I will be a man. My monthly appointment with the doctor is the day after tomorrow. I'll take you with me, and you can see for yourself that what I'm saying is true. I want you to be by my side from now on, always. I need you so much. You won't regret this. I'll make you so happy in our life together."

"You're speaking as if you're already a man."

"Actually, I am."

Suddenly, I realised that he was very easily leading me to exactly where he wanted me to be. I decided to take a step back. I told myself I had to put a stop to things right then and there, even if I knew deep down I wanted to hear more. There were so many things that drew me to Ali, but we were not suited to each other, even if he did transition. First of all, I'm a decade older. And his complicated life won't get any less complicated. He supports a very large family. His entire life became tethered to them after her father's passing. His life is so difficult, and I don't want to get pulled into that labyrinth. On top of everything else, he's Arab. When he transitions, he'll be an Arab man, and Arab men are known for cheating and polygamy—that's practically common knowledge. No, I won't let myself go down that dark path.

"We aren't suited to each other, Ali."

His face fell. He became surly and visibly sad.

"I love you like a friend, and I'll be your friend so long as you're you. Even after you transition and get married, we'll stay in touch—like the closest of friends," I continued, trying to get my message across.

But he interrupted me, waving his hand, asking me to be quiet for a moment.

"Why such a rush? I'm not asking you to respond right away, or today even. Take your time to think. The surgeries won't start for a year or two. Why decide right now? All I wanted to say was that I love you. I really, really love you, and I have from the first day I met you. But at the time, I didn't know all this about myself, so I wasn't able to speak up about my feelings. I couldn't tell you until I'd confirmed the truth of who I was."

This comforted me. Before I even knew what I was saying, I quickly followed up with, "But where would we go from there?"

With lightning speed and a wide smile, he said, "I want you to be my wife," as if he'd rehearsed this line countless times.

A foggy image of what my life with him in the future would look like—even if he transitioned—forced me to ask him to leave this alone, to stay friends. But he insisted that I give it a chance before deciding definitively. I conceded.

"My love for you is no ordinary love. I'm crazy about you. If you're not with me in the next phase of my life, I feel like I'll die. I love you madly, Amira."

I smiled. Why did I smile? Something was happening that I couldn't explain. There was some strange kind of magic in the air.

Things moved quickly after this. He grasped my hand on the morning of 21 November 1994, and we took the train together to Hammersmith Hospital, where he introduced me to Dr Montgomery. He assured me that Ali was fully a man, in every way. He told me that the operations he was meant to undergo would restore him to the condition he should have been in for the past twenty-eight years. He tried to explain this to me in detail, "He will be able to perform sexually—there's no need to worry about that."

He stopped talking for a moment and brought over a plastic model of the male reproductive system. I felt really embarrassed and out of place. I wondered why I had to be here and see all this. Even at that moment, I hadn't yet decided what I wanted the rest of my life to look like.

The doctor finished his thought, "But I must inform you both that performing sexually is one thing and being able to have children is another. In Ali's case, we can't be certain until we know the condition of the testicles. There is a possibility that the damage done to them is too great and they cannot be brought back to full function."

I couldn't figure out what to do; the days passed in a blur. I don't know why I decided, or rather why my heart decided to give in to him, do as he asked, and promise him he could be my man. I also never fully understood why I felt I had to choose this obscure, mysterious path to an unknown future when I could have lived with another man, even if he wouldn't have had all of Ali's qualities. But if Ali wasn't able to have children, I would give him up to be able to start my own family.

I couldn't imagine living without children. This was and still is one of my main lifelong dreams. I've always hoped to have a family with at least two, three, or maybe even four children: two boys and two girls. I'd like to have the girls first, preferably twins—or, if not, then with no more than two years between them. I want my eldest daughter to have a sister to be her lifelong companion and friend, especially in childhood. I don't want her childhood to be lonely, like mine was. I spent my whole life alone at home, without a sister or brother, no one to talk to except my mother, my father, and my dolls. My capricious, overbearing mother controlled everything. She was harsh and cruel to the people around her, including me. She never made me feel like I was her friend or that I could have ordinary conversations with her. She never gave me the chance to be close to my father, either. The poor man so badly wanted to avoid being in a room with her that he even searched for an evening job to follow the one he did during the day. This meant he came home only to sleep. He was weak and unable to negotiate or discuss things with her. He simply was defeated and withdrawn and lived his life in misery. He died before he'd even reached the age of fifty.

I lived the worst imaginable childhood. And so I swore that my children would have a calm, gentle, peaceful life, free of shouting and anger. They would live in a house full of love, understanding, kindness, and support. I also swore that I wouldn't marry any of my mother's bad-tempered relatives so that my children wouldn't inherit her family's traits.

***

As the days passed, so did our life together, calmly and peacefully. We kept things private from the rest of the girls in the apartment until the time was right. At the end of January 1995, I took my exams and defended my doctoral dissertation in physics. This meant I had to return to Malaysia.

I went back to Penang and immediately took up a job as a professor at the University of Science Malaysia. At the beginning of 1996, Ali came to visit me and stayed a whole month. Then, a year later, I returned to Britain, on a year-long academic sabbatical. After that I kept flying back and forth between Penang and London whenever he needed me there. He had enrolled in a PhD program at the University of Leicester, which was in Leicester City, a place I didn't like.

His father died at the beginning of 1997, and so he had to travel to Yemen. I begged him not to go for fear he wouldn't be able to come back, especially after the university cut off his research stipend when they learned of his decision not to return to Sanaa. They stopped his scholarship payments, even ordering him to pay back what he'd received from the university while he was studying in Swansea. I feared that they would detain him, but he was able to return to Britain one week later, saying, "I am Ali now. They are making claims against Alia. Alia is dead." Ali had already transitioned in his official paperwork, without informing anyone at the university. But that summer, he was struck down by a strange and sudden fever, which landed him in hospital for more than a week. The correspondence between the hospital and the university forced him to inform the college about his situation, including the fact that he had transitioned.

I lived with him in his small apartment in a 20-storey building for foreign students. He supervised both the building and the students. I found a different Ali there than the Ali, or Alia, I had known in Swansea. Busy as a bee, he never stopped working. He was like a burning flame that never dies out, despite all the tragedy weighing heavily on his heart.

He used to wake up early, sometimes even before sunrise. He'd always be the first one at college. He did what he had to do, and then left for work in the afternoon. He did anything and everything he could to earn the money that he might someday need. And he was right about needing it. He would call me out of the blue to inform me that he'd be working in a restaurant or pub for a while. Or that he was cutting the weeds in someone's garden, or on the way to drop someone off at the hospital, or the train station, or the airport in London or Manchester. On the day he became president of the International Student Union, he had accumulated so many responsibilities that we sometimes didn't see each other until late at night. They called him at all hours, for any reason at all—if, for example, a student was sick or estranged from his family. If a new student needed help finding a place to live, he would go with them to buy furniture and other things they needed.

I grew cross with him more than once and doubled down on the blame, especially for volunteering to do things that weren't part of his duties. He would organise events or arrange parties that he wouldn't even go to himself.

"I'm having fun and filling my spare time while also earning some money."

"I'm killing time until I can have my operations."

He'd waited impatiently for the National Health Services in London to approve financing his treatment, which was supposed to start at the beginning of 1998. When they informed him it wouldn't happen before September 1999, he plunged into a state of grief and despair. He stopped going to the university for several days. He then decided to use all of his savings and borrow the rest to pay for the first operation and have it as soon as possible. He was no longer able to live in peace with his breasts, which were a constant reminder that he still was presenting as a woman. "I can't keep binding them, it makes me feel disgusting."

Dr David Paul performed the first surgery in the middle of the day on Wednesday, the 10th of March 1999. He went into the operating theatre with two spectacular breasts (I wished they were mine) and came out without them. It was a "tedious and exhausting surgery," as the doctor put it, lasting more than three hours, "But Ali was strong. His body showed incredible determination."

He's even stronger than he should be, I told myself. *The average person needs at least two weeks to heal before leaving hospital.* But even after I had exhausted every possible means to convince him to stay longer than he wanted to, Ali left the hospital only eight days after his surgery. The almost childish joy that coursed through his entire body extended visibly to his face, especially when he stared at his chest and no longer saw his breasts. The joy he experienced was indescribable. It allowed him to ignore the pain left by the sharp blades of the surgeon's scalpel, the scissors, and the sutures. This is especially true where they'd reconstructed the nipples. I looked at the lines on his chest and felt dizzy.

"Thirty-four years old, and not one of them counts," he said right after the surgery, his voice shaky and exhausted. He added, "I used to say that my true birthday was the day I arrived in London the first time—the 1st of July 1990. But that's no longer true. My actual birthday is the 10th of March 1999." Three months after this operation, he insisted on formally proposing. I asked him to postpone until he was finished with the operation that made his penis and testicles descend from his abdomen. But he refused to hear my pleas.

He reasoned, "I want to get engaged to you, and then get married. You must be my wife according to the laws and customs of God and His Prophet when I come out of that second surgery. I'll be fully a man then, and you can't stay with me according to our laws and customs if I'm not married to you."

This was perhaps the most offensive thing I'd ever heard from him. I tried to match his offensiveness. "I promise to marry you no matter the result of the operation. I'm even prepared to sign a paper swearing to it."

But Ali was quicker than me. "I can't wait until I go to Malaysia for us to get engaged. I'm afraid I'll do something forbidden with you before that."

I felt he was trying to guarantee that I would stay with him no matter the outcome of that operation. But I was so drawn to him. I'd never find such a sweet and gentle face, such rosy cheeks, and such a pure heart in anyone else.

We got married on the 8th of June, 1999. His mother and sisters flew in from Aden. Jawaher, his mother, is very kind and gentle. I wish my mother could be like her. She was the happiest person at the wedding party and insisted on recording it all. Her voice brimming with joy, she announced, "When I go back to Yemen, I am going to invite all of Sanaa, as well as Khobar, Aden, and Taiz to my house. Everyone should know that Alia has become Ali and that she was a man from the very beginning."

Then her demeanour changed a bit. Her eyes glistening, her voice not untinged by anger and hurt, she continued, "Sharaf's mother especially must watch this wedding tape. If she doesn't come, I will deliver it to her myself, so she knows that Alia and her mother haven't lied to anyone. Alia is indeed a man." Then she added, recalling faces that she knew, "Haifa's mother, that hypocrite, must also hear this news. Then it will be her turn to die of resentment, just as she tried to kill me with worry and anguish."

At that, she collapsed onto the sofa, sighing in agony.

"We are husband and wife now, so we can be patient and wait nine more months like the doctor advised," I told Ali.

Just six months earlier, Ali had undergone another small, unplanned surgery. But he had to have it done before the other major operation would help descend the testes and penis. That was in July 2000. David had removed a node that was a tiny remnant of a uterus, the size of a bean. David referred to it as an "incomplete uterus."

On that day, I begged him to postpone the main operation until the nine-month period recommended by the doctor had passed. But he insisted. He wouldn't budge. He was very confident in the resilience of his body. David wouldn't take my side either, as he had no doubts that Ali's body could take it.

There was a six-month period between the removal of the ovaries and the other, bigger operation. Ali spent these six months doing the extensive hormone treatments needed to help reorganise the functioning of his organs and how they operated in his body. They needed to be prepared to interact with the "dangerous and complex postoperative period," as David described it. He also said, "The operation to bring out the penis and testicles requires extraordinary effort on the part of doctor and patient alike. The urinary tract must be reconfigured to be sure that the urine is able to pass through a tube out of the penis. There are some aspects of the anatomy we will only discover once we have opened up the abdomen."

Amidst all his great fear and anxiety, Ali's smile never left his face. With courage and confidence, he kept repeating to me and the doctor, "It doesn't matter. My life means nothing without this operation." I couldn't but admire him and his resilience. Still, I was worried about him, and I didn't want to be there on the day of that particular operation. I begged him to excuse me from being by his side. "I'll pass out, Ali, I can't take it."

But he insisted.

"You have to be there with me. If you don't come, I'll die," he said, manipulatively, but David swooped in and saved me. "She cannot enter the theatre at all," he pronounced, cutting off any further attempts by my husband.

Thursday the 4th of January 2001: the day of reckoning arrived. The operation Ali had been waiting for so impatiently, the operation I was also quite breathlessly anticipating, finally took place. Ali was even more confident than David that the operation would be a success. He was certain; I was terrified. My heart was filled with dread and my body shook in fear. I had only twice heard David describe in detail what he would do to Ali's body under anaesthesia. Both times, I felt myself consciously dissociate from the part of me that had heard David's heart-wrenching description—it slashed straight through my chest. I'd draw just enough energy from that part of myself I'd left intact to give the shaken part of me the strength to expel whatever food and drink was in my stomach.

I'd rather die than undergo a surgery like that, I thought, envying Ali's strength.

At that point, I longed to feel the full pleasure of intercourse, having patiently waited for so long. My experienced girlfriends had described the feeling, the orgasm that comes from him moving inside me. For so long, we had just been having oral sex, which was more torturous than pleasurable.

I'd married very late. I had been waiting for a man—any man—to propose, but it never happened. Why? I don't doubt for a moment that it was my mother. Anyone who heard about her would surely run in the opposite direction. Only a fool would take the risk of proposing to my mother's daughter. In my small coastal town of Kulim, connected to Penang by the famous Penang Bridge, people refer to my mother as a "weapon of mass destruction". She would crush any man who dared propose marriage to me unless he first agreed to submit to her and her constant demands. They joked that, "Anyone who wants to marry Amira must sign a declaration on the day of the engagement that he has become her mother's servant." They are also certain that my father didn't die of natural causes, but rather from the worry and stress my mother heaped upon him.

Even I have to admit that I am not the most beautiful of women. After growing a moustache and beard to convince his friends that he had truly become a man, Ali was still much better looking than me. You simply can't describe what I have as beauty. My breasts are so small that they could pass as little lemons. I sometimes wistfully wish that I'd asked the doctor to stick the breasts he'd taken from Ali onto my chest. My skin is sallow, and my face is etched with despair, which ages me by about a decade. Looking in the mirror, I'd swear I was over fifty. My little eyes are the size of the bean removed from Ali's abdomen. My face is droopy. The skin on my cheeks has expanded and hangs down like a desiccated rose, its leaves dried out and withering away. Above and beyond all this, the years between us are not just a few.

On the day he confessed his love to me, I admired his madness, the way he could sacrifice the life he had. What did he see in me? I was at a point in my life where he should see me more as a mother than a wife! But I felt true joy. His words seeped into every cell of my body. My heart welcomed his love, even if at the time the situation was awkward. He was simply the first person to ever say that they loved me. I had never heard this from anyone, not even as a teenager. I can even almost say that, if he hadn't transitioned and had remained a woman, I would have loved her anyway, after this declaration of love.

I used to compare him to the men in Malaysia, and he stacked up well.

Though his eyes might be considered small, they are much larger than those of the men in my country. He has the most beautiful smile and a refined and heartfelt laugh. But the loveliest thing about him is his perpetually rosy cheeks, which blush not only out of embarrassment, but even when touched by an icy gust of wind in winter, or a hot breeze in summer.

When he insisted on travelling to get engaged and married, I started to imagine our wedding night. I would wear a white dress and a thin, gauzy veil to cover my face. He would stand next to me in a navy-blue suit, white shirt, and burgundy necktie. He would lift my veil and sit next to me on the velvet chairs reserved for the bride and groom. Our guests would come up to congratulate us while a band played lively music. I would walk past my girlfriends at the end of the evening, parading by, as they jealously watched Ali and me head toward our marital chamber. And that is exactly how our wedding night unfurled.

When David left the operating theatre after six full hours of surgery, he reassured me that the operation had been a success. I was awash with relief. My soul filled with joy and my body surged with energy. I practically danced through the hospital's corridors. Before I knew it, I was hugging David and the nurses who'd assisted in the operation. I thanked them over and over as tears of joy streamed down my face. This was a new kind of joy, totally different than any I'd previously experienced—like when I'd finished my PhD or gotten married. Only now did I really and truly see Alia as Ali: in reality, not as a possibility.

Because Ali wasn't scheduled to wake up for at least twelve hours after the operation, I decided to go out, high on this happy feeling. I roamed the streets of London that freezing cold evening, feeling warm inside. My body danced; my hands fluttered every which way with childish glee. I was a conductor leading an imaginary orchestra that played vibrantly as I passed through the wide, open spaces of Piccadilly Circus. I became a colourful bird hopping between the dried-up branches in Hyde Park. Feeling like a bride once again, I told myself we'd have a second wedding celebration here in London or in Leicester. We'd invite all the friends Ali had talked about, but Nasser and Meshal first of all. The two of them really should see Ali in his fully male form.

***

"I'm sorry to be the bearer of bad news, but Ali will not be able to produce sperm. This means he won't be able to have children. It was simply too late to save the testicles," David said as we watched Ali regain consciousness. But he added encouragingly, "I hope that this news isn't too sad. The most important thing is that he is now fully a man, and after a short time he will be able to achieve full sexual performance." Those weren't the words I wanted to hear as I sat there, watching my lifelong dream wither and die before my very eyes. How would I live without children?

We stayed in the hospital for three weeks, until he had fully recovered and was able to walk. He continued to suffer from various pains of differing intensities. The worst, by far, was the pain associated with the changes to his urinary tract. The sight of all the tubes was awful. They entered and exited every part of his body—his mouth, his nose, and his wrists. The most annoying were the two synthetic testicles implanted below his penis, and the plastic bag that hung below the bed to hold his urine at the beginning, before it became his companion wherever he went. Despite this, he kept smiling through it all, not believing he was now truly and genuinely the man he should always have been.

But he was sad, maybe even sadder than me. He'd always dreamed he'd have "at least ten children", as he liked to say. When he heard the news, he couldn't stop crying. Every so often, he asked me if I still wanted to be with him.

"I won't be angry with you if you decide to leave me. It's your right. You shouldn't have to suffer through this bad luck, too," he muttered weakly.

"It's my mistake," he added. "When I confessed my love to you and asked you to stay with me, I dared forget that I was jinxed. I haven't been lucky in life, nor will I ever be. I'm sorry, please forgive me."

I cradled him, holding him to my chest. Trying to ease him out of his misery, I gently rubbed his back. "There are children in the world without parents. We'll welcome one into our home and become a family. Perhaps this is God's wisdom. If everyone bore their own children, who would look after the orphans?"

After this, I stayed by his side in hospital and helped him with everything. I was a little envious of his boundless patience. He was in severe agony, especially when his painkillers wore off. His face would grow paler or darker, or even turn blue. His wounds would seep. But he never complained about being in pain, not even once. He kept painting that smile on his face, repeating, "Soon this will all be over, and we'll live as we dreamt we would. We'll adopt four children—two girls and two boys, just like you always wanted."

I was with him for the full three weeks. I slept in a narrow white bed next to his. I gave him his testosterone pills every day, the ones that would give him male features. Every passing day made me admire him and his courage that much more. Even David described his courage as rare. He said he'd seen it in one in a thousand cases. Every single day I spent with him made the love in my heart grow deeper.

I will never forget the day, three months later, when we had intercourse for the first time. I was nervous and flustered, and he was dripping with sweat. Neither one of us had ever had proper sexual intercourse before. We'd spent more than an hour searching Google and Yahoo for all the information we could find about intercourse, from searches like: "What you need to know about sex," "How do you make your partner comfortable during sex," "Having proper sex," and so on.

That first time wasn't comfortable for either of us, but it got better the second and third times. For a short period afterwards, he would be in pain, because the plastic supporter that helped him get an erection had shifted. So we went back to the operating theatre for a fourth time. We left the hospital only four days later. I hoped with all my might that we would not have to go back a fifth time. But we soon returned, only three months later, because he could feel a tear in the area connecting his thigh and penis, and the tear was growing daily. Looking at it was painful and disgusting. I worked around the clock to keep it clean and remove the pus oozing between his thighs, before the operation could fix it.

We stayed like this for five days, until he recovered. As usual, he never stopped smiling, even when he was in excruciating pain. He regularly apologised to me for the trouble he'd caused: "I promise you that this will be the last time you visit the hospital. Next time, and I hope there won't be a next time, I won't let you come with me. You deserve better."

I tried to dispel his fear that I had grown weary of his situation, reassuring him that I would never abandon him. "We're already finished with the most intense and dangerous part. All of this will pass. We'll get through the tough times together."

This is what I said aloud, while secretly I was praying to God that it really would be the last time.

***

The pilot announced that we were about to land at the Muscat International Airport: "We will begin our gradual descent about a half hour from now." Ali woke up during the announcement. I'd hoped he would sleep through to the end of the flight. He'd been passed out in a deep sleep and snoring audibly. I knew that only happened when he was absolutely exhausted.

"Why didn't you sleep?" he asked with a tired voice, looking dizzy.

"I didn't feel like sleeping. I'm too excited to see Muscat and Nizwa."

"But you're usually asleep now, it's late in Malaysia."

"No, don't worry. I'll have a proper rest when we land. I hope Nasser doesn't forget what time we're landing."

"I don't think he'll forget."

He fell back to sleep, and I went back to reading the magazine I'd found in the seat pocket in front of me. By chance, Nizwa—the City of Numbers—was featured in the inflight magazine, *Wings of Oman*. I assiduously read what was written there about the city: about its fortress, city walls, market, ruins, and the customs and traditions of the people, including their clothes. It didn't seem that Nizwa was a city, as they referred to it, but more of a large, ancient village. It has no large buildings, shopping malls, or intersecting roads. Perhaps Ali and I would enjoy this village life, especially since the apartment we would be staying at was on campus. "It's less than a three-minute walk from the residence to the college," Nasser said. "This will save us a lot in our expenses," I told Ali, adding, "We want to save as much money as we can, so that the Orphans' Association will allow us to adopt."

I was excited for this new adventure—joy and anxiety mixed together. Joy at being away from my mother and her never-ending quarrelling. Fear of not finding the specialist hospitals for Ali in Nizwa or Muscat, where we could seek treatment if something were to happen. What if there were complications? What if the pains that still afflicted him every now and then resurfaced?

We arrived in Muscat at half past seven in the evening on Thursday the 13th of August 2009. Nasser was waiting for us, but Ali was suffering from the same pains again, so we had to stay in Muscat for three days on a quest to find someone to treat him. My fears had not been misplaced, and we couldn't find anyone to treat him in Muscat. His pain grew so intense that he couldn't sleep for the three nights we were in Oman. He had to let me go on to Nizwa with Nasser, while he got on a plane back to London.

"I'll be back soon," he said, hugging me tightly. Sadness was etched on his face. Choking up, he continued, "If I could stay even one more day, I would take you to Nizwa and make sure you'd settled in. But the pain is like a knife slicing into my intestines."

"Perhaps I should come with you. Nasser can put in a word for us at the university and apologise on our behalf until we can return." I said this, shooting a meaningful glance at Nasser, so he would help me persuade Ali.

"Of course. If this is the only way, I'll do what needs to be done, don't worry," Nasser assured us. He was visibly concerned for Ali. But my husband insisted on travelling back alone. This was not the first time. He had vowed to never again let me go to the hospital with him after that operation to mend the tear.

He bade us farewell and insisted that Nasser not leave my side until he was satisfied that I was completely settled in Nizwa.

Jawaher
Sanaa

Like the Yemeni poet Husayn Abu Bakr al-Muhadir said, "It's impossible to return to the past/ so as to alter the present." Had it been possible, I would have acted differently. But my regret came too late. After speaking with Dr Abdel Ghaffar, I should have insisted that Abdel Rahman leave Khobar sooner and seek out treatment for Alia. I shouldn't have listened to Umm Mishari and married her off. I was going to marry a man to a man.

The day Ali called to tell us that the doctor in London had confirmed indisputably that he was a boy and had been born male, I was flooded with pangs of regret for every minute I had spent doubting Alia's behaviour. I cried. I prayed. I asked for God's pardon and forgiveness. But Abdel Rahman's regret was even greater, and he spent that sorrowful night in tears. "If I could get my hands on Abdel Ghaffar right now, I'd throw him into a fire," he lamented.

I spent the following day telling everyone about Ali. I knocked on all my neighbours' doors, and I called those far away in Hodeida, Aden, Taiz, and Khobar. "Alia has become Ali." I spent more than a quarter of an hour on the phone with Sharaf's mother in Khobar. She couldn't believe what she was hearing and responded sarcastically, "I'd like to see his children then."

"You will see, Umm Sharaf, time will reveal the truth," I answered confidently.

However, Abdel Rahman's sudden death, and Ali being forced to return to Sanaa while still in a woman's body, meant that my words were wasted. I lost face in front of everyone. The state that he was in—with his breasts still there—meant that he couldn't wear the traditional men's thobe and receive male guests in the men's section of the funeral. But because he had already become a man, he couldn't sit in the women's section either. In the end, he was confined to a room at home.

Rumours started flying again, until the news reached Sharaf's mother. She didn't hesitate to contact me and share her hateful thoughts, "I told you that God restrains only the monstrous," and, "The truth will come out sooner or later, Umm Alia." She kept spewing nasty things, and I tried to explain the situation, but she didn't care for what I had to say. "God doesn't strike us with a stick, Umm Hamed. The punishment should fit the crime," she repeated.

As for Ali, he was already speaking and moving differently, in a more masculine way. But despite these differences, it seemed like he was still taking his first awkward steps toward becoming a man, steps that his father and I had witnessed together. He remained in an in-between space, neither fully male nor fully female, a bit confused and not yet ready to fully become a man. He still spoke to his sisters as if he were one of them. With his brothers, he was just as he had always been—their eldest sister. He mentioned Arwa, calling her his friend and girlfriend, and recalled his conversations with Haifa and how she was jealous of his rosy cheeks and small, round lips. The day he came home, after greeting us all, his feet automatically led him toward his sisters' room. He would not have even noticed his mistake had it not been for one of their packs of menstrual pads, which he'd always been disgusted by, left strewn on the bed. After that, he was confused about where to sleep—with one of his brothers, or with his sisters? Finally, he decided to solve the dilemma by sleeping in my room.

Ali is not to blame, I told myself, when I saw him kissing his sisters' and brothers' cheeks the same way. At the end of the day, he'd been raised amongst girls. He'd spent most of his life with girls; even at university in Britain, he'd lived with female students. How would he have learned the ways of men?

"Your father asked me to tell you that he'd hoped to live to see the day when you became a man," I said when we were left alone in the room.

His eyes misted over out of grief at his father's passing.

"Baba didn't live the life he deserved. His work, especially at Aramco, consumed him and stole the best years of his life. I too hoped he would live to see the birth of his first grandson Abdel Rahman, named for him."

Abdel Rahman died young; he was barely sixty-two years old. His weakened heart gave out, and he decided to stop fighting. Before his death, he had been lying prostrate in bed, paralysis slowly creeping over most of his body.

"He said that you would be a worthy successor and that you would never abandon us. Will you?" He made no comment, but simply shook his head, No. After this, when our sadness had waned, he told me his story with Amira and how he loved her. He talked about her intelligence, her strong morals, and how she'd also had a difficult life. He talked about her overbearing mother and how afraid he was that she would refuse his request for Amira's hand in marriage.

"So why don't you find yourself a Yemeni girl to marry?" I asked, hating Amira's mother before I'd even laid eyes on her. He replied quickly, "No Arab girl could ever live up to Amira."

I told him that Arwa and other girls like Henaa had been asking after him, even after they'd gotten married.

He understood that I was trying to remind him of the beautiful girls he'd known. He said, "Arwa is the most beautiful woman I've met in my entire life, but Amira is just amazing."

Still, he could not readapt to the old life he'd led here for a quarter of a century, and one week later he went back to London, protesting, "I no longer belong to this place. I feel like I'm suffocating."

He came and went so quickly that he let me fall prey to the vicious tongues that tore at my flesh. He'd begged me to tolerate what was being said and be patient for a while. So I waited two years, and then he sent me a photograph of himself after his double mastectomy, when he was able to grow a beard and moustache. I enlarged this photo and made two copies, which I framed and hung up—one in the men's sitting room, the other in the women's. Below each picture, I had printed in bold typeface: **Dr Ali Abdel Rahman Ilwan**.

When I came back from Malaysia after attending the wedding, my heart was filled with joy. I invited the whole neighbourhood to a wedding banquet one evening. I hung a canvas cloth on the door to our house, saying: "Everyone is invited to celebrate the wedding of my eldest son, Dr Ali Abdel Rahman Ilwan." I bought decorative sparkling lights, which I strung along the walls and roof of the house. Wedding music rang out in the courtyard, and I let the wedding video play on a loop in the living room. I danced amongst the guests with my daughters, something I rarely do. Later, the whole house came alive with people dancing, as if we were at a real wedding. Haifa, the first to arrive and first to dance with me, whispered jokingly in my ear, "I would have left my husband had Ali proposed to me."

Of course, I didn't waste a minute sending a copy of the wedding tape to Sharaf's mother in Khobar, along with many pictures of the wedding. On a sheet of white paper, I scribbled, "Soon I will send you photos of my first grandson, Ali's son Abdel Rahman, whom you are no doubt eager to see. She who laughs last, laughs best, Umm Sharaf."

Ali
London

It's December 2017 and here I am, going back to London for the tenth time. I need to have another surgery to correct the placement of my implant and stitch up the abscess that keeps reappearing. Whenever I think I'm done with one pain, another just like it recurs. Only six months ago, I was here in London, getting treated for a serious inflammation of the same area.

I'm in the Departures area at Heathrow's Terminal Four, sitting at the Bridge Pub and Restaurant, waiting for my friend Nasser and his wife Fatima. They're leaving London today after having been here for a short holiday. I haven't seen Fatima in person since I transitioned, and I haven't seen Nasser since I bade him farewell in Muscat when I was there with Amira. I visited Oman twice during the year Amira spent in Nizwa, but Nasser wasn't in the country either time. At the end of 2010, Amira returned to her University in Penang, and I came back to Britain.

So much has happened in the last seven years—between 2011 and 2017. But the biggest change is that I returned to Saudi Arabia. This time, I settled in Riyadh, not Khobar, and I entered on my British passport, not my Yemeni one. Because of this passport, I've been able to earn a much higher salary, more than three times as much as my Yemeni colleague, though he's a bit older than me. He reminds me of my father in his hatred of the British, and, because of the difference in our salaries, he decided that he would hate me, too. His heart was filled with spite and jealousy. He told everyone that people like me were sell-outs, "loyal to Elizabeth and traitors to our land," which we had handed to the occupiers along with our dignity.

Behind my back, he told everyone he met that my father was just one of many cowardly British agents who'd sided with the enemy against the brave heroes of Yemen. In his words, these heroes "were able to defeat the cowardly invaders and drive them out of the beautiful lands of Aden." He even claimed that the Queen of England had awarded me and my family British citizenship because we'd betrayed our homeland. I was deeply upset when I found out he was saying these things about us. How could my father, God rest his soul—a man who had been pursued by the British military and forced to flee the country for which he'd fought—possibly be called a traitor? *Oh, the irony*, I muttered to myself. As soon as we returned to Sanaa, we were scornfully labelled "children of emigrants" and treated as second-class citizens, closer to traitors than citizens in our own right. And now, with British passports, they called us traitors and said we were only "loyal to Elizabeth". How amusing life can be, when there is no justice.

Though I'd gone back to Riyadh, I really had no desire to return to Saudi Arabia. It was not a country I'd ever thought I could live in. But fate reunited me with Meshal after we'd not seen each other for a long time. It felt as if he wanted to atone for how he'd wronged me and make up for accusing me of having deceived him. He tried to help me find a job with a good salary. Before our meeting, he'd seen Nasser, who'd told him the truth about all the hardships I'd been through. Perhaps his conscience had told him he'd been too quick to blame me back then. But no matter the material temptations, I never would have accepted this job had it not been for my family—especially my poor mother—and the fact that I'd promised her and my father I would support them when he no longer could.

After the events of the 27th of January 2011, the new reality in which my mother, sisters, and brothers found themselves was unbearable. Ear-splitting battles were taking place over our home in Sanaa; there were warplanes, missiles, and bombs all around. Many of these bombs exploded right near our house. The explosions hit everywhere, obliterating houses and lives, decimating weddings and celebrations. Our region, which had been one of the most beautiful in the world, became bleak and scary, filled with fear, barbed wire, and death. Our family home was especially affected. It was quite close to President Saleh's house; the distance between them was no greater than the distance between Heathrow's Terminals 4 and 5. This was what finally pushed me to accept Meshal's offer. The very day I arrived in Riyadh, I started my new job and began looking for someone who could help me get my family out of the hell they were living in. For a huge sum of money, I found someone who said they could deliver my family to the desert border between Yemen and Saudi Arabia. And I left it in their hands.

On the day I met them at the border crossing, my mother was on the verge of collapse. She'd been stuck waiting in the scorching July sands for too long. I got there in time for my brothers and sisters, but my poor mother had already succumbed to extreme fatigue, emaciated as she was from a lack of proper nutrition. Her diabetes and high blood pressure only made things worse. She lost consciousness and slipped into a coma, and she didn't wake up until a week later.

This meant I had to accept Meshal's pity and return to Saudi Arabia. That was four years ago, and I stayed there, rooted in place, unable to do what I'd dreamed of doing during the years I had left on this earth. My dreams were not that big. It wouldn't take much to achieve them. Everything revolved around Amira. She had a heart kinder than that of all the rest of humanity put together. She was patient and gave up everything for me. She believed all the promises I made her about the happy life we would share together. Always serene, the wonderful Amira is worth her weight—and more—in gold.

What could I possibly do for Amira to make up for everything she's done for me? I've asked myself this so many times, and I can never find the answer. What she has offered me is beyond anything I could have imagined. Put quite simply, she's devoted her life to me. Nothing forced her to continue in this bland, tasteless existence with me. She lived four thousand miles away, all alone, with an exhausting mother who was taking years off Amira's life. What exactly did she gain from being with me? What had I offered her other than hardship and tears? She could have changed her destiny and lived a more dignified and decent life in Penang.

But Amira doesn't get angry. She doesn't get sad. I don't remember ever seeing her enraged. She's only ever gotten cross with me once. It was when I was far away. Her voice sounded different on the phone. I wasn't able to see her face, though I wish I could have in that moment... Ever since I met her, I'd begged her to get angry with me, even if just once. "I'm sure you're even more beautiful when you're angry," I would say, trying to fuel her rage, but she'd just laugh. I witnessed her fury only once—never before and never since. It came when my brother Hamed and his family decided to spend their summer holiday in Penang. They stayed at her house. His crazy children climbed all over her furniture and drew on her walls with coloured markers; they even reached into her fishpond and pulled out her ornamental goldfish, leaving them to lay there until they were stiff and dead on the ground. That was what pushed her over the edge. She rang me in Riyadh and begged me to do anything I could to get Hamed and his family out of there and back to where they'd come from. But despite her anger, she didn't shout or yell like anyone else would have. She said what she said in a voice that—very simply—lacked its usual serenity, which told me that she was, indeed, angry.

Life before the surgeries was torture. Living through the surgeries was torture. And life after the surgeries was torture, too. Such was God's will. It was as if someone in my family had sinned again and again and I alone had to pay the price. Then there was Mourad, the Mama's boy, the last of the bunch. The crazy one. He didn't appreciate my miserable, beaten-down state, and he decided to add to my burdens, very masterfully bringing me even more misery, right up until he got married. Even then, his marriage was a trap set out for me. He had only married at my mother's insistence—she had thought this would put a stop to his antics, and she wanted to see him wed before she died. But he threw the burden of this marriage onto me. I kept paying the rent on his flat, as well as his daily expenses, so that his landlord wouldn't have him thrown in prison. He was lazy. But my mother stood by him and spoilt him.

My brother Assem wasn't any more sensible than Mourad. He was the only one helping me pay for our family's household expenses, but one day, he went mad and decided to leave his job and go back to Sanaa, at a time when everyone else was fleeing. No matter how much we tried to reason with him, he wouldn't listen. He insisted on doing exactly as he pleased. And he did, although only to discover that life in Sanaa was unbearable. He called me one day in tears, sobbing, begging me to help him come back. He sounded utterly mad as he pleaded with me. I continued to send him as much money as I could, but just as he never thanked me for it, he also never thought it was enough. My mother was sending him the bulk of the money I gave her, too. And then there was Hamed, the eldest of my brothers. Ever since he'd gotten back from Malaysia, angry at Amira and me, he had resolved to live far away from all of us. He went to work in Jeddah. From that point on, we had no more news from him. One evening at my mother's insistence, I visited him to see how he was doing. He threw me out, ordering me never to visit him ever again.

My sister Anoud married a poor, older man who locked her up in his dilapidated mud house. The dank, musty air got into her lungs and those of her only child. My mother extricated her from his grasp, and she and her child are now living at home with me. Nuha, my sister the doctor, who'd gone to work in Dhofar, couldn't really help with our expenses because of the high cost of living in Oman. My younger sisters Suha and Shazza still lived with me, too; both were unemployed and unable to find work.

I couldn't count on my three brothers for any support at all. They saw me only as a bank, an ATM that provided the money they needed to carry on living as they always had. I can't say that this didn't make me angry. Sometimes, in a fit of rage, I'd yell, "I'm not giving you another penny! Learn to support yourselves, I'm not your servant!"

"You're their elder brother and have to stand in for their father," my mother would say, as my anger swelled.

"They're lazy and apathetic because of you, Mama. You've spoilt them, you raised them wrong!"

"If your father were alive, he wouldn't complain about them like this."

"But I'm not their father. I have my own life, but because of you all I can't live it!"

"But your father entrusted you with this duty."

Then came a day, at the beginning of 2015, when I definitively decided to send my brothers and all their children back to Sanaa. My mother and sisters would stay, but the rest had to leave so that Amira could come live with me. But it was just my luck that on that very day, war erupted between the coalition forces and the Houthis in Yemen, and our living situation remained unchanged.

My mother was never the same after my father's death and her collapse while crossing the border. She'd started to change even before that, back when a bomb fell near our house and crushed our neighbour's son. He had simply been in the wrong place at the wrong time. She withdrew into herself and was constantly worried about something terrible befalling her children. She defended my brothers even when she knew they were wrong. She didn't mind that they lay idle at home all day. I never once heard her shout at them, or urge them to leave the house and make their own living.

I implored her, "You've made them into undependable, unreliable, weak men!"

"Don't say that about them. When the time comes, you'll see."

"But now is the time. Why do you let them lie around and sleep all day long? They aren't kids anymore!"

"I don't want them to work in Riyadh. You know what I'm saying."

"No, Mama, I don't know. Everyone works in Riyadh. No one will treat them differently."

"You say that because you have British citizenship."

"Dozens of Yemenis work with me."

Whenever she realised how angry I was, and that I was going to stand my ground, she'd whip out her usual retort, "If you're going to tell me what to do, then just send me back to Sanaa!"

But the years were passing by, and life is short. Amira and I hadn't been together in the same place for more than a month at a time since she'd gotten back from Nizwa and I'd gone to Riyadh.

"Do you think we'll ever be together?" she asked me before this trip to

London. Her voice was heavy with grief. Before this, we'd spoken at length about our life together thus far, how it had gone, and how separation and worries were most of what we'd gotten out of our relationship. I promised her that, as soon as the war in Yemen ended and my family was back at home in Sanaa, I would resign from my job and she and I would live together in Oman. I assured her that Nasser had promised to look for jobs for us both, and that he would be true to his word. I also told her that if it didn't work out, I would come to Penang and live with her there. I could open a little electronics shop with whatever money I had left, and we could live off of what we made from the shop.

I curse and blame myself sometimes for involving this angel of a woman in my life. It was selfish of me to insist that she stick by me and marry me. I had stupidly believed that all the tragedy in my life would surely end one day.

***

An email notification blinks on my mobile phone. It's Dr David. I open the message, expectantly.

Dear Ali,

I'm so sorry to be the bearer of bad news. But we already knew this was a possibility. You're a strong and resilient person, and you've been through worse. This situation is just another difficult thing you will have to overcome. Your test results from the day before yesterday have come back, and they revealed the presence of a tumour at the base of your penis, near the area connected to your thigh. We are not completely sure what kind of tumour it is yet, but we believe it is still benign. The good news here is that it is extremely small and new. But, for peace of mind, I've sent a sample of the tumour to the laboratory for further analysis and a biopsy.

You should know that we believe the primary cause of the tumour to be the penile implant—the pump you are using to boost your erections. Truth be told, we're seriously considering the permanent removal of your implant. Your body appears to be continually rejecting it. You have now suffered from no less than six infections in the past two years, which is both uncomfortable for you and worrying for us. Though we are still not sure about this, we believe that your repeated, painful, weeping abscess is related to the pump.

If indeed the tumour is confirmed to be benign, then it can be treated. But the implant will have to be permanently removed, and we will replace the missing tissue with some taken from another part of your body. You should also know that things are likely to worsen if you decide to postpone the surgery.

In sum, my dear man, I want to reassure you once more that we doctors here at the Hammersmith Hospital have met and consulted to discuss your case. We agreed unanimously on the following course of action:

1) remove the tumour.
2) remove the implant and pump that give you an erection.
3) suture up the abscess area.

Your hospital stay may last only 10 days. We just need to be sure that you have made a complete recovery before we authorise you to travel. Please note that we advise you to stay near the hospital for at least a full month after this surgery.

We leave the final decision to you.

I'll be expecting you in my office at one p.m. sharp, to explain everything and discuss this further. I hope that before we meet, you will have been able to carefully consider your decision. Please know that we will support you, however you choose to proceed.

Please accept my best regards.

Yours faithfully,
David

I'm shocked by his message. Despite myself, I smile and wonder, *Do I have anything left to help me cope with a new surgery?* I laugh involuntarily and with such force that the waiter hears me and smiles at me from a distance, gesturing to ask if I need anything.

In any case, David's email isn't far off from what I was expecting. On the contrary, I anticipated something like this. Removing the penile implant and pump is a course of action I felt would inevitably come. David himself had prepared me to accept this fact when we discussed it two days ago. But I wasn't expecting a tumour. The pain isn't any different from what I've felt before.

Instinctively, I thank God for everything I have. But my tears overpower my will and quietly slide down my cheeks. I quickly wipe them away, because from where I'm sitting, I can see Nasser and his wife Fatima approaching. We talk for about an hour about all kinds of different things, but I don't tell them what I've just read. They bid me farewell and head into the airport terminal, after Nasser promises to speed up his efforts to find work for Amira and me in Oman.

I sit there alone, staring at the constant movement all around me. This place is brimming with life. People rush about in throngs—if only I could tell what was going on in their minds! Has anyone experienced more suffering in their life than I have? Has anyone else endured such loss and pain since their very birth? Is there anyone out there who has seen this other side of life—the dark, disgusting, cruel, violent, destructive side—and not yet taken matters into their own hands to end it?

During the hour I spent with Nasser and Fatima, I wished I could live like him. I wished I could *be* him. I don't think I've ever seen him hurt or in pain. He's never once whinged about anything to me. What's more, he knows how to get on well with English people. I've seen him play football with them... He's very athletic. He's so good-natured, and everyone appreciates his funny stories. I saw him a few times, sitting in his usual chair under the walnut tree, or in Victoria Gardens, smoking peacefully and happily, kindly smiling at everyone who passed by. And his wife is as lovely as he is. She's also cheerful and clever. As long as Nasser is by her side, she too seems not to have a care in the world. The two of them are so lucky, why couldn't I have had just a bit of that luck?

Then I think of the people like me—those whose sorrows overshadow their joy. I think of poor Bouthaina, stripped of any opinion by her overbearing, arrogant husband. She was a skilled paediatrician. She was such a good person that it was almost as if she could heal wounds just by touching them, a sort of miracle worker. But she lived an unhappy life, until her husband finally agreed to divorce her. Only then did she find some relief. I also think of Fakhera Saeedi, the Omani woman who came to teach in our Master's course after earning a doctorate in Women's Studies. She got divorced as well, after her husband's abuse and humiliation nearly drove her mad. She would spend nights on end wailing as her mind flooded with memories of the wrongs her husband had done her, while also suffering from serious thyroid infections. Sometimes she deliberately refused to take her medication, which made it seem like she intended to harm herself or even take her own life. All these people opened their hearts to me, told me about their problems and preoccupations, their pain and sorrows, their deepest secrets. But not once did they ever think to ask what burdens I was carrying.

If only what was wrong with me was like what was wrong with them, I tell myself, then I'd be willing to live with it. Those kinds of problems come and go... they don't last. Though your heart may ache, and you might be in great pain, that lasts only a few hours, maybe a few days—weeks at the most. I'd put up with these kinds of problems—one a month, or even one a week. I'd endure them gladly and be the happiest person on earth. I promise I wouldn't complain like they do. I swear. Their kind of suffering, even increased tenfold, is nothing compared to what I've lived through. I've always yearned to talk to someone about the traumas of my life. But I'm afraid that, once they heard my stories, they would be ashamed to tell me about their everyday problems.

As I sit at the airport café, I notice the waiter walking up to me. This takes me back to a wild dream I had about going into a pub in Piccadilly Circus and ordering a beer. "Are you okay, Sir?" He seems anxious because I haven't moved, even though Nasser and Fatima have left.

"I'm fine, no worries," I answer. He asks if I need anything. I nod straightaway. "Yes, a pint of whatever my friend here was drinking."

He brings me a pint of Blue Moon Light. I am going to do what Nasser does, or at least drink the beer he drinks—perhaps it's why he's so happy.

I knock back two glasses without noticing the bitter taste. I take the Underground back to my hotel, but before I walk down the corridor to my room, I decide to go back out to a nearby pub. I drink a third pint of beer and chase it with a fourth. A sense of calm euphoria washes over me. Only then do I make my way back to the hotel, promising myself to drink more after I get out of hospital. I'm going to ask Nasser what kind of drink would deliver me to this state of euphoria the fastest, right from the first sip.

***

Sitting across from David the next day, I'm not afraid. He greets me with a nod, asking me to be brave and strong, as I always have been. With a half-smile, he adds, "This may be a blessing in disguise. I can guarantee that if we do this operation, you'll no longer have to worry about painful tears and abscesses. You'll be able to live your life without all these trips to London and so many stays in the hospital."

I have no choice, do I? I won't tell Amira about any of this yet. I won't allow myself to worry or scare her. I'll tell her that it's a routine operation, just stitching up the abscess like usual. I won't go back to Riyadh straight after the operation. I'll travel to Penang and meet her there. I'll extend my holiday by a week or two: I might be able to spend a full month with her. I'll ask her to put her life there on hold—her mother and her teaching especially—and come unwind with me. We'll fly together to the nearby island of Langkawi, where I'll rent us a chalet by the seaside.

I'll tell her that I love her very much, that I've done my best to fulfil my promise to her, and that she can peacefully live the rest of her life as a princess, the Arabic meaning of her name. I'll tell her every detail about what happened and ask her to forgive me for how difficult things have been, for the beautiful dream that we imagined together, and for my promise to her, which God did not will to come true. I'll ask her to choose what she wants to do with the rest of her life—stay with me or bid me farewell. I'll let her decide. The rest of my life will be all illness and fatigue. I leave that choice to her.

David looks up at me and says, "We'll wait for the lab results, as I told you. We must be absolutely certain that the tumour is not malignant. You do understand what I'm saying?" He repeats the question twice, to be sure that I've gotten the point. My heart is thumping against my ribcage; I feel David is hiding something from me. My voice suddenly shaking, I ask, "What happens if the tumour is not benign?"

He looks at me with silent eyes before shaking his head. "Let's hope that it's benign, shall we? If not, we will have to amputate the entire penis and build an artificial one with reconstructive surgery."

What more do you want from me, God? I don't know if I should laugh at how awful what he just said is, or cry at my bad luck, which will seemingly never change. What did I do to deserve this? For a moment, I'm unable to speak or think or even lift my eyebrows in surprise. What is the appropriate reaction to what I've just heard? I tell myself, *At this point, what's the difference between having the penis and losing it? Once they take out the implant, its only use is to urinate. After this, nothing matters anymore, Ali. You've run out of energy. You don't have any left.*

***

In the hospital room, I notice the movement of the clock's pendulum, indicating that it's exactly twelve p.m. on Friday the 15th of December 2017. I realise that in three or four hours, I will be leaving the operating theatre for the twelfth time since my very first surgery. But this time, I will come out different. I will never be able to have sex again, even though I'll still be a relatively young man. If I count the day of my second surgery as the day I was born, then today I am still a teenager. And I actually do feel like one—or, at least, I did before today. Even Amira describes me as boyish, as "someone trying to make up for an unhappy childhood," as she likes to conclude.

I didn't really have a childhood, or a young adulthood for that matter. In some ways, I wasn't even really a man for long, after living in misery for so many years. I lived my first childhood feeling different and anxious about the strange urges and feelings that other girls my age didn't seem to have. I kept wondering who I really was, why I was different. I lost my entire childhood searching for the answer. My young adulthood was also lost searching for a treatment and cure, and in a short while my manhood, as a "complete man", will be over. I'll go back to where I was after the first surgery—a man, but not quite.

I squandered more than three decades searching for my truth. But it has just turned its back on me, in a way that feels premeditated and unapologetic. Here I am, once again, fated not to be my true self. I spent most of twenty years—from 1997 to 2017— haunted by pain that would always attack me by surprise. I underwent so many agonising and exhausting surgeries, and these left dozens of scars on my body. I've got a chunk of flesh missing in one spot, crisscrossing scars in another. I had two breasts that were never really mine and now I have a penis, and even though it's small, I didn't manage to keep it for long. Every morning when I go into the bathroom, take off my clothes, and look in the mirror, all of these outward manifestations of my past flood me with reminders. Each time I say, *Okay, at least now I can really start living.* I'd hoped to live to a hundred so I could make up for what I've missed. But I've deluded myself that God would recompense me with a future brighter than my past. At first, I used to be glued to the Internet, closely following the news of medical developments. Perhaps there would be an earthshattering discovery that could restore my ability to produce sperm, and these could fertilise Amira's eggs, instead of watching them be flushed away every month.

I was tormented but patient, hoping that one day my misfortunes would end. Consumed by this fantasy, I gulped down litres of medicines and swallowed hundreds, perhaps thousands, of pills. I've also had dozens of stitches sewn into my body; I spent countless days in hospital rooms. But I've still wound up back at square one, as if I'd never done any of this. Twenty years washed down the drain.

As if this torture weren't enough, it then caused illnesses that stayed with me for years and would now be with me forever. I've put up with constant pain. Every day, I take a thyroxine pill to treat my hypothyroidism and two metformin pills to control my blood sugar. If I forget to take them, I feel so fatigued I can't even move. Worst of all is the heavy needle full of testosterone, which I inject once every two weeks. When the thick fatty liquid enters my bloodstream, it always makes my stomach churn.

Now here I am once more, ill and waiting to be sliced apart and patched back together again. I wake up and get out of bed slowly and carefully; I lower my legs to the ground and prop up the wrist that's connected to the IV pole, which I drag with me toward the window. Then I pull back the curtains and stare outside.

People pass by the old Victoria Station as usual, everyone on their way somewhere. I raise my eyes toward the cloudy sky and speak to Him for the hundredth time—maybe He'll finally listen.

God, I wonder what sin I committed against You that You would do this to me? Why did You choose me to endure this and not someone else? Why have You tortured me so much? Do You hear me, or did You judge me long ago and are no longer paying attention? Don't You forgive all sins? Aren't You compassionate and merciful with Your servants? I am Your servant, what crime did I commit to deserve such torment?

I've tried to recall all the sins and misdeeds I've committed, but I can't come up with any that would deserve such treatment. I've even tried to think of those committed by my father or mother. I thought I was perhaps paying for their sins. But I couldn't think of anything they'd done that was worthy of mention.

It's going to rain, maybe even snow soon. Such is winter in London. In a few days, everyone will be celebrating Christmas. Snow will fall then for sure. Santa Claus will come, spreading good cheer and gifts for the children. Everyone will be filled with holiday joy. I'll be discharged from hospital the night before Christmas Eve, and I'll go looking for Santa in Piccadilly Circus. I'll ask if he'll let me come with him, to help distribute gifts to the good girls and boys. How I wish I had two or three children myself, though I haven't even been able to have one. I'll ask him to help me—to speak with God and ask Him to forgive me, to save me, to come and take me and Amira by the hand—she deserves the best this world has to offer...

After I'm discharged, I'll go to church. I'll tell the priest my life story and ask if my sins deserve such punishment. We believe in the same God, after all—perhaps he can help me find the answers. I then draw the curtains on the scene before me: a woman pushing her baby in a pram with one hand, the other holding a small Christmas tree, her little dog running along beside her.

I go back to bed, and Amira is standing there in front of me, smiling. She's waiting for me to speak. I cover her cheeks and forehead with kisses. Please don't be sad, things won't be that bad Amira, my princess. I suppose it's a good thing we aren't teenagers brimming with sexual desire anymore... especially if you decide to stay with me. I'm nearly in my fifties, you in your sixties... Now that we're older, we'll change our lifestyle a little. We'll forget about sex and remove it from our daily lives—we'll focus on other things instead. From now on, we'll vow never to live apart from each other, to never leave each other's sight. We will make an unbreakable pact. I'll send my mother and everyone living at home back to Sanaa. You'll leave your mother in Penang. We'll look for a new place to live together. We'll put all our old memories aside and start again. We'll take in a child or two and live what's left of our lives far from anything that could hold us back. We'll eat our favourite Malaysian dish every day—Nasi Dagang.

***

It's exactly one p.m., and the snow is starting to fall. I'm waiting for the nurse to come take me to the operating theatre. What a magnificent sight it is: the tops of houses and buildings covered in white powder. Looking at it, my heart swells with an overwhelming sense of peace and calm. I wish I could be out there, sitting at a café, sipping coffee and contemplating the beauty of life. It has no meaning without joy.

Life loses so much of its value when the soul is tormented, not only by pain but by fixating on its arrival. What can the value of life be, really, if one feels scattered, haunted by loss and the loneliness of living far from home? Having beauty right before your eyes but not feeling it, losing sight of beauty altogether, as you wallow in misery and despair—that's no way to live.

But there is vast beauty out there. I see it. It dazzles in its many forms. Tell me, though, how can someone like me take pleasure in such divine splendour when my life has been destined to be utterly miserable and bleak?

Questions simmering inside me bubble up to the surface: Was I born to be unhappy? Was I ever truly happy, just happy, even once?

The answer is no. Since birth, I've never known true joy—not the kind that I saw in Nasser and Fatima's faces, nor the kind I've seen on Lissi's. Why was I even born? Does my life have any purpose? I know Nasser's does—when I sit with him, I can see the palpable delight and cheer he brings to the table. I see how he makes people happy, how he helps them forget their troubles and worries. But me? Find the purpose of my life, I dare you. Tell me the meaning of what I've lived through.

What is the story of my existence? Every person who is born and dies on this planet has a story. So what's mine? If I gathered up all the details of my life and laid them out before me, what would I take from it? It's a series of symbols—a painting you can see but can't interpret, like a Picasso. I've always looked at life with longing. I've spent it as a fighter, refusing to be defeated. I've been an exemplary model of someone who's tireless and in-defatigable, who stops at nothing to get what he wants. And I haven't been selfish along the way, either: I've offered help to anyone who's asked. Indeed, in one way or another, I must have helped every single person who's passed through my life. But in the end, here I am with nothing, empty-handed.

I remember what my father told me one day in the Singleton Gardens in Swansea, how sweet his words were and how much they affected me. But Baba, what you said wasn't true—leaving Khobar for Sanaa wasn't as you said it would be, at least not for what I needed. You were wrong. I couldn't find treatment in Sanaa. Instead, my pain and loss intensified. Remember, Baba, your promise to do the impossible and get me to London? I remember you asking me to get a British passport. Did you think I wouldn't under-stand what you meant back then? May God forgive you. You were another one of those people who believed I was gay, just like that stupid Sudanese doctor. You wanted to send me far away so your reputation wouldn't be tar-nished. Did you think I was so silly not to understand that you were trying to lessen your burden by passing it onto Sharaf? You wanted to marry me off to him and relieve yourself of me and your promise to help me find a cure.

Did you really mean to do that? Or have I wronged you somehow? For-give me if your intention was to let me live a life that was suited to my mis-erable state. I loved you so much, Baba, and I would have loved you even more if you'd done the impossible as you promised and flown me out here. If instead of squandering your money, you'd sent me here back then, I'd be okay now. But you were blinded by greed; you lost your properties, your health, and you almost died. If you hadn't made those mistakes, I would have fathered many children by now. And you wouldn't have died. Your heart wouldn't have stopped beating. You would have been alive to see your grandchildren, the first of whom would have been named Abdel Rahman, after you.

Did my mother hurt me by trying to do the impossible—shaking the eggs loose from my body? How many medicines did I inject into my thighs, how much male frankincense did she burn for me? She had it brought especially from Hadhramaut, but it did nothing. Yet my poor mother committed no sin. She did everything she could think of at the time.

Mama, Baba... It doesn't matter anymore. Neither of you meant to do me any harm. It's life itself that did me wrong. I'm haunted by a curse. But I don't know who cursed me. I just don't.

I feel lost and orphaned. Faces and images jostle in front of me. I'm a small boat that's gone off course in the middle of a vast, murky, desolate sea. The midnight sky is empty—no stars, no moon—and the deathly waves relentlessly toss me every which way in the obsidian unknown.

Afterwards, I retract into myself and ask God's forgiveness. I beg Him to forgive me, spare me, and excuse me for any transgressions. I no longer know what the truth might be. I'm tired, and I've endured a lot for very little hope, a mere flicker of hope. In vain.

Forgive me, God! Inspire me, guide me, and deliver me from evil. Please pardon my sins. You who sit on the heavenly throne, You are the Greatest, the Most Loving and Most Forgiving. You are the one who says something will be and it is. You can do as You please. I am asking You by the very light that fills You and the heavens to forgive me and pardon my transgressions, to guide me to the right path.

***

Two hours before the operation is set to begin, the nurse comes in to apologise first for the delay, and second because she must inform me that the surgery will have to be postponed for a day or perhaps even more. She also informs me that Dr David will come in and talk to me soon.

Reeling, I think, *God, is this how you respond to my hopes and pleas?*

Here I am, once again, without.

Acknowledgments

Translations never happen in a vacuum, and as this novel was translated during the physically distanced COVID pandemic and in the heavy shadow of the apocalyptic Beirut blast, we owe a debt of gratitude to those who made it possible. Our first thanks are to the author of this important work who was gracious, thoughtful, and helpful in responding to our queries about the text and what the story means on a larger scale. We would also like to acknowledge Nasser Albadri and the team at Dar Arab, who approached us with the translation and gave his full support to this important project. M Lynx Qualey was an excellent editor, and we appreciate her work that helped put the final touches on the manuscript and truly brought everything together.

We spoke to and consulted many people to think through the different elements of how to translate this work. Our most important debt of gratitude is to Hajar Assaad who read and thought through the entire text with us. Her close readings and deep knowledge of Arabic terms and phrases were helpful all along, thank you Hajar. Sasha Elijah also read through the novel carefully and helped us think through some of the conceptual issues particular to this translation. We would also like to acknowledge others with whom we have been in conversation about this text in one way or another: Farah Khan, Alison Slattery, and Elissar Haddad. We also owe deep gratitude to those who helped us power through the difficult realities of life that formed the backdrop of this translation. Tameem and Liliane, thank you.

Michelle Hartman & Caline Nasrallah

Translators

Caline Nasrallah is a Master's student at the Institute of Islamic Studies at McGill University, where her research focuses on language as a feminist tool. She also works as a translator, mostly from Arabic to English, and has an MA in Translation from the École de traducteurs et d'interprètes de Beyrouth (USJ).

Michelle Hartman is Professor of Arabic Literature and Director of the Institute of Islamic Studies, where her research focuses on language, literature, and the politics of translation from Arabic to English. She has published several academic books, as well as a number of literary translations of works by Arab women authors.

Caline and Michelle have one other co-published translation, Nawal Qasim Baidoun's Memoirs of a Militant: My Years in the Khiam Women's Prison (Interlink, 2021).

Younis bin Khalfan Al Akhzami
The Author

A writer from Oman, born in 1968, participated in many local, regional and international literary forums. Head of the Short Story Writers in Oman in 2006 and 2007, and one of the founders of the Society of Writers in Oman. He holds a Masters degree in Information Systems Management from the USA in 1994 and a PhD in Geographic Information Systems (GIS) from the United Kingdom in 2000.

His publications include:

- Alnatheer (The Forerunner, short stories, International Press, Muscat, 1992)
- Habs Alnawras (Locking the Seagull, short stories, Arab Foundation for Studies and Publishing, Beirut, 1996)
- Humma Ayar (Fever of May, short stories, Arab Foundation for Studies and Publishing, Beirut, 1999)
- Nuqoosh (Inscriptions, short stories, Nizwa book, Muscat, 2007)
- Al Sawt (The Sound, Novel, Dar Al-Intishar, Amman, 2012)
- Bar Alhekman (Novel, Part I of the Arabian Sea Trilogy, Dar Question, Beirut, 2016)
- Kahf Adam (Adam's Cave , novel, Dar Arab, London, 2017)
- Ghabta Hashish (Novel, Part 2 of the Arabian Sea Trilogy, Dar Arab, London, 2018)
- Bedoon (Without, novel, Dar Arab, London, 2019)
- Ras Madrakah (Novel, under printing, third part of the Arabian Sea trilogy)

He has been a judge for many local literary contests for both story and novel scripts.